STEALING STANLEY

BlackCanoe

ISBN: 978-1-7390126-0-1

Dedication

Pour ma blonde.

1

"What. Was. *That!?*"

An excellent question. It was asked, in a wavering voice, by the woman with the flaming red hair and flowing skirts. But all of us in the elevator were no doubt wondering the same thing. What *was* that horrific bang? The sound was loud and sharp and seemed to have come from somewhere above us. The obvious, though pessimistic view, was that it was exactly the sort of noise that a cable snapping under tension would make. It was certainly the only idea that I could come up with. My hands tightened their grip on the pizza carrier. My stomach dropped. The elevator kept rising.

"Whoa!"

"No! Really! What *was* that!?"

"I knew I should've taken the stairs."

"Are we going to die?"

"Well, we just passed the eighth floor. So, ya, probably."

"Whoa!"

Despite having my nose pointed at the doors and my back to everyone else, I had no trouble identifying who was saying what. Being the last to get on, there had been some jostling around to make space for me and the large Hawaiian pizza that I was trying to keep flat. Which was eons of time for me to make a detailed inventory. I'm good that way.

Off my left shoulder was an older man holding a spectacular bouquet wrapped for delivery. He wore a rumpled old-fashioned suit and a look of resigned fatigue.

Which gave the impression of someone arriving sixty years too late for the prom. Beside him were a mother and son (judging by their matching pale freckled skin and red hair). Before the interruption, the two of them had been engrossed in a lively discussion about missing dental elastics and the unreliability of both orthodontist office hours and ex-husbands. She was in West Coast hippy chic with layered skirts, a hemp woven carryall, and an uncountable number of scarves and shawls. The son wore a striped tie and a private school crested jacket.

"It's an Otis Gen3 elevator. They're usually fairly reliable."

"Usually? What does that mean? *Usually*!?"

The last bit was from the two on my right. One was a woman in orange coveralls with eyes, skin, and hair all in complimentary shades of espresso. I guessed she was maybe ten years older than me, somewhere in her mid-thirties. With her outfit and toolbag, I put her down as an electrician on the job. The other, somewhere on my right, was Thimoty 'Tim' Angulalik, a cyber security specialist originally from Inuvik. We'd never met before, but I knew all about him. Tim was the guy whose computer I had come to steal.

From outside, three more bangs followed in rapid succession—each louder and sharper than the one before. There was some whimpering behind me, but most of us seemed to have held our breaths. Still, we didn't plunge to our deaths. The elevator just came smoothly to a stop, and the doors slid open on the ninth floor without a hitch.

As I'm short, I wasn't blocking anyone's view of the two serious men in dark suits standing in the lobby outside. One of them was bald and huge. Not just absurdly tall, but proportionally broad in all directions with the solid build of a rugby forward. His hands were so massive that the cellphone he held by his fingertips looked like a toy.

The other guy was much more regular-sized, though decades older. The deep lines of his face seemed permanently etched with a world-weary expression. He wasn't holding a phone. Instead, he had a large and very shiny chrome-plated handgun.

And they weren't alone.

Blue-grey smoke drifted over a third man. He was sprawled in a wheelbarrow. It was parked so close to the elevator that I could only just see him over the edge of the pizza carrier. His body lay inside with all four limbs hanging limply over the sides. Like the other two men, he also wore a dark suit, though in his case the light-coloured shirt underneath was mostly a splotchy brick-red.

There was a frozen moment of complete silence.

Then, a small squeak of protest came from the pizza carrier as it crushed under the clench of my hands. The next sound was the crinkle of the bouquet's plastic wrapping when it brushed my shoulder, as the old man leaned forward for a better look. And finally, a piercing shriek rang out from the mother or the electrician, or maybe both together.

Aside from a slight lift of his eyebrows, the man with the gun hardly even altered his expression. There was a scuffle of shoes and I sensed space opening behind me as everyone tried to back away, even though there was nowhere to go. I felt an ice-cold rush of goosebumps from head to toe as the man slowly raised the gun away from the wheelbarrow, higher and higher until it was level and pointed straight at my head. At that angle, the shiny chrome disappeared and all I could see was the end of the barrel, looming black and huge.

This was a moment for clear thinking. The kind of scenario that my Uncle Rupert had lectured me about so many times. When things go sideways, you have to stay in control. Be calm. Be cool. Above all, don't do anything rash or impulsive.

Solid advice.

So I hucked the pizza carrier as though it was a frisbee—as hard as I could—straight at the gun.

2

My uncle Rupert thinks the pizza delivery gag is too brash. He's fond of telling me: *Margot, you just can't go wrong with a hard hat and clipboard.*

With those two things, he maintains he can go anywhere, at any time, and nobody so much as raises an eyebrow. But then Uncle Rupert is male, burly, and old. And I'm definitely none of those things. So while he can play dress up and effortlessly look the part of an engineer, or HVAC repair technician, or even, god-forbid, a city health code inspector, I could never pull any of those off. The few times I tried, people just seemed to think I was a little too old to be out trick-or-treating. And I've yet to do a job for Uncle Rupert that actually fell on Halloween. Pizza, however, is year-round. Everybody loves pizza. And nobody cares who's delivering it. At least that's true most of the time.

In this case, however, my pizza delivery woman disguise was being tested in a completely new way. I'm not sure what I thought throwing the carrier was actually going to accomplish. But there was nowhere to go, or time to hide. So I just chucked it, closed my eyes, and fell back against the cluster behind me, bracing for the shot that never came. Maybe the gun had run out of bullets? Maybe it jammed? Whatever the reason, the bullet-deflecting properties of an extra-large Hawaiian were never put to the test.

Instead of a deafening gunshot, all I heard was: the muffled thump of the pizza carrier hitting something, a collective gasp from those behind me, frantic clicking as someone hammered on the panel buttons, and finally an electronic *bing* as the elevator doors closed. And then…we were moving.

"Well, that was unexpected," the old man mumbled.

I opened my eyes in time to see the floor indicator lights over the door change from nine to eight. Hands were aggressively pushing on my back. In the pile-up, the shoulder strap of Tim's laptop case became tangled at my feet. He must have dropped it or set it down, but I had to kick it toward the doors to be able to stand up properly. I'm not keen on being touched by strangers, and it seemed like a reasonable time to ignore elevator etiquette, so I did a quick spin to face them.

"Holy crap," the electrician said. A patch on her coveralls was embroidered with the name 'Maryam Satvika'. "Did we just see what I think we saw?"

"Nope," the mother said in a much quieter but equally shaky voice. "I didn't see anything. We didn't see anything. Nobody saw anything."

"Whoa, that dude in the wheelbarrow got *toasted,* huh!?" the kid said, just in case the rest of us were starting to have any doubts.

"No Colin. He didn't," his mother corrected. "It didn't happen. Can't this thing go any faster?"

"Nice throw," the kid said. He did a slow-motion punch toward me, but I passed on the celebratory fist bump and reached over to press the fourth-floor button—just in time. The elevator immediately whirred to a stop.

"We have to get down," the mother said with a shriek.

I heard the doors slip open behind me, and I backed out with shuffling steps.

"What are you doing!?" Maryam said. She'd managed to

keep her voice level, but her eyes were wide with a manic glint, so I assumed shock was already settling in. The kid was still giddily slack-jawed while the old guy had fallen completely silent, presumably turning inwards to process what we'd all just seen.

My own freakout was going to have to be postponed until a little later. Being able to compartmentalize is just one of my charmingly useful personality quirks. As I grew tired of explaining to my parents and teachers growing up, *I'm not getting distracted…I'm just focusing on something else.*

I knew that I still had a job to do. So I automatically shoved the panic and shock of witnessing a murder into the background of my mind to deal with at a more convenient time. This is why, rather than sensibly ride the elevator down to the ground and flee with the rest of them, I just kept backing my way out of the elevator.

"Sorry, I don't do well in groups," I said. "So. Ummm… bye."

The mother stretched over and frantically jabbed at the 'close door' button. I stood facing them, fixed in place just clear of the elevator doors. Partially, that was just in case I had second thoughts about jumping back on…but mostly it was to hide Tim's laptop bag that I'd been pushing with my feet. Uncle Rupert would be proud.

There was no time for a premature celebration. As soon as the elevator was gone, I scooped up the laptop bag and zipped over to the reception counter. There were two computers in the bag, but only one was warm to the touch. When I opened the screen, it sprang to life, prompting for an unlock code that I didn't have, but also didn't need. I rummaged in my shoulder bag until I found the pouch for the USB sticks. I located the one marked with three Z's—which meant it was the right one to use for a sleeping computer—and stuck it into an open USB port (not bragging, but I got it in the right way up on my first try). Then I just stared at the little light on the end while it flashed and blinked and strobed while it did whatever evil digital things it was supposed to do.

It was still working away when a thunder of footsteps came crashing from the stairwell. I looked over in time to see a flash of dark suits zip past the door window. One. Two. And then...a third. None of them paused to see who might be lurking on floor number four. A few seconds later, the flashing light on the magic USB stick turned to a steady green, which was my cue to unplug it and move things along.

According to my original plan, all these sorts of computer shenanigans were supposed to have taken place in the peace and quiet of Tim Angulalik's empty office. Now, despite things having gone dramatically sideways, I'd got the job done. So I was feeling pleased with myself as I repacked the laptop and set the bag on the floor just outside the elevator. I gave it an artful nudge with my sneaker to scuff the side and help sell the idea that it had been accidentally abandoned. With that done, I put the USB stick back in my bag and swung my focus toward other issues.

When I did a quick mental replay of recent events, all the smugness evaporated. It was replaced by a sick-to-my-stomach feeling that was only partially due to seeing a dead body in a wheelbarrow. When I got to the part where I'd heroically saved the day with my quick-thinking pizza toss, I realized there was a problem. Uncle Rupert was going to be far less pleased with me than I'd been imagining.

It wasn't losing the pizza so much as the bag it was in. I'd got the carrier off Amazon. Super cheap. It came with a comfortable carry strap, a rigid liner, and a nifty graphic of a

—now somewhat ironically—flying pizza on the cover. It also had a clear pocket on the flap for holding business cards. Though my name is Margot, I had a bunch of cards made up with 'Danny Delivers' on them. This wasn't about being sneaky, but had everything to do with the logo on the Vespa scooter I had parked outside. I have no idea who Danny was, or what she or he delivered. Who knows...maybe it was pizza? But I got the scooter complete with the 'Danny Delivers' paint job for next to nothing at a police auction. This is something—given the sometimes dubious legality of my employment—that probably qualifies as another source of irony.

The business cards, I felt, gave an air of professionalism. But they were also handy for those slow times when jobs for Uncle Rupert were scarce and I did *actual* courier work as opposed to just the pretend variety. So while the name Danny was fake, the phone number was very real. In my mental playback, I could picture the bright white business cards tucked into their little pocket as the carrier spun away from me. Which, maybe, wasn't a *huge* problem. I don't have a lot of friends and I could always get a new number. But the issue I was now envisioning had more to do with whether the guys in the suits had contacts with the cellphone people, or maybe they were just highly skilled at computer things. Either way, that number could link them to my real name and real address. I try not to be snobby, but they didn't seem like the class of people I wanted to see dropping by my apartment unexpectedly.

What to do? The stairs were at least temporarily off the table as a safe route out of the building. The elevator was not worth considering. Then the thought occurred that if everyone had run down the stairs, the ninth floor might be empty. So maybe, just maybe, there was an opportunity to salvage my pizza bag.

A minute later, I was three flights up the stairwell and climbing. Above the fourth floor, the air was thick with drywall dust and the smell of primer. The building was brand new. While accountants and lawyers and orthodontists (and even cyber security consultants) had already moved into the lower floors, each grimy stairwell door window above them showed only empty spaces still under construction. Even the stairs were carpeted with a thick layer of construction grit. I had to go on tiptoe so my sneakers made only the slightest scritching sound with every step. I was tempted to find some satisfaction in my stealthiness, but I knew Uncle Rupert wouldn't have approved.

In our line of work, sneaking around is only for idiots and ninjas. And you're neither of those. Always try to look like you reluctantly belong. Think of it like you're at the doctor's office for a flu shot. You're there only because you have to be, but you're not thrilled about it. Don't skulk in the shadows, sulk in plain sight. Simple really.

Simple for him and his clipboard, maybe. I couldn't think of a clever cover story to explain myself to anyone I might run into, so I kept on my toes the whole way up to the top floor.

With my new focus shifted over to recovering the pizza carrier, I'd sort of mentally skipped the whole dead body thing. But with a peek through the ninth-floor stairwell window, I saw the wheelbarrow still parked near the elevator and recent events came flooding back. I felt a rush of goosebumps from my scalp to my toes at the memory of the gun.

Hurriedly, I took a tiny step to put the wheelbarrow out of sight. The new angle gave me a different view, but it was equally depressing. There was the same sort of reception counter area as there had been back on the fourth floor. Only this one had my pizza bag and a razor-thin blonde in a stylish pantsuit perched on it.

She struck me as being one of those too-thin model types. All cheekbones and hollow eyes darkened either from makeup or rigid dieting. I watched her critically appraise the cuticles of one hand while she helped herself to a big slice of Hawaiian with the other. She took a few healthy bites, so maybe the dark eyes were all about the makeup after all.

I loitered in the stairwell for a few minutes, alternating between standing quietly and sneaking peeks through the window, all in the hopes she'd disappear. As much as I tried to ignore it, the wheelbarrow of death kept drawing my attention. It took me a few glances to realize that the wheelbarrow was completely empty. Or almost so. There seemed only to be a blanket left inside, like one of those that movers would use to wrap furniture in. Probably it was there to soak up the splatter. Which got me wondering about what they'd done with the body.

Only one of the elevators seemed to be working. Seeing as the building was still being worked on, maybe the other elevator was still just an empty shaft. Which, if true, could be super handy for emptying the garbage bins or...maybe dropping bodies down. Now that was a grisly thought.

There was the squeak of shoes on tile and I risked another peek through the fire door window. I caught a glimpse of the blonde disappearing down the hall past the reception counter. She was carrying the cardboard pizza box under one arm at a ridiculously jaunty angle. This was *not* a good idea. Something topping heavy—like that Hawaiian—was bound to slide itself to destruction. She was going to wind up with a naked crust and a massive, cheesy, pineapple and bacon ball of goo. But I was far more concerned about my pizza carrier bag that she'd thoughtfully left behind.

The fire door had the same standard Schlage deadlock set I'd encountered back on the fourth floor. Lots of new builds are going with fancy electronically controlled options these days, but these locks were the cheaper old-fashioned variety. Spin the key one way to make the door open from both sides. Spin it to the other and it would only open from the inside. The one on the fourth floor had been set to open. This one was not. I gave the thumb latch a quiet but firm press but it didn't budge. Which wasn't a problem. Or shouldn't have been.

I had barely unzipped the shoulder bag to dig for my trusty lock-pick kit when the metallic sound of a door slamming came zipping up the stairwell. The echoes were still reverberating when I heard a rumble of deep voices and the hurried slap of leather shoes on gritty concrete steps.

Precious seconds ticked past while I stood frozen in panic. Not enough time for me to jimmy the lock and no way down. Which only left one other direction.

The concrete dust was thicker on the final set of stairs leading up from the ninth floor. At least the crash bar on the roof access door was well-oiled. The catch opened with only a muted click, but the hinges squealed in protest. I froze and held my breath to listen. The plods of heavy feet had slowed their rhythm in time with some pretty laboured panting. Still, they seemed to be only a few flights away. I slipped through the gap and eased the door closed as quietly as I could. And then waited.

Ten long minutes crawled by and all I heard were the sounds of street traffic from below and the squawk of some passing gulls above. Aside from a plastic chair and a metal coffee can half-filled with cigarette butts, the only other structures on the roof were air conditioning units of various sizes scattered here and there. There was no external fire escape or any other obvious way to get safely back down to ground level.

On the plus side, the view was spectacular. It had only just turned June, so even now, at the end of the workday, the sun was still high in the sky. The snowy tops of the Olympic Mountains across the water on the American side felt so close I could almost reach out and touch them. Closer to home, downtown Victoria was spread out below me like a display at the miniature museum. From this height, the people and cars on the streets, and the passenger ferries and seaplanes in the harbour all looked toy-like. The Empress Hotel and the Legislature building beyond were doll houses. So that was all fun, at least.

Still, as heights are not one of my comfort areas, I kept well back from the edge as I made a cautious approach to the street side of the building. I got just close enough to check that the Vespa was still where I'd left it: on the sidewalk propped against a bus stop shelter. Not technically legal parking, as far as Victoria City bylaws go, but the kickstand had fallen off some months ago, so leaning it against stationary objects was the new procedure. My main concern was that, at least from this angle, the logo on the rear of the scooter was mostly hidden by a garbage can. If the man with the gun had found my business cards in the pizza carrier, I didn't want him to realize that 'Danny Delivers' was still in the area.

But there was no sign of menacing men in dark suits, or even anyone running around in a blind panic screaming for help that I could see. If one of the elevator gang had made a 911 call, it didn't seem to have had any effect. I retreated to the safety of one of the smaller air conditioners, a coffin-sized box of aluminum, and used it as a bench seat. I could see the sports centre in the distance. I used it as a landmark to strain my eyes and ears in the general direction of the police station. No obvious flashing lights or blaring sirens were headed my way. Something for which I was typically very grateful, but at that moment, it gave me mixed feelings.

Besides the view, there was one other bright side. Since I'd entered the building, I had had no reception at all, but now my phone was showing full bars. What to do with that wasn't clear, however. As tempting as it was, I had a deep aversion to contacting the police myself. At least not yet. First, I needed to get safely down and gone. Then I might figure out how to make an anonymous 911 call.

Looping Uncle Rupert in on how the operation was proceeding was one idea, but only in so much as that I'd acquired the target's computer bag. Little things like stories about witnessing a murder would spoil his dinner. And much more importantly, it would lead directly to a *'You're fired for your own safety'* sort of situation. He takes the Uncling thing fairly seriously when he wants to. Besides, I've always waited to contact him until a job was done and I was safely off-site. Despite how sticky things had become, I was still hoping to keep that tradition alive.

With the police and Uncle Rupert in limbo and no immediate safe way down, I needed to do something to keep myself distracted...so I texted my roommate instead. Harley is a canine adventure experience coordinator. Or, as the rest of the world knows it, a professional dog walker. Most of her four-legged clients are in the neighbourhood around James Bay where we live, but she has a few over in Cook Street Village. This meant that if she was on her usual schedule, then she would be somewhere in Beacon Hill Park by around now.

Harley has little idea of what my job entails beyond

'running errands' for my uncle, and it's important for me to keep it that way. So as much as I wanted to text her factual things, I got my thumbs working and went with the lightest and most random thing I could think of: *Dude. You'll never guess where I am!*

Hopefully, some silly banter would pass the time until things quietened down below me. The phone began buzzing in my hand barely a moment after I'd pressed 'send'. As that was Harley's usual response to an interesting message, I answered without bothering to check the display. Big mistake.

"Harley! I'm literally on the roof of a building downtown," I said. "Wild, huh!? The next time the city has fireworks, we totally need to come here. The view is ah-mazing!" I hoped the extra bounce I was forcing into my voice wasn't too over the top. Typically, she is a waterfall of words, and I braced for the deluge. Instead, a long silence followed. Until…

"Hmm. Danny Delivers? Yes?" The voice was male, deep, and heavily laced with an Eastern European accent. Most definitely *not* Harley.

"So, view is nice on the roof, is it? Good. Stay. Enjoy. Valery will be there to get you in a moment."

3

Valery, as it turned out, was not the skinny blonde who'd been scarfing down my pizza. Valery was the huge bald guy. He showed up all of twenty seconds after I'd frantically pressed the end call button of my phone. During those brief moments, I did a few things. First, I sprang to my feet. Then I hurled my phone over the side of the building.

It was the same sort of instinctive throw that had been behind the pizza toss. No thought, just action. I wanted to get the voice that wasn't Harley as far away from me as possible, and so, over the side, it went. If I'd *really* been thinking, then I would have unstrapped my go-bag and chucked it over as well. Though, in my shocked state, I might have considered adding myself to the list of falling objects. Depressing stuff, but then panic will do that.

Panic also started me running—even though there was nowhere to run to, and nothing much to hide behind. Something that sunk in only after I'd done a quick lap around the air conditioner. With no other ideas, I dropped into a low crouch behind it. Squeezing myself into a ball just in time to hear the crash of the access door flying open.

A half minute or more ticked past and all I could hear was my heart pounding so fiercely that I thought my ears might explode. Eventually, I remembered to breathe.

I dropped my hands to the rubbery surface of the roof, fingers spread wide for balance. Gingerly, I tipped forward to risk a peek around the end of the air conditioner. The access door was propped wide open. An inviting sight was it not for the impossibly massive shape of the bald-headed Valery looming in front of it.

"Pizza girl! Where are you?" His voice was a guttural rumble. Deep and thickly accented.

He seemed to be alone. Though that was a small comfort. A cold feeling of dread ran through me as I watched him start to spiral his way across the roof. Despite his bulk, he moved in a remarkably silent and fluid manner—like an oversized panther. While his steps were slow and halting, his head was in constant motion. His eyes scanned the rooftop like a radar antenna, left and right, back and forth. Once he even twisted to look back at the roof of the access building in case I might be hiding up there.

There were a few other small air conditioners like mine at seemingly random locations over the roof deck. But there was a single, much larger unit, about the size of a mini-van, that seemed to draw his attention. To reach it, he was going to pass in clear view of where I was hiding. Maybe, if I timed it absolutely perfectly, then I could duck-walk my way around the end of the air conditioner and keep out of sight. So long as he never got too close, we could theoretically play hide and seek like that all day. But I wasn't feeling that lucky. So instead, the instant his bald head glided into view, I popped up like a Jane-In-The-Box and flew on adrenaline-soaked feet straight towards the open access door.

I didn't look back. Not once. Just sprinted flat out all the way. I reached the door on skidding feet and made a desperate grab for the coffee can beside the chair. Cigarette butts went flying. I hauled the door shut behind me. There was a flash image of Valery bearing down like a charging bull. His quick feet and much longer legs had closed the distance faster than I'd dared imagine.

The door slammed, and I wedged the coffee can under the

crash bar with barely an instant to spare. The door frame shuddered while Valery wrenched on the handle from the other side. I watched in alarm as the can bucked and jumped...but it stayed in place.

For how long? I didn't wait around to find out. I flew down the first set of stairs, envisioning a breathless run all the way to the ground floor, but it was not to be. My feet skidded to a full stop on the small landing outside the ninth-floor door. Patiently blocking the stairs down was the man who'd been holding the gun. He wasn't waving it around now, but he wore a very hard and angry expression, which seemed equally dangerous.

It was like a bucket of ice water had been dumped on my head. Above came resonating booms so loud the air seemed to vibrate. It sounded like Valery had found a sledgehammer.

"Go back up and let Valery in. I'll wait here."

He responded to my nervous glance at the stairs behind him with a slow shake of his head. "Go! Before he gets angry."

My stomach felt tight and my legs were numb. With no other obvious options coming to mind, I plodded back up the stairs and did as I was told.

A minute later, I was being closely escorted into the offices of the ninth floor. There was no sign of the blonde with my pizza, but if I was feeling nostalgic, there were some familiar faces in a conference room at the end of the hall to make up for it. Everyone who'd been along for the elevator ride was now clustered around one end of a ridiculously long table. The boy, his mother, and the electrician were on one side, while the old guy and Tim were on the other. Their reactions to my arrival seemed to range between annoyance and disappointment.

Of all of them, only the old guy gave me a look and a sad but hopeful smile. "Hey, shorty, any chance your name is Polina Pavlova?"

"No," I said. "Why?"

"Flowers were for a Polina on the fourth floor," he said and gestured to the bouquet that the mother was now holding. "I gave it to Saffron here to cheer her up. I guess you're just a delivery person like me then? Was the pizza for Polina too?"

"And here we thought that you'd got away," Saffron said.

"She's the reason we didn't," Maryam grumbled, giving me a squinty look. "I hope you realize that if you hadn't stopped us on the way down, we'd all be free right now."

"Ya, what was the point to that?" the kid asked, in a surly tone that Saffron didn't bother to correct.

Given the temperature, I opted to sit at the far end of the table.

"Well, to be fair...Benny's van didn't start," Tim said with an apologetic look at the old guy. "And, also, they'd closed the garage gate. So that might have been a problem."

"I told you we should have got out on the ground floor," the kid added.

I leaned back in my chair to close my eyes as they bantered back and forth.

"Well, to be fair...that idea came up only after we were in the van."

"The dampness. Probably got some drainage problems in the garage, too much moisture in the air. Carburetors don't like that."

"How far do you think you would have gotten, Colin? Your Mom said you took the bus."

"A bus would be better than that piece of junk."

"Easy there, sonny. The 1962 International Metro is a classic."

"You should drive an electric anyway. Only fossils use fossil fuels."

"Well, to be fair…"

"Oh, Tim, stop with that! There's nothing fair about this!"

It was nice that they all seemed to be on a first-name basis. Still, the bickering probably would have continued, but the gun-dude, as I was calling him, walked in. My eyes opened, and all heads turned. Just like that, everyone found a reason to shut up.

Maryam made a rambling plea along the lines of: 'We saw nothing, we won't tell anyone, just let us go, and it's like we were never here' kind of thing. He just held up a hand in a stop gesture and gave each of us long, uncomfortable stares, ending with me.

"You. Phone. Wallet," he said, and snapped his fingers at me. I wasn't sure how well pleased he was going to be if I told him I'd misplaced my phone and the only ID I carried in my go-bag was more of the business cards that he'd already found. Which just left all incriminating tools of my trade that I'd stupidly not dumped when I'd had the chance. This had not been one of my better outings.

I unstrapped the shoulder bag and chucked it down the full length of the table. Or tried to. It skidded to a stop barely halfway there, and the others had to pass it hand to hand along the rest of the way.

"You're better at throwing pizza," the kid said.

Valery gave a supportive grunt in agreement as he took the bag and hefted it once or twice as though appraising the weight before handing it to the gun-dude. The two exchanged some words which I assumed were of the '*make-sure-they-don't-leave*' and '*don't-worry-I-won't*' variety. Not that anyone was likely to make a dash for it with someone the size of Valery standing in the way.

After the gun-dude left with my bag, we sat in brooding silence for a half hour or more. When he returned, he was wearing half-moon-style reading glasses, and a slightly puzzled expression. "You. Pizza girl. Come."

I felt like the class troublemaker getting called to the principal's office. A few nasty glares from the rest of the elevator gang did little to suggest otherwise. Unlike grade school, though, I didn't have to wait on a little bench out in the hall. Instead, gun-dude ushered me right in and I got a comfy chair and everything. His office had floor-to-ceiling windows, which might have impressed me had I not just seen the more panoramic version of the city from up on the roof.

Aside from the great view outside, there was a West Coast landscape hanging on one wall that was all molten shoreline and ocean under a swirly sky. I suspected that it might even have been an Emily Carr. Beneath it was a small table holding an orderly pile of cellphones and wallets, which I assumed were the property of my elevator buddies next door.

I found it far easier to let my eyes wander over the surrounding office than it was to look at the man directly, but eventually, I relented.

Up close, the lines of his face seemed to be etched even deeper. The eyes that I'd seen as dark and menacing were actually a soft grey, almost pleasant really. Though the look he was giving me was anything but. My go-bag had been thoroughly emptied, and the contents arranged in neat piles over his desk. He did a few minute adjustments to my business card with a perfectly manicured fingertip. Nudging it this way and that until it lay in perfect alignment with the top edge of my well-used Peterson Ghost limited edition lock-pick kit.

"Danny Delivers. Danny? Yes?" he asked, with maybe a trace of skepticism, though it was hard to be sure with the accent. "This is a boy name. No?"

I took a long breath to steady my nerves. "Well, I didn't want to say anything. But since you bring it up...in *this* part of the world, Valery is *always* a girl's name. Do you want to be the one to tell him? Or should I? He kinda seems like the type that would have problems with a challenge to his masculinity. Looks like a bit of a gym rat? Am I right? How do you think he'll take it? You know...I can tell him if you'd like. It might be better coming from me, but you decide. Where are you boys from, anyway?"

He ignored all that. Clicked his pen once, adjusted his glasses, and then tried again. "Your name? Full name, please."

"Danielle Anderson," I lied. "Danny is short for Danielle. See? Regular girl's name."

The 'Danny', of course, had come from the scooter. As for the 'Anderson'—I'd googled that in anticipation of just such a crappy day as this. I had once looked up the most common surnames in my part of the world. Smith and Brown were way up there, of course, but those are the sort of names that sound fake unless you are one. Lee and Chan were also insanely popular, but creeping into the top ten was Anderson. And based on my bland Caucasian genetics, it sounded plausible enough, to me at least.

"Okay, Danielle Anderson, tell me, what is all this you have?" he asked. The personal things that he'd scrounged from my shoulder bag: the lip balm, bubble gum, protein bar, hair elastics, and so on, were in exile way over to one side of his desk. He wasn't talking about any of that. Instead, he hovered a finger over the other items, one by one. The lock-pick kit. The lipstick cameras. The microphone bugs. The fancy USBKill v5 Tactical Kit that I wasn't entirely sure how to use.

"No idea," I said. I gave an exaggerated shrug and held up my hands in wonder—though I quickly dropped them back on my lap when I noticed how badly they were shaking. "All that is just another courier job I was supposed to drop off right after the pizza. Danny Delivers! That's me. All your small courier needs. Packages. Run to the liquor store for ya. Pizza…you name it. Speaking of which…did Polina eat *all* of that Hawaiian? I mean, she looks like she needs it. But if not, maybe you could have Val bring whatever is left to the rest of the gang. They're getting noticeably hangry. Is it okay to call him Val?"

"Hangry?"

"Hangry! Like, hungry and angry mixed together. You know, so hungry that you get angry. It's a thing. Sounds almost like Hungary now that I think of it. One of those European countries…have you been?"

He lifted his pen to make a note, but then thought better of it. "Where is your phone?"

I made a show of checking my pockets. "Dang. I *know* I had it earlier. Wait, wasn't it in my bag? You don't think Val nicked it, do you? Is he the sticky-finger type?"

He narrowed his eyes a fraction and gave a small lip-pursing motion. "Address?"

"Address," I echoed, as I did a few time-delaying nods of my head. "Wow, you're going to laugh at this. Though I'm glad you brought it up! I'm just between places right now and actively looking. Do you know of anything? Seems to be lots of empty floors in this building. Are they converting any of that to apartments, do you know? What does it cost to rent here, anyway? But seriously, I don't need anything crazy big, and it doesn't need to be downtown like this, though near the beaches would be awesome. And affordability is important. I'm on a bit of a budget these days. I was sharing some space in a basement apartment with these university students. Where were they from...Czechoslovakia? Or was it... Romania?"

If any of those countries rang a warm bell of familiarity with him, he was hiding it well. He let out a breathy sigh. "Okay. So you have relations?"

I stole a glance at his notebook. So far, all he'd got down was my pretend name and my real phone number. "Wow, relationships!? We're getting a tad personal now, aren't we? But okay...let's see...I was dating this one guy not so long ago. Just on and off, nothing serious. He was a foreign student at the university. Russian, I think? Or was he Slovakian? We didn't hit it off. Did you want to hear the details? Oh, wait... unless you were asking for yourself? But yikes! I mean...I'm what? *Half* your age? More? What's that they say about snow on the roof, though? You have some grey coming in—if you don't mind me saying."

That seemed to throw him for a second. He shifted back in his chair and dipped his head to stare at me over the rims of his glasses. Which was more of a reaction than when I'd slipped in the guess about Polina's name. Though that hadn't been a huge stretch of logic. True, the flowers could've been for someone working at the dental office. But Polina Pavlova seemed like a name that fit in well with wherever these guys were from. And I've seen 'nines' look like 'fours' in my own handwriting countless times, so it wasn't a big jump to imagine the flowers that the old guy had been delivering should have come to this floor all along. I didn't feel bad for her. She missed out on the flowers, but she got my pizza.

"No. I am not asking this. I want the names of your parents. Brothers. Sisters. Relations."

"Ah! Gotcha. Nope, none of those. Quite tragic, really. If Sister Agatha at the orphanage was to be believed, my mother was a struggling pastry chef and my father was a longshoreman from Latvia. Or did she say Estonia? Might have been Estonia...or what's that other one?"

Normally, I'm the somewhat weak, and very much silent type. Though you wouldn't guess the quiet aspect from all the blabbering I was doing. Something about being scared out of my wits had caused my mouth to keep flapping, and the lies to keep flowing. The guy in the wheelbarrow had been the first dead body I'd ever seen. And aside from those strapped to the hips of police officers, it had been the first gun I'd witnessed up close. It was certainly the only one to have ever been pointed directly at my head. Those facts also led to the final first...I was sitting an arm's length away from an actual murderer. Someone who had coldly taken a life and was now casually sorting through my effects while he presumably pondered my fate. It was a lot to take in, and my mouth was trying to distract my brain from having to deal with it. I sat on my hands while I kept spewing nonsense to keep myself together. But the nerves were now taking over and I couldn't stop my right leg from pumping up and down.

"Stop." He held up one hand palm first towards me and placed the pen in his other hand down on the desk with slow and meticulous precision. A phone was ringing. I looked over at the pile of cellphones, but he reached behind him to where an old-fashioned landline telephone was sitting. It had a small caller display, which he examined with a nostril-flaring intensity. He picked up the receiver with one hand and with the other, he pointed me to the door. "Go."

So I went. Valery was hovering in the hallway, so I didn't even get time to contemplate a mad dash to freedom. My legs seemed to have reached a wobbly state of uselessness, which wouldn't have gotten me far. As it was, I was happy enough to stagger my way back to the far end of the table, which put a buffer zone between me and the others, who also seemed to have reached a meltdown state of mind. On the bright side, at least my mouth seemed to have run out of smart-ass things to say. The others, however, were all still relatively chatty. I sat back and observed the chaos. After another hour had crawled passed, I'd developed a theory that—just like the stages of grief—there is a similar timeline for processing the stages that follow witnessing an execution.

"We didn't see anything!" (Denial)

"This is ridiculous! You can't keep us here like this!" (Anger)

"Look, just let us go and we won't say anything about this to anyone, ever." (Bargaining)

"This whole thing sucks." (Depression)

"Oh god. They're going to kill us all." (Acceptance)

After that, everyone fell into a brooding silence. Reflecting, presumably, on their mortality, or maybe just the wisdom of choosing stairs over elevators.

Valery had left the door open, but I could see him lurking in the hallway from time to time. At one point, he seemed to disappear for a long stretch, but there was rarely anyone not keeping an eye on us. The 'ding' of the elevator coming and going became a regular occurrence. A few other suits, mostly of a younger demographic, slipped past, carrying laptops and such.

Time passed slowly. There was some lamenting about what had brought each of us to the building that evening. Saffron was unhappy that Colin had forgotten his dental elastics. Colin was unhappy that the fourth-floor orthodontist's office had been closed. Both of them found ways to blame Saffron's ex-husband for the situation. Maryam had worked on most of the new buildings in the area, including this one. She'd chanced into Tim at the bagel shop on the corner where he had brought his laptop because his office lights wouldn't stop flickering. She had offered to help and had regretted it ever since.

Benny and I just stayed in quiet reflection. I think I dozed off at one point.

According to the wall clock, it was shortly after 9 p.m. when the gun-dude finally reappeared. Valery followed right behind, pushing an office cart laden with our cellphones and other items piled beside a stack of file folders, each thick with paper. Saffron sobbed audibly while Maryam gave it one last go. "Look," she said. "You don't need to keep us. None of us is going to do anything. We'll all swear we didn't see anything. Just let us go."

Benny pitched in as well. "We don't know who you are. And I don't particularly care. I'd just like to go home."

The man just held up a single finger, which was enough to quiet the room. "You don't know who I am? Please forgive me. It's been an unusual evening, yes? I forgot introductions. My name is Alexander Yevgeny Mironov. This is my associate Valery Yakovlevich Mikhailov. We work for a group of Ukrainian...let us say...businessmen. And as of this moment, you now work for us."

4

Ukrainian! Dang it! I couldn't believe I'd missed that one. And I didn't feel I deserved any bonus points for having guessed the organized crime involvement—that had been obvious from the start.

"Okay. Let's begin," Alexander, our new mob boss, said. He clapped his hands together with something close to enthusiasm. Almost like he'd just closed a huge real estate deal but was trying not to brag about it. "As I say, I am a businessman. I like simple communication. I will be open and honest, and I wish the same from each of you. Okay? Now, first thing...Kirill Bondarchuk. The man in the wheelbarrow? You remember? Kirill was my second cousin. Nice guy. Good worker. But he did something that angered my boss. What Kirill did is not important. But my boss was not happy. He tells to me to take care of Kirill, which, as you all saw, I have now done."

If Alexander was deeply moved, or even a teensy bit upset about shooting his cousin, he was hiding it well.

"What size of service are you thinking of for him?" Benny interrupted. "I have a few very nice funeral packages. I did that Enid Bellwether memorial just last month. The philanthropist? You maybe saw it on the society pages? No? It was beautiful. All top of the line. From our *Eternal Garden* casket spray to the fifteen bouquets around the hall, all the way down to the small arrangements for each mourner to take home or leave at the gravesite. Almost a hundred of those! It took me days. Extravagant? Sure. But *very* tasteful.

You want something like that? I can probably work the numbers a bit—get you a deal."

Alexander gave a slow blink. "No."

"Sure, okay. Budget's an issue. No problem, I can do something small. Our wreaths are quite special. There are over twenty styles to choose from, or I can do something customized for you. Either way, they come with a stand and everything. I'm sure you'll be very happy."

"No! No funeral. No grave. None of this!"

"I see. Not so much of a *close* cousin then? What about his next of kin? I'm sure his wife would appreciate something. Was he married? Family man? Girlfriend, maybe? I could send her something like what Saffron is holding. Very classy, and really...quite affordable."

"They are very lovely," Saffron said. "My horoscope said that I was going to have a memorable emotional encounter, which might be the source of some extra zeal today. This must be it. I'm a Capricorn, of course...I suppose that's obvious."

Alexander turned to Valery and gave what sounded like a short rant in what was presumably Ukrainian. If I had to guess, it was probably running along the lines of: *My god! Does nobody ever just shut up and listen anymore!?*

Whatever he said, Valery just gave a massive shrug in response. The movement of his shoulders was like watching an earthquake in slow motion. It put an alarming strain on the seams of his suit jacket. Amazingly, no buttons popped off. But maybe he had them sewn on special with Kevlar thread or something.

"No flowers. Understood?" Alexander pinched the bridge of his nose and then gave his forehead a quick rub as if to clear his thoughts. "Perhaps you thought that what happened to Kirill would also now happen to each of you? As I say, I wish to be open and honest. So I tell you this is still *very much* a possibility. But I don't want this. This kind of solution always creates more problems than it solves."

There was clearly loads of experience behind the statement as Valery began nodding sagely in agreement.

"Or maybe some of you were thinking that you now had some kind of power over me? Yes?" Alexander continued. "You saw me do this to Kirill. If I let you go, you will tell the police. They would come and visit me. I tell you now to forget this idea! Even if they believe you, they would find nothing. So, this does not worry me. But maybe your story makes them curious. The police start to pay attention to my business. This I would find inconvenient. My boss would not be happy. I must work very hard to keep my boss happy. So now you must all work very hard to keep me happy. If we all do this, then everything will be fine."

"I don't like you. And I already have a job," Benny said.

Alexander gave him a flat, unwavering stare as he dipped his hand into an inner pocket of his suit jacket. For a scary moment, I thought he was reaching for his gun. A thought that was apparently shared as there was a collective sigh of relief when Alexander's hand emerged, holding his reading glasses. He held out his other hand toward Valery, who quickly selected one of the file folders from the stack. Only when Alexander had opened the cover did he finally shift his eyes away from Benny to the pages inside.

"Benjamin Schlesien. Eighty-one years old. One hundred sixty-eight centimetres tall. Weight, seventy-two kilograms. Sole proprietor of the florist business, his late wife started. Wonderful. No children, but three nieces. Each with families of their own now and what's this I see? Soon you will have another great-grandnephew? How exciting! My fingers are crossed for you that all continues to go so well, Mr. Schlesien. Benny The Jet? The Rocketman? Yes?"

All the colour and energy seemed to have evaporated out of Benjamin Schlesien. Somehow, I doubted it was just the weird Elton John song references. A moment ago, he'd been the feisty old guy and now Benjamin was collapsing into his chair as though he was hoping to disappear completely.

Alexander closed the folder and set it down on the table so carefully you might have thought it was an unstable explosive, which, in some ways, I suppose it was. He gave the cover a two-fingered tap. "You have knowledge of what I did. But now I also now have knowledge. I have your wallet identifications. My team go into your phones and from that onto internet and now I know where you live, where you work. Your banking information. Medical records. Your taxes. How much you owe and to who. All your social media contacts and silly postings. Your emails. Where you shop. To what schools you went. The vehicle you drive. Where you've travelled. All your relations and all of your friends. Everything. Everything about all of you."

"So...what?" Maryam asked. "Are you threatening us?"

"Yes! Exactly so!" Alexander beamed at her like she was the star pupil. "You. Your families. Everyone you know."

Alexander let those words sink in for a full half minute as he slowly circled the table. "What is done, is done. I'm sure we all wished things had been different. But, that ship has sunk...I think is expression? Yes?"

"Not exactly, though I have to say that your version has more punch," I said and instantly regretted giving him a reason to have his attention back my way. The empty stare of those pale eyes was unsettling.

"We'll get to you in a minute," he said, and then turned

his attention back to the group. "As a businessman, I must always be looking for opportunities. So now we must all pull together to move forward. We can help each other, so let us look on this bright side."

"Oh sure, I can tell that you're a real glass-half-full kinda guy," Maryam said.

Alexander held out a hand to receive a folder from Valery in response.

"Maryam Mitra. Thirty-seven. One hundred seventy centimetres tall. Weight..."

"Is that really necessary?" She tried to interject, but Alexander plowed on, undeterred.

"...seventy-one kilograms. A contract electrician currently employed by Richard & Sons out of Sidney. Oh my! So many relatives I hardly know where to begin. None more special than your younger brother Badal, though. I hope you get that promotion you wish for so you can manage a crew of your own. The extra money would be helpful for his upcoming surgery, I think."

He set the folder in front of her and reached out a hand for another. "Thimoty Angulalik. Twenty-nine. One point seven-two meters...and eighty kilos. Our resident computer security specialist. Prefers to go by 'Tim', though his sister calls him 'Ookpik'? Cute. An impressive resume I see. You've come a long way from Iqaluit. To think, this morning I had no idea you existed, never mind worked right here in our building, and now...I know everything about you. Hmmm. Yes, interesting. Maybe I may have a real job for you after we finish with this current situation....but we'll see."

Alexander circled back around the far end of the table and gestured to Valery. The last two folders were handed over.

"Saffron Hendricks and her dear son Colin. Saffron works part-time at a health food store and sells candles through craft websites on the internet. Hmmm. Saffron, this ex-husband of yours? I have to say I don't like what I'm seeing here. Let me know if he misses an alimony payment or anything like that. I'll send Valery to visit. He can be very… *motivating*. As for you Colin, math is very useful. You should study harder at this. And delete all your social networking things—you waste too much time. Ah yes, I almost forget. Valery? You have something for Colin?"

Valery rummaged in a pocket and extracted a small white plastic bag. For a second I thought it was a very odd drug transaction, but then Colin gave a metallic grin in thanks and, in the next moment, was yanking elastic bands onto his braces.

"We overheard you mention this, and Valery ran an errand. You see? We can help each other. For now…go home. We have all your information. Valery will contact you when I need you."

"Why?" Maryam asked. "What do you want from us?"

"This is a good question. You see, between us right now, we are out of balance. All of you have this knowledge of what I did to Kirill. For me, I have only threats against you and your family. These are not the same. But," Alexander continued, raising a finger in a gesture of triumph. "I have a solution. You will do something for me that will fix this. Then balance is restored. No need for threats. And we can all go back to how we were. Simple. Okay? Now, those folders are yours to keep. Take your phones and things. Have a nice weekend. Just remember, if the police show up here, I will blame you. And you will all be joining Kirill. Is this clear? All understood?"

"What about her?" Maryam said, turning an accusatory

glare my way. "How come she didn't get a folder?"

Indeed, I hadn't. While everyone else got a fancy cover filled with reams of paper, mine was just a single sheet that Valery had slid in front of me using all his meaty fingertips to hold it flat, as though he was concerned the tiniest breath might have blown it away. I recognized it as the same piece of paper Alexander had been writing on in his office. It had only two bits of information: the fake name of Danielle Anderson, and my phone number. There was a single heavily weighted question mark bracketing the two lines as though his pen had drawn the symbol over and over.

"Yes. I don't have information for her because I don't know who she is. Clearly, she is a liar, and I think she came here to spy on me. So, for this very good reason, I was thinking of having Valery kill her. This would be a nice example for the rest of you. It would also set a serious and professional tone for our new relationship—which I would like." Alexander nearly made all that sound like a completely sane and rational business decision. I noticed nobody was jumping in to argue.

"But...it's getting late," Alexander continued, giving his watch a hard look. "I have already wasted far too much time on this whole problem. There is a baroque recital at the Alix Goolden Performance Hall. Have you been? The acoustics are wonderful. I have tickets, and I have already missed the first half. So, yes, the pizza girl is a problem, but now I make her *your* problem."

"What does *that* mean?" Maryam asked. She threw another glare my way and rolled her chair back from the table to put some more distance between us.

"It means you are in this together," Alexander said. "If *any* of you contact the police, you will *all* be joining Kirill. No exceptions. This is clear, I think. Yes? So, if you don't want this…and why would you? Then you will all work to keep the pizza girl quiet."

"And…how do we do that?" Tim chipped in. I had to hand it to him. Despite the near-death experience we'd been collectively dancing around, he had managed to keep a lazy grin on his face the whole time.

"That's up to you. Lock her in a basement somewhere—not here, please. Kill her if you want. Or maybe even get her to tell you the truth. You figure it out, I don't care. Okay. Bye-bye. Valery will show you out. Polina!" He yelled as he left us with a lazy wave. The blonde must have been hiding in another office somewhere as a moment later there was a flash of her running after Alexander toward the front lobby.

"Hey, has anyone seen my bag?" Tim said.

Yikes, I'd almost forgotten about that.

"Probably in my van," Benjamin said. "I know Maryam left her tools there. Didn't you?"

"Is that where they found you guys?" I asked, eager to steer the conversation in a different direction. I was clearly still in the doghouse as everyone just ignored me and started collecting their things from the cart. If it had been my fourth-floor stop that delayed their escape, then I could hardly blame them for feeling that way.

I didn't bother to check if they had restocked my bag. I just grabbed it off the cart and followed the rest of them out to the lobby. We had to wait for the elevator to return; I suggested taking the stairs, but Maryam was having none of that.

"You're not going anywhere just yet," she said.

So we waited because when could taking an elevator ever go wrong? Or maybe we were all just secretly hoping the cable would snap for real this time and put us all out of our misery. Valery herded us inside when it arrived and then squeezed in after. Which would have been impossible before, but I didn't have the pizza carrier anymore, so that helped. I ended up in a back corner.

"Well, this is awkward," I said.

"What do you think he'll want us to do?" Tim asked. He seemed to ponder the question as though it was a coding problem or something else academic.

"Something illegal," I said. "Obviously."

"No! Why!?" Saffron said, dragging an uncooperative Colin towards her in a firm hug.

"Because that *has* to be the point of it," I said. "He knows he can't just threaten us indefinitely. At some point, one of us is going to break. So he wants to have something on us that will never go away. Right now, all he knows about us is that we're six fairly boring law-abiding people...more or less. He needs to be sure that we'll all just go away and keep our mouths shut. We know he's a murderer. He wants to have the same sort of leverage on us."

"So we should all go to the police together. Right now?" Saffron said.

"Whoa, whoa. Hold on now," Maryam said. "Let's not do anything rash."

"She's saying that we have to kill someone," Saffron said, pointing at me.

Valery had opted to stand with his back to the door. Not socially conventional perhaps, but it did allow him to better follow the conversation. Something he was doing with obvious amusement.

"No, I didn't. We're not going to kill anybody," I said. I gave Valery what I hoped was a warm smile. "Nobody is killing anybody. Anymore. Okay? I just meant that whatever he'll want us to do will certainly be something shady. Mind you, the body of his cousin, wherever that is, probably needs some hiding. Maybe he'll want us to bury it?"

"Oh, is t*hat* all!?"

"Could be smuggling maybe?" Tim said—a tad optimistically, I thought. "Like driving a carload of drugs over the border. Something easy like that."

"Oh cool! Road trip!" Colin said.

Maryam gave a nod toward me. "You're forgetting something."

"Oh, ya? What's that?" I asked, knowing full well where she was going.

"You said he knows all about us. But that isn't true. Is it? None of us knows *anything* about you," she said.

The elevator whirred to a stop, and the doors opened into a damp underground garage. Valery went off to open the security gate while the rest followed Benjamin over to an ancient fifties-era muted green delivery van. The words *Edna's Fine Flowers* over a pastel bouquet were painted on the sides.

I watched from a distance as Maryam recovered her tool chest and Tim had an inexplicably futile search for his laptop bag. For the first time, his perma-grin seemed to be slipping. The others fell into conversation about giving lifts and drop-offs and so on.

Tim excused himself to ride the elevator back up to his office in hopes of finding his bag. I wished him good luck because sometimes I try to be a team player.

"What about her?" Saffron asked.

"I have a basement we can use," Maryam offered.

"No, no, enough of that sort of talk. There's a simple solution," Benjamin said. He fished out a clipboard from between the seats of the truck and handed me a pen. "Okay, shorty. Let's have it."

"Let's have what?" I said.

"All of it. I don't know what your story is, but it's time for you to tell it. You need to write down all the sorts of things that these guys know about us. We'll give it to Valery. Then all of us here will feel a whole lot better that they'll know how to find you, too."

I looked from one face to another.

"That's only fair. Isn't it?" Benny said.

Ya. Sadly. It probably was. I gave Colin the keys to my scooter and sent him off to collect my wallet from where I'd stashed it with my helmet in the seat trunk. Might as well show some proof to back up the rest, I thought.

"Okay. My name isn't Danny. It's Margot," I said. "Margot Croft. I'm twenty-six. I'm five foot two-ish and the last time I weighed myself was ages ago, but I think it was around a hundred and fifteen pounds—I have no idea what all that is in metric—though I know I should. Sometimes, I work as a courier. Mostly, though…I'm a professional thief." The last part was sort of another lie, but it gave them something to chew on while I wrote down all the rest.

5

It was nearly dark before I found my phone. I had to search all on my own as nobody had volunteered to stick around and help out. Not that I'd asked, mind you.

Once I had finished writing out my CV, there'd been something of an exodus. Benjamin had immediately left in his flower van, along with Saffron and Colin. Well, at least immediately *after* he'd had to do something that had involved booster cables and Maryam's pickup truck. Once it was running, the van popped and spluttered its way off in one direction. Maryam had followed him out from the parking garage in her pickup truck with barely a glance my way. Tim, however, had given me a triumphant wave from the passenger seat. His enthusiastic grin had been firmly back in place since he'd returned from the fourth floor with his laptop bag in hand. If he'd been curious about why or how it had ended up where it did, then he'd kept those questions to himself. Last was Valery, driving a whisper-quiet metallic blue electric Audi—the folded papers of my memoir protruding from his breast pocket.

I don't wear a watch as I generally have my phone to tell me that sort of information. But my guess was that it was getting close to ten. The sun had set long ago, but there was still that leisurely late spring twilight period. I gave the top of the building a squint and tried to triangulate a likely cellphone trajectory. How far from the edge had I been standing? What direction was I facing? How hard did I throw it? Questions that directed me to the west side of the building. The one that the landscapers had ignored and was now just a broad and wild swath of post-industrial nature.

I was spurred on by my promise to the rest of the group that I would find it, and so have a phone to be easily reachable. Well, that, and the fact that there was still a year left of monthly payments. I certainly couldn't afford a new one. Even so, I probably would have given up if Harley hadn't called. I was crawling around under a massive blackberry bush when I saw a light flashing from a short distance away.

I always keep my phone in silent mode. Partially out of intentional sneakiness. Mostly because the little switch had become glued in that position thanks to an encounter with some maple syrup at breakfast one morning. For messages, it just vibrates, but when a call comes in, the little light flashes on and off as well. I followed the blinking like a hyper-focused moth.

"Okay, I give up!" Harley said, by way of a greeting.

It took me a second to remember what I'd texted her when I'd been on the roof hours ago.

"I'm across the harbour," I said, as I dragged myself clear of the blackberries and into the rear car park. It was empty aside from a black BMW sports coupe. The glow from a lit cigarette gave the man in the driver's seat a disturbing film-noir quality. "I'm slumming with the nouveau riche. You?"

"Huh!? Your text made it sound far more exciting. What happened to dinner, by the way? I thought you said you were bringing pizza?"

Oh right. "Ya, sorry I got a bit...delayed. I'm heading home now, though. I can pick up something on the way."

"No worries! And I'm just about to leave, anyway. I was calling because a guy came a few minutes ago looking for you."

"Oh, ya? Chiselled jaw? Shining armour? White horse? Not *that* guy again?" It was an old joke between us that never got a laugh. Just one of those silly roommate bonding things that had become so entrenched it was automatic.

"No. Like for real! He was more...no neck, cheap suit, and a dark sedan. And huge! He just about banged the door down, asked if you lived here, and then took off. It was weird."

I suppose I shouldn't have been surprised that Valery was checking up on me already. After all the whoppers I'd been spinning to Alexander, physically confirming the address I'd written down seemed like an obvious first step for them.

"Ya weird," I agreed. There was no point in scaring Harley with the sordid details of my evening from hell. "Don't sweat it. Probably just a Jehovah's Witness. I hear that they are *really* changing up their game these days. New approach entirely. They're dropping the first half of the whole passive-aggressive thing they used to do."

"Riiiiight. Sure, whatever. Anyway, I'm taking off for the weekend. Some of my surf friends are heading up to Tofino and I'm tagging along. They're leaving super early in the morning, so I'm heading over there to crash on their couch. You'll have the apartment all to yourself. Don't have too much fun without me, though! Okay?"

I assured her that I would try not to, hung up and had a glance back to make sure the cigarette guy in the Beamer was staying put, but his corner of the parking lot was already out of sight. Still, I kept up a brisk pace until I was across the street and back on my Vespa, just in case. Having a gun pointed at me for the first time was making me paranoid.

It was only when I was digging out my helmet and putting the phone away that I noticed the list of missed calls. There were fifteen or so, all from one number that I didn't recognize. Which seemed a tad persistent even for a spam-type robo-caller, so I had to assume they were from Valery. The times matched when I'd noticed him take a long break from his hallway loitering. Presumably, in addition to scrounging dental elastics for Colin, he'd been dialling my number, hoping to track it down from the ringing. But that was before he found out I was going to write everything down for him, anyway.

The Vespa grudgingly spluttered to life on the third try. It was something that normally set my teeth on edge, but right then, I was fully empathetic. I felt dog-tired. I was mentally exhausted, my nerves were fried, and I was starving.

It took all my concentration just to keep a safe distance from the cars speeding across the bridge. But then a flood of pedestrians along Wharf Street had the traffic bumper to bumper and all stop and go. Mostly stop. The foot traffic slowing things down seemed to wear Vancouver Canucks jerseys, so I had to assume that a hockey game had just ended. There are not any real sports bars downtown, but when something significant is going on, a few of them will tune their TVs to whatever is happening. Judging by the volume and degree of drunken giddiness around me, I had to assume that the right team had won and that the victory was somehow significant.

I'm not a huge sports fan in general, and as a devoted non-team player, I tend to only follow those sorts of solo activities that I enjoy myself. Which is a short list limited to crossword puzzles, disc golf, and picking locks. Not all of those are technically sports, and none of them are regularly televised, at least as far as I know.

I got squeezed between a panel van and a city bus—which was claustrophobic, and the diesel fumes were killing me. There was no option of passing, what with drunken revellers clogging the crosswalks and sidewalks and generally making a nuisance of themselves. The bike lane was relatively free, though. I could argue that the Vespa is technically smaller than most bicycles. And certainly, it's slower than the fancy e-bikes. So at that moment, the bike lane seemed like a reasonable option. I did get some unfriendly looks from a few actual cyclists going the other way, but they were lightweight scowls compared to what Maryam had been able to serve. So I wasn't terribly moved.

Going straight home was the most tempting idea. The takeaway food graveyard that was our fridge wasn't so appealing, but the long hot bath I could soak in would be wonderful. I considered that doing so would only delay the unpleasant chore of debriefing with Uncle Rupert. I always try to meet up with him face-to-face right after I've completed a job. Normally, it's something I look forward to, as I can boast about how very clever I've been, and not have to weave together a stinky pile of half-truths. There was also the lure of my Aunt Stacy's cooking to be considered. There are always yummy leftovers to be had. And even this late at night, I knew I'd be welcome. It was a hard choice.

I let the stoplight by the museum decide for me. Green or even a stale yellow and I would have continued straight on through in the direction of the attic apartment that I call *Chez* Harley-Margot. But it was a very bright, cheery, and determined red. So I hung a right and puttered my way into the depths of James Bay.

"Well...?" Uncle Rupert drawled from his favourite chair an hour later.

Eleven p.m. had come and gone and we were both sprawled in the living room after having done a heroic effort to polish off one of Aunt Stacy's lasagnas. She makes it in one of those foil pans that's about the size of a small canoe. Uncle Rupert had already had his dinner long ago, but he didn't want to see me eat alone. So we were both stuffed to capacity. He was lying collapsed with his feet up on the matching overstuffed ottoman. I was in a similar position on the couch. Aunt Stacy and their dog, Pretzel, had gone out for a pre-bedtime lap of the neighbourhood, which gave Uncle Rupert and me a chance to catch up. Aunt Stacy knows we wander across the line of strict legality from time to time, but she thinks it's more about not paying for parking or stealing reception counter pens. She prefers not to know more than that, and we oblige.

"Well....?" Uncle Rupert prompted for a second time. "How'd it go?"

"Piece of cake," I lied. "I was lucky on this one. The wrapper was just leaving when I arrived. There was a bit of kerfuffle with the elevator and I took advantage. I got access to his laptop in the confusion and then USB'd it easy-peasy. So whenever he next logs in, you should be good to go!"

"Hmmm. I see. Well, that's good. Isn't it?"

I knew there was a pretty close to zero chance that I was 'good'. Uncle Rupert can smell deception from several time zones away. He let me simmer and stew for several agonizing minutes, knowing that he-knew-that-I-knew-that-he-knew something was amiss.

He sipped his coffee. I sipped my tea. The gas fire danced merrily.

Finally, he cleared his throat. "Kerfuffle? Hmm. Of what sort? Exactly?"

"Ohhhhh...hardly worth mentioning," I lied. "Just one of those things."

He gave me his 'accountant look'. It's a special mix of head tilt, eyebrow pucker, and lip bite. Typically, he puts it on when some mis-configured formula in one of his spreadsheets tries to tell him that one plus two actually equals seventy-eight or some such.

I tried to adopt a look of mildly confused innocence. "We were just a few too many people in the elevator. A bit of pushing and shoving happened. You know how that goes! So I got out, and, when I did, I saw a chance to nudge the wrapper's bag with his laptop in it along with me. And voila!"

'Wrapper', by the way, is the term we use to refer to whoever is holding the object or information of interest. Uncle Rupert thinks that names like 'target, and 'mark' are too on-the-nose, so to speak. His point is that seldom do we care about the person in question...it's just what she or he *has* that we're interested in. So he likes the idea that they are just the holders or 'wrappers' of what we're after. I admit that sometimes it makes what we do more palatable. And, as a side bonus, when Aunt Stacy overhears us, she thinks we're just discussing the sort of music that they play on the sort of radio stations she never listens to.

"I see," he said. "Hmmm. I probably shouldn't tell you this because it's been useful to me. But I've noticed that your lexicon tends to expand whenever you're fibbing, or intentionally leaving something out. For instance, I've never once heard you use the word *kerfuffle* before. So are you sure there's nothing that went pear-shaped I should know about?"

"All round and smooth," I said. "Just been doing the cryptic crossword a lot recently. Real vocab booster. You should try it!"

I was saved from more lies, as Aunt Stacy and Pretzel have exquisite timing.

"We're back," she called out. "I'm ready for bed myself, but if you two have any room, there's still some pie left over."

Uncle Rupert and I exchanged a glance that said pie won hands-down over any further discussion on a topic neither of us *really* wanted to pursue. So we let it drop.

"Only if you're done with your shop talk, though," Aunt Stacy added.

The 'shop' that she was referring to is one of the larger accounting firms in town: Johansson, Abernathy, Bartlett & Associates. JAB & Ass (as I like to call them because I'm sometimes childish like that) work almost exclusively for lawyers. They're not picky, either. Prosecutor or defender is all good to them, so they're rarely short of work. Most of the time, they can easily handle all the number crunching, Googling and whatever else, all on their own. But not *all* the time. Now and again there is some little nagging problem that gets firmly stuck on the *other* side of that imaginary line between the completely legal and the...maybe not so much. Which is where we come in.

Uncle Rupert *is* an accountant. Has a degree and everything. But he financed his way through university by working for a locksmith. As things played out, the locksmith eventually became his father-in-law, but it was a small operation and never brought in enough income for two families. So Uncle Rupert struck out on his own to join the number-crunching workforce. With his still-damp diploma, he landed a job with a slippery character by the name of Ted Bartlett—later destined to become the 'B' of the aforementioned JAB & Ass empire. Uncle Rupert's locksmith abilities were strongly encouraged back in those early days, and he quickly distinguished himself as a guy who gets things done. Now, some thirty years later, he is still very much a valued employee, despite no longer officially appearing anywhere on the company payroll. Some arm's length distance is desired between a now respectable firm and any kind of potentially murky shenanigans. I believe he shows up on their books under Miscellaneous Expenses. I can only assume I got filed with Petty Cash.

I don't mind though. The work is at least never boring. And most of what we do is fairly harmless. Like say, there's a messy divorce and one side is hiding funds from the other. When all the money is just ones and zeros on the internet, we're not typically needed. But what about when some of those digital dollars get mysteriously converted into trinkets like gold bars or fancy watches and then squirrelled in a safe or deposit box? Well then! The lawyers involved often find such knowledge to be *super* handy.

Or maybe some character has pictures or files that they shouldn't. Blackmail is an ugly, ugly thing. As I see it, our job is helping to beautify the world.

Despite my fatigue and a belly full of Aunt Stacy's cooking, the brisk night air on the drive back to the other side of James Bay had left me wide awake. With Harley gone, our upper-floor apartment felt depressingly lifeless, and I was in no rush to crawl into bed. There was also the spectre of Alexander's flat grey eyes haunting me. I gave the kettle a poke and fired up my laptop while I waited for it to boil for tea.

'Alexander' and 'Valery' put together in a Google search didn't amount to very much. He'd announced their full names, but I couldn't remember any of it. I'd got lost in all those triple-barreled syllables. The heck with just 'Margot'. Maybe I should start introducing myself as Ms. Marguerite Penelope Croft. Maybe not.

There was one name that had stuck in my head. At first, I wasn't sure. Google didn't find a ton of pictures and they were mostly all taken from a distance. But then came a nice close-up, and the resemblance was undeniable. She was standing with her hand looped through the arm of an elderly gentleman. They were both dressed formally and had toothy, though somewhat forced, smiles for the camera. The article was from a Russian online newspaper and had been handily captioned in both Russian and English: *Leonid Yakovlev and his granddaughter Polina Pavlova enjoy a visit to the grand opening of the new Usmanov museum in Saint Petersburg.*

Even after I used the Cyrillic versions of their names, Google didn't have much more to say about Polina Pavlova, but there were loads and loads on Leonid Konstantinovich Yakovlev. But then that wasn't a surprise. You don't wind up being one of the wealthiest Russian Oligarchs without attracting a smidge of press coverage along the way.

Still, other than now knowing that Ms. Pavlova could certainly afford to buy her own damn pizza and flowers...I had no idea at all what that meant.

But it was certainly curious.

6

The weekend held one major victory for me. And it arrived first thing Saturday morning.

I was midway through performing the bizarre ritual needed to coax our coffee machine into action when Uncle Rupert called to let me know that Tim Angulalik—the friendly cyber security dude whose laptop computer I'd messed with—had logged in.

Which, in itself, maybe doesn't sound radically exciting. But the breath-holding bit was that not only had Tim turned on his computer, but he had followed that up by diligently working away *for over an hour.* This was hugely significant. It meant that whatever security software that a professional like Tim would have running (and you would expect there to be tons of that) had been successfully duped. No small feat. But then Uncle Rupert's computer geek friend Marty is, so he claims, the very best at what he does.

"So good job there, Margot," Uncle Rupert said. "I guess everything went fine. Just like you said, huh?"

I didn't answer right away. Besides all the other things I had held back from telling him about last night, there was one new, additional, tiny hitch to add to the pile. When I'd woken, I had discovered all my personal bric-à-brac floating around inside my go-bag, but none of my tools of the trade. No lock picks, no electronic gizmos, not even the USB thumb drives. I'd been too frazzled by everything that had happened or I would have realized last night that it was lighter than it should be.

"Maybe not entirely fine. Marty might be a shade upset with me," I said. "It's possible that I misplaced some of his toys."

Marty is Uncle Rupert's oldest childhood friend, but somehow the two of us have never hit it off. I have yet to nail down exactly why. What is clear to both of us is the fact that one of us is amazing and irreplaceable and the other is a pain in the ass. If I ever develop any doubts about which of us is which, I have Marty to remind me—something he does every time we meet. As such, I try to keep visits to his basement lair in Oak Bay to a bare minimum.

"Is that all?" Uncle Rupert chortled. "You had me worried. I'm sure Martin will be only too happy to get you the latest and greatest replacement. He loves to upgrade. What is it you lost?"

"I'll have to check," I said. I couldn't find it in me to say: *Everything*.

"Uh huh," Uncle Rupert said. The skepticism of last evening was back in voice. "Well...I'll call him later and soften the news. I wouldn't want to interrupt him just now while he's happily working away on the job."

I hadn't got the full rundown on what the job was all about, but I'd gathered that it had something to do with system log files and a corrupted hard drive. All of which belonged to whoever was on the other side of the legal dispute in question. The client on our side of things had been informed that one Tim Angulalik, an independent cyber-security consultant, had been enlisted to help sort things out. Being lawyers and all, our clients naturally assume that everyone involved is always lying. In this case, they suspected that Tim hadn't been hired by the opposing council to try to recover information so much as to make sure that it was permanently erased. They tasked me with providing access to Tim's network so that Marty could peek over his virtual shoulder and ensure that everything Tim did was all tickety-boo (as we professionals in the industry like to refer to such things).

The important part, as far as I was concerned, was that with Tim's laptop now in sneaky communication with Marty's system, my job was done. With that good news out of the way, Uncle Rupert and I wished each other a nice weekend, and I returned to pondering the coffee situation.

Harley nicknamed our machine Lucifer—Lou for short. She'd found it at a rumble sale a local church was holding. That there was a religious connection gave rise to our working theory that the low sale price, of what should have been a very expensive machine, is the result of demonic possession and a failed exorcism. It's ridiculous. Obviously. Though, on my frequent outings to the library, I do find myself giving the church a wide berth…just in case.

Uncle Rupert didn't explicitly mention it, but when a job gets done successfully and quickly, there is usually a bonus in the form of a little extra in my paycheck. With that in mind, I let the coffee machine score another victory, got dressed, and took my crossword book to the little bookshop-café around the corner. I was sufficiently buoyed by the thought of positive cash flow that I splurged on a cranberry muffin to go along with my cappuccino.

"New boyfriend?" the owner asked as I fumbled for my wallet.

I visit the Black Canoe Café just often enough to be recognized with a smile and a nod. That I knew she was the owner, and that her name was Hannah, was only because I'd overheard conversations with the real regulars.

"How's that?" I said.

Hannah leaned over the counter towards me to stage-whisper. "The hunky guy waiting outside? You two are about the only ones here, not at retirement age. He's only had eyes for you the whole time you've been in line. Is he not with you?"

When I turned, I caught a blur of someone disappearing from the open doorway. Just an impression of average height, medium build, darkish hair, and a leather jacket. It could've been almost anyone. But it definitely wasn't a massive Ukrainian named Valery, which was a relief.

Still, to be on the safe side, I slunk my way over to the lounge area by the book racks for a stakeout. There was an overstuffed chair by the window where I could sit half-hidden behind a fern and watch the sidewalk outside. After ten minutes of watching regular people having a regular morning, I realized I was being an idiot. Whoever it was, they had probably just mistaken me for someone else. Assuming they'd even been looking at me at all. Hannah did have something of a matchmaker vibe to her. Ridiculous. I opened the crossword book. Drank my coffee. Ate my muffin.

I was doing okay in my little bubble of denial until I ran into: *Take small bits out of tipsy cake lacking yeast (4)*. The answer—if you remove the letters of *yeast* from *tipsy cake* and do some rearranging—was: *pick*. Which brought to mind my missing lock tools, and had me mentally replaying the events of last evening all over again.

In the familiar comfort of the café, surrounded by the buzz and hum, it all seemed just like a very strange dream. One of those where you wake up and for a moment you have a problem separating out reality. The missing tools were real enough. So I suppose the rest of it was as well. I wondered if anyone in the elevator group had enough common sense to ignore the threat and call the police anyway—I know I didn't.

The thoughts followed me around for the rest of the day, and I was still moping and brooding about it Sunday morning.

Lou the coffee machine took pity on me and produced a double shot on its very first try. As it spluttered and barked out my espresso, I was reminded of the fateful bangs on the elevator.

We'd all heard the shots. But what had we really seen, anyway? A guy in a wheelbarrow and a guy with a gun. Both of which were now presumably buried in wildly separate locations. Alexander had been right to say he wasn't really worried about us. He shouldn't be. So, he scared us. He had his fun. There wasn't going to be any phone call to have us do some mysterious errand. He would just let us all quietly cower in fear. Probably for years to come.

It was annoying, but I didn't see any solution aside from trying to pretend it hadn't happened.

I set my jaw and opened a fresh browser tab on my laptop. A replacement pizza carrier took me less than two minutes to locate and order. The electronic doodads were Marty's, so I'd deal with that only when I had to.

Replacing my lock picks was a more vexing challenge. It was a kit that had taken me years to put together. A perfect mix of the latest and greatest, together with the tried and true. There were even a few tension levers that had once been Uncle Rupert's. They were the first ones that he'd given me back when I was learning. I kept those more for the good luck charm aspect than their functionality. But they were linked with warm memories of the two of us in his den, shoulder to shoulder, facing whatever challenge he'd mounted on his workbench. The picks, combs, rakes, tension levers, extractors, and other tools—all neatly lined up like surgical instruments before an operation.

For a heartbeat, I considered breaking into the office building to retrieve them. Of course, if the doors were locked, then I was in a textbook catch-22 situation. Since my futzing with Tim's laptop had been successful, I saw no reason to return to that building. Or see any of them again. Ever.

I gritted my teeth and ordered a standard covert kit from an American company that I've dealt with a few times. They're crazy expensive, but they're also one of the very few companies that make tools that are actually useful in the field. Most lock picks are angled perfectly so long as you're sitting comfortably at a well-lit worktable, or if you're happy kneeling. When I'm actually working, neither of those things is true. So I entered my credit card and crossed my fingers. My bonus was taking a serious hit before it even reached my bank account.

With that done, it was time to put all of that off my mind and move on. I grabbed my bag of discs out of the closet and set off on the Vespa, heading north and out of town.

Disc golf is just like regular golf. But instead of a ball that you whack with a club, you have a selection of small Frisbees that you throw by hand. And rather than a tiny hole cut in the ground, you aim for a basket. Typically, those are a sort of steel and chains contraption that often looks something like a medieval scarecrow. The course I was heading to used a different design. The 'holes' are simple poles that stick up high out of the ground and give a pleasing 'gong' whenever a disc hits them. Otherwise, the general concept of regular golf and disc golf is identical—the better you are, the less time you spend playing.

On my first time around the nine-hole course, I'd been

caught by a pair of lanky women in matching ball caps. They were both grimly focused and threw their discs with astonishing distance and accuracy. I watched them power their way right past without so much as a glance my way. Which wasn't rude, or even surprising, as I was completely out of sight at the time. My aim is getting better, but distance is still a weakness. And the harder I throw, the more I find myself enjoying little adventures digging through the forest underbrush, searching for errant discs.

Hoping for a better score, I took another lap around the course and got stuck behind a mixed group of four who appeared to be downing a beer per hole. They were just teeing off on the seventh hole when the clouds that had been darkly threatening all afternoon finally decided to follow through. A misty drizzle sent them wobbling toward the parking lot. I hoped one of them was sober enough to be a designated driver, but I had my doubts. It seemed safer to let them get a head start on the road, so I stayed on. Besides, I always like to finish what I start.

The rain was coming down properly when I got back to the parking lot. The only vehicle left was my Vespa, sitting alone and damply forlorn beside a pile of smouldering cigarette butts someone had dumped from their ashtray. At least they'd taken their empty beer cans with them.

When I opened the seat trunk to get my helmet, my phone was buzzing and flashing underneath. It showed five missed calls from a number I didn't recognize. The same number had sent a group text. "All of you come to office. Now."

The sender had then considered the possibility of confusion as he'd followed up with a second message. "This is Valery."

So it wasn't over after all. It was difficult not to feel

disappointed.

I drove back into town and this time parked the Vespa right by the front doors of their office building. I ignored the elevator and trudged my way up the stairs. If there was some cosmic relationship between playing nine holes of disc golf and then climbing nine flights of stairs, the significance was lost on me. Perhaps nine was in my horoscope. I made a mental note to ask Saffron.

"Finally! We were starting to worry about you." Benny said, by way of greeting.

They were all clustered near the far end of the reception counter. A spot that was equidistant from where the wheelbarrow had been, and where Alexander and Valery were standing like a pair of hounds guarding the gates of hell. Tim and Colin each gave me a small wave. Maryam just narrowed her eyes. And Saffron was looking as though she was wishing she was anywhere else—which was a sentiment I deeply shared.

"I have made a decision," Alexander said, brandishing a folded newspaper like a conductor's wand. "If you all do one thing for me, then I promise our business together is finished."

"And what is that?" Maryam asked.

"Through here," Alexander said and directed us to follow.

He led us past the conference room where we'd spent so many fun-filled hours waiting on Friday night. At the end of the hall, a door opened into what was presumably the office lounge. It was a windowless rectangle, painted in a sombre dark green. The centre of the room was dominated by a soft leather couch flanked by several matching reclining chairs around a low live-edge style coffee table. A long bar stretched along one wall with more than enough alcohol to start up a nightclub. All of it was clearly there for one purpose—to enjoy the big-screen television that did its best to fill one wall.

"Get me this..." Alexander said and pointed to the television.

There was a long pause as we all stared blankly. Valery, or someone, had been watching the sports channel as it was paused on a wide shot of the interior of a stadium somewhere.

"That?" Benny said. The relief in his voice was almost overwhelming. "Just that? Exactly the same? I mean, the one you got looks fine. That's a great TV."

"Sure," Maryam said with a chuckle. "What is it...a Sony? Ninety inches maybe? No problem. I mean, they're making over a hundred inches these days. We can get you an upgrade. Probably two or three thousand, but we can all chip in. Right, gang?"

I watched Alexander drop his head forward and rub his forehead against the heel of his hand.

"He's not talking about the TV," I said. My chest tightened as the realization washed over me. It felt as though I'd just chugged a gallon of ice water.

Alexander took a few steps closer to the screen and pointed up to the centre of the screen. He muttered something in Ukrainian under his breath before saying more audibly; "No! Not the television. That. There."

"But...that's Madison Square Gardens. In New York," Tim said, uncertainly.

As if on cue, we all leaned closer to the television. The arena was set up for hockey. Along the bottom, a pair of Zamboni's were frozen in place, their paths visible like snail trails across the ice surface. Retired jersey numbers hung from the starburst rafters along the top of the screen. Other than the half-filled seats with fans coming or going, the only other notable object was the jumbotron display.

"You can't mean...*that*!?" Maryam said, pointing to what was filling the screen of the jumbotron.

Alexander nodded in agreement. "Yes! Go get this for me and bring it here."

Tim's expression was a deer-in-the-headlights look of wonder. "He wants us to steal...the Stanley Cup."

7

Alexander paused to glance at his wrist. His watch was one of those thin and elegant ones that you see on models in high-end fashion magazines. That kind that seem to do very little besides tell the time, though this one apparently had a date function. "You have ten days."

"What!?" Maryam yelled. "You can't possibly be serious. Ten days or ten years. Nobody is going to steal the Stanley Cup. I mean…how?"

"Of course I'm serious," Alexander said. "How you do it? I don't care. And I don't wish to know. Just have this trophy here on Wednesday after next."

Tim and Benny were exchanging nearly identical open-mouthed blank stares of incomprehension.

"But that's a crime," Saffron said. "No, no, no. I don't want to commit a crime. We can't do a crime. Colin can't be involved in a crime. He has school."

"Then, I suggest you don't get caught," Alexander said. He threw in a small shrug and an eyebrow lift to clarify that this really should be very self-evident. "Just do it and don't bother me until it's done."

"But how?" I asked.

"Here, take this," Alexander said and handed me the newspaper. "Call Valery if you have problems. He'll give you the number. Out you go now. Bye-bye."

Saffron wrapped her son in a protective hug and all but ran him out of the room. For his part, Colin let himself be pushed along, though he was in a zombie-like state with an expression of almost rapture.

"Oh, my god. This is *so* cool," he said.

The rest of us followed them out to the elevator in varying stages of numbness. Only Tim seemed to have already moved past the shock and incredulity stage and reached the practical planning step. He turned to me as we piled into the elevator.

"So? How do we do it?"

"How do we do *what*?" I said.

"You're the thief, aren't you? Isn't that what you told us?"

Right. I had said something like that, hadn't I?

"Not exactly. But I can see now where you might have gone off on that tangent."

"You *literally* said you were a professional thief," Colin said. If he was trying to keep the disappointment out of this voice, he failed spectacularly.

"Yes. Maybe. In truth, I've never actually *stolen* anything," I said. "Or at least I've never taken anything that actually belonged to whoever had it. I'm more...surveillance and recovery. I sometimes need to go places where I'm not technically supposed to, but that's it."

"It doesn't matter," Saffron said. Her face was flushed and her eyes had gone wide in a slightly manic way. "We're not stealing anything. Right! Right?"

The elevator bonged to a stop on the ground floor.

"It's dinnertime," Benny said, as we piled out. "I'm hungry. Let's all go get something to eat and we can talk about this...situation."

Victoria has more restaurants by population than any other city in Canada. There are loads of them. One restaurant for every two hundred and seventeen people. This means that, in theory, providing everyone communicates and staggers their mealtimes, the entire city could eat out for dinner on the same day. This was apparently what was happening when we got downtown. Only the important 'everyone communicates' part had been completely ignored. There were lineups outside every restaurant that we could find that met our collective criteria.

Benny wanted steak. Tim had a hankering for sushi. Colin required either pizza or spaghetti. Saffron would only consider a strictly vegan menu. Maryam and I saw eye to eye for the first time—we didn't care in the slightest. At least we didn't care so long as it was a licensed establishment. I'm generally not much of a drinker, but discussing how to deal with Alexander's fantasy was going to require something more bracing than just a cup of tea.

After thirty minutes of wandering the downtown core with no luck, we were all getting cranky. Benny had been lagging further and further behind with each block. We waited for him to catch up and I noticed the slight hitch in his step that he was trying to hide.

"I'm not sure this is working," I said.

"All the places that can make everyone happy have lineups," Maryam said. "Why don't we just pick one and wait?"

"I'm hungry now," Colin said. "Why can't we just go to someone's house and everyone can order delivery?"

"The kid's right," Benny said, as he joined us. "My shop isn't far. The design room in the back has a big table we can use. Everyone go get whatever you want."

An hour later and the heady floral scents of Benny's flower shop that first overwhelmed us were crushed by the aromatic weight of various outsourced greasy foods. I had made a halfhearted effort on a fish taco, but my appetite wasn't up to the challenge. While the rest of them finished eating, I cracked open the newspaper Alexander had given me. He'd left it open on the sports page—a fluff piece about all the varied and exciting places the Stanley Cup has visited. I'd had just moved on to the crossword when Maryam took charge.

"How do we get out of this mess?" she said. "Just blurt out whatever comes to mind. Blue-sky thinking. No ideas are bad."

She'd run out to a local liquor store while we were waiting for the food orders to arrive. Now she was wielding a can of cider in one hand, and an erasable marker in the other. She began by writing each of our names across the top of the whiteboard that Benny used for bouquet design.

"Shouldn't we just call the police?" Saffron said.

"Okay, maybe some ideas are bad," Benny said.

"No, listen," Saffron said. "I have a cousin who's a cop. We could explain everything to him."

"Ummm…Trevor rides a scooter and gives out parking tickets. He's a meter maid, Mom."

"Parking enforcement officer," Saffron corrected.

"No police," Maryam said. "We've been over this! He has all that information about you—about all of us—and he has people who will do whatever he wants. Alexander isn't some petty thug. He's a mob boss, for Pete's sake. Even if he got sent to jail, he could still make our lives miserable…or worse."

A moody silence followed as we all considered what form 'or worse' could take.

"We might think about it like a security challenge," Tim said.

"A what challenge?"

"When you're trying to protect a computer system, you

have to think about all the obvious ways that someone might get in, but also you need to try to imagine the *less* obvious approaches. Because there's never a fully secure network, someone will always come up with something you didn't think of. Some completely different angle."

"Does anybody know what he's talking about?" Benny asked.

"Maybe we can find one of those ideas," Tim continued, undeterred. "The key is that you need to define, as accurately as possible; the goal, the challenges, and what success will look like."

"Oh, I think we got all that covered," Maryam said. "The goal is to steal the Stanley Cup. The challenge is that we have no flipping idea how. And success will look like none of us dying."

"It's not *exactly* that though, is it?" Saffron said. "The goal I mean. Alexander wants us to steal the Stanley Cup because that will make him happy. So, isn't it just that we need to make him happy? Isn't that the goal? Maybe we can come up with some other idea that would make him happy."

"Hey, ya. That's good Mom," Colin said. Mother and son exchanged smiles and even a fist bump.

"Great!" Tim said, his grin firmly in place. "So, how do we do that?"

"I was at a workshop in Oregon once," Saffron said. "We had a session to dream up new ideas to combine natural elements with soaps and candles. So they split us into groups of two. *Powerpods,* they called them. They said it's better for brainstorming than trying to do it alone or with more than two people! Why don't we do that? We'll take an hour in groups of two and then pool our ideas?"

"Soaps and candles?" Maryam said.

"It's worth a try," Benny said. "Maybe it will come to that. I mean, aside from a Stanley Cup, what do you get for the mob boss who has everything?"

Saffron waved a hand as though she were hailing a cab. "What's everyone's star sign?"

"Oh god no," Benny muttered under his breath.

Being Scorpios, Tim and Colin were paired together, while Maryam went with Saffron as Taurus and Capricorn are both earth signs. Which left Benny with me.

"Margot is a Leo, which is a fire sign," Saffron said.

"Obviously," Maryam agreed. Apparently serious.

"So fire and air are compatible. It all works out!"

"Wait," Tim said. "Benny is an Aquarius? How can *Aquarius* possibly be an *air* sign?"

"It doesn't seem right to me either," Benny said. "But I'll take my chances. C'mon Leo, let's go upstairs."

Benny led the way up a narrow metal stairway that ran along the brick of the rear wall. We could hear Tim trying to point out that even if there had been some weird correlation between what constellation the sun was passing through and personality traits, over the centuries axial precession had messed it all up long ago. In reply, Saffron announced she and Maryam would work best elsewhere and would go find a café.

Benny's apartment above the flower shop turned out to be a simple three-room layout. The stairway opened into a long combined space that served as a kitchen, living room, and office. There were two doors side by side that opened to a bedroom and bathroom. Along the opposite wall were three equally spaced windows that overlooked the street below. The furniture was an eclectic mix of elegant mid-century modern and rough but functional country-cottage.

Books, magazines, and newspapers filled every available shelf or table. It wasn't hard to guess how Benny passed the time. I sat at a well-worn kitchen table made of thick planks and sipped my cider while Benny made himself a cup of tea.

I'd offered him a can of cider from Maryam's six-pack, but he declined.

"I gave up alcohol years ago. It became a bit of a crutch. But I was never an actual alcoholic or anything."

I must have looked skeptical.

"No, really, it wasn't like that. You laugh all you want. Edna and I knew what we were doing. We had a lot of great years. So many great years...but not enough."

Benny's always expressive eyebrows seemed to sag. I sipped my cider and looked around to give him a moment. There was a single framed black-and-white photograph on the wall near the bedroom door of a woman standing in a field. She was dressed in coveralls, holding a clipboard, and wearing an open-faced helmet of some kind. The look on her face was one of youthful, mischievous excitement.

"When did she...you know...pass?" I asked.

"Pass," he repeated with a sigh. "Never liked that one. But I suppose it's better than some others. Edna left me twenty years ago now."

"I'm sorry."

"Ya," Benny said, nodding slowly. "Me too."

We shared a long silence that grew increasingly awkward. I was starting to fidget when Benny gave a little shake of his head, as though to clear some thought. "So...the Stanley Cup. Why is that?"

"Why is what?"

The lines around Benny's eyes furrowed in puzzlement. "I've been thinking. I read a lot. All sorts of different things...

fiction, history, all that. From what I gather these days, organized crime activities are usually organized, but not always a crime."

"Huh? You sure? It's, you know, kind of in the name."

"I've read about guys like him—this Alexander whatever-his-name-is guy. It's like what he said. He thinks of himself as a businessman. The Russian mafia, or Ukrainian mafia, mafia this...mafia that...whatever. They're all about making money. If they find some angle that turns a healthy profit, they'll do it—legal or illegal, they make no distinction. It could be flipping fine art, or importing wine, things that are all completely above board. Or...not. Stealing cars, selling drugs, or god only knows whatever else. They don't care."

"Still not quite with you," I said.

"Well, ask yourself...how is he going to profit from having the cup? Where's the angle here? The Stanley Cup is one of the most, if not *the* most, recognizable sporting trophies in existence. So what's he going to do with it?"

"Sell it maybe?"

"To who? For how much?" Benny batted the idea away with a wave of his hand. "It's like boosting the Mona Lisa. Sure, it's valuable, but nobody other than a crazy person would buy it. I'm not seeing it. And if it's just to make us do something illegal and stupid so he'll have something on us in case one of us panics and tries to sell him out...well...there's got to be simpler things he could have us do?"

"Maybe he's just a hockey fan, and he wants it for his lounge?"

"Maybe," Benny said and chuckled as he nodded. "Sure was a nice television he had. I mean, why go to a game when you can watch something like that?"

"You know, I'll bet if you lose the whiteboard downstairs, you could squeeze a TV like that on the wall between the coolers."

"And then you could break in and steal it?" He said it with a chuckle, but then he gave me a squinty look. "Alright, let's have it. You're a thief who's not a thief. What's all that about?"

I took a last sip of my cider and rolled the empty can in my hands.

"It's pretty simple, really. My Uncle and I work for a company that helps lawyers. Sometimes that means blurring a few legal lines."

"How'd you wind up doing that?"

"My parents split up when I was young. They both work in aviation. My Mom flies float planes and my dad's a helicopter mechanic. They were both often gone, particularly during the busy summer months when I was off school. So I used to spend summers with my uncle and aunt here in town. My uncle was trained as a locksmith. Playing around in his workshop became my summer camp."

"And he taught you to steal things?"

"No, no, no. Just how to open locks."

"All locks?"

"Anything that uses a key. And most things that don't."

Benny thought about that for a long minute. There were some muted yells of excitement from the flower shop below.

"What about filing cabinets? I got one in the corner over there. Edna hid the keys somewhere. It used to be unlocked, but one day I guess I pushed it closed."

It was a standard three-drawer filing cabinet with a single push-button style key lock at the top. One of those where you don't need the key to lock it, you just have to push the entire key cylinder flush. A simple lever and bar mechanism holds the drawers shut. There are a few ways to get them open without even needing to look at the lock, but where's the fun in that?

"Got any paper clips?" I asked.

Five minutes later, the lock popped open with a satisfying 'chunk' sound. It actually took me only about half a minute of fiddling. Filing cabinet locks, even the quality Richelieu one that Benny had, are not the most challenging. If I'd had my tools, it would have been much quicker. But paperclips or not, I could only start after I'd given a thorough explanation of how locks worked and why I needed two paperclips and not just one like in the movies because Benny wanted to know. I left the drawers closed and stepped over to one of the windows to what I hoped was a respectful distance.

Outside, I could see Maryam and Saffron crossing at the street corner and heading back our way. When I turned to tell Benny, I saw him standing transfixed beside the filing cabinet, one hand moving so gently across the top that it was almost a caress. I thought he was about to open the drawer, but with a quick, decisive movement, he reset the cabinet lock with a firm push with the heel of his hand.

"Another time. You're okay kid." Then he added, "I don't care what the others say." Which kind of ruined it.

Benny and I had somehow avoided doing anything that anyone would consider remotely constructive. When we rejoined the others, I was having flashbacks to that adrenalin rush I used to get in high school when I'd show up for class without my homework. Maryam was holding a notebook that was filled with an impressive amount of text and little drawings. Though when I peeked closer, it seemed most of it was scratched out by a flurry of scribbled lines.

"Who wants to go first?" Saffron said.

"We will," Tim said. Only he and Colin seemed upbeat. Though with Tim's usual half smile, it was hard to tell if that was just the status quo or whether there was something to actually be happy about. Colin, on the other hand, was clearly bursting at the seams.

"We've done it!" Colin said.

"What have you done?" Saffron asked with a healthy dose of motherly angst in her tone.

"Colin's idea," Tim said. "The rest of you each owe me eighty-seven fifty."

"For what?" Saffron said.

Colin gestured with both hands at Tim's phone lying on the table. "We went online. We bought it! We bought the Stanley Cup!"

8

If Tim and Colin were expecting the rest of us to be dancing for joy, then they had *way* overestimated our processing speed.

"What in the world *are* you talking about?" Maryam said. Which was pretty much my question as well.

"We bought a Stanley Cup. Not *the* Stanley Cup. Obviously," Tim said. "A replica. There's a fair variety of them out there on Amazon and eBay. I guess Amateur hockey leagues buy them for fun, and there's probably a home market for those fans hosting viewing parties."

"Overnight shipping too," Colin said. "It'll be here tomorrow. Not as much fun as actually stealing the real one, of course. But, problem solved!"

"Most of the replicas out there are mass-produced cheap plastic things," Tim said. "But we found this guy on Craigslist in Calgary that has one in real silver. It looks exactly like it. It's amazing."

"Look," Colin said, holding up Tim's phone like he had pulled Excalibur from the stone.

He scrolled and zoomed, and then we all huddled around to see the image of a shiny trophy. I had to admit; it did look pretty good. Some views were slightly out of focus, but most of the angles showed a Stanley Cup sparkling under studio lights on a bed of black velvet as though it were a high-end jewelry piece.

"This was how much?" Saffron said.

"Four hundred and thirty-seven dollars and fifty cents,

with shipping," Tim said. "A bargain when you think about it."

"Tim said that you and I count as one, Mom. So he split the total five ways, not six."

"If that's alright with everyone else?" Tim said.

Benny gave a rumbly sigh. "That part is fine, but what makes you think that this Alexander fellow is going to be fooled—even for one second—by this fake one?"

"It looks pretty real in the photos," Maryam admitted. "I saw the actual cup a few years ago when I was in Montreal. They brought it out between periods. I wouldn't say this one was any different. And I doubt Alexander has been any closer to the real one than I was."

"A Habs fan, eh?" Benny said. "Edna was from Montreal. We never missed a game."

"No, Leafs. I flew out to see Toronto blank them four-zip when they were together in the first round a few years ago."

"Ah," Benny said. I noticed his mouth briefly pucker as though he'd just tasted something unpleasant.

"The playoffs are just about to start," Maryam said. "Which is maybe why he thought we could pull it off. That was the last game of the Western Conference he was watching. It's the New York Rangers and Vancouver Canucks in the final. So the cup will be close by at some point."

"Won't Alexander wonder about how we got the trophy so fast?" Saffron said.

"He said he didn't want to know the details, remember?" Tim said. "Besides, we don't have to give it to him until next week. I had it sent here to your flower shop address, by the way. Is that alright Benny? I thought giving my office address wasn't a good idea, as they're in the same building and all."

"That's fine," Benny said. "But there is the one other pesky issue that we've sort of glossed over."

"Which is what?" Maryam said.

It wasn't hard to guess where Benny's thoughts were going so I jumped in. "Assuming we get a perfect replica that fools Alexander. What happens later? When he watches the next hockey game and sees the real one on display? He's bound to be a tad curious. No?"

"I'm actually concerned he'll be more angry than curious," Benny said.

"Maybe not," Colin said. He was slouching back in his chair with his cellphone in both hands. Eyes glued to the screen. "I mean there's three of them. Well, two really. He'll probably just assume he's got the other one."

"What!?"

Colin briefly held up his phone and gave it a waggle, which I was beginning to understand was teenage shorthand for 'I looked it up'. Then he went back to scrolling.

"It's all here on Wikipedia," he said. "The original cup was just the bowl part. Lord Stanley bought it—The Dominion Hockey Challenge Cup—to give to Canada's best amateur team. Over the years, they added bands underneath it to hold all the winners, but it got so long it was known as the 'stovepipe cup'. So they redesigned it and now every thirteen years they retire one of the bands, so it stays the same size."

"Honey, what does that have to do with anything? You said there were different ones?" Saffron said.

"I'm getting to that. The first cup was from eighteen ninety-two...like over a hundred and forty years ago, and it all got too delicate. So that one got retired in nineteen sixty-three when they made a copy."

"A copy?"

"Ya, the new one is what everyone sees getting carried around on the ice and things. They call that one the presentation cup."

"But you said there were three?" Tim asked.

"Then they made a copy of the copy. Because the presentation cup travels most of the year, they wanted something for visitors to the Hockey Hall of Fame to look at when the other one is gone. So there's the original cup, though that one is on display in pieces, and then there's the presentation one that you see on TV, and then there's the display copy they just put out when the presentation cup isn't there."

"So…if Alexander knows any of that," I said slowly as I worked it through. "Then he wouldn't think there is anything weird about seeing a copy."

"Well, there we are!" Saffron beamed and gave Colin's shoulder a motherly squeeze of pride.

"I guess it's job done, then?" Maryam said. "Nice work, you guys."

I got home to find Harley wobbling on a surfboard in the middle of our living room. Our modest collection of hand-me-down and thrift store-sourced furniture had all been piled to one side. She'd stripped the couch of cushions, pillows and blankets and had jammed them all under the rug in a fair approximation of a wave.

"Cool huh?" she said. "I bought it off a guy I met on the beach. It's a little beat up, but I got it for next to nothing. Want to try?"

Did I want to pretend I was surfing as though I had

regressed to middle school? As though I was playing the floor-is-lava game or some other childish thing?

"Of course I do," I said.

This is why I keep her around. Harley can't cook or clean or remember to buy toilet paper. But she's fun. On my own, I'd have gone to bed early with my crossword or a book. Or spent the rest of the evening re-aligning the contents of my sock drawer. Instead, we spent an hour taking turns practicing our questionable balancing skills, which involved countless wipe-outs and nearly continuous laughter. We kept it up until a thump on the floor from Mrs. Carter's broom handle told us it was past her bedtime.

"So good weekend?" I asked, taking an out-of-breath seat on the floor beside her.

"Ya, it was fun. You should come next time. There wasn't room in their van for another body, and I know you don't like new people. But maybe we can borrow a car and go on our own? It's kind of a long way for your scooter...although that'd be fun to try! How about you? What'd you get up to?"

With the fake trophy on order, it almost felt like the whole weird debacle had been sorted out and the danger was gone—I nearly confided everything to Harley right then. This is another reason why I value our friendship so much. She is the only person I've ever known who is completely honest in word and thought. With the rest of the world, I tend to miss the conversation cues that others seem to find so easily. Apparently, my radar for sarcasm and subterfuge is wonky. With Harley, that never matters.

"Oh, gosh! I forgot to say, when I got back, another guy was looking for you. No, not Prince Charming," Harley quickly added when she saw my expression. "Or that gigantic bald dude, either. He was kinda...studly."

Studly guys don't generally follow me around. Nor do hunky ones either, I realized. Which brought me back to Hannah's comment about the man who'd been spying at the café.

"What did he look like? What did he say?" I asked.

I must have put more edge in my voice than I intended because Harley did this side twist with her mouth that she does when things aren't adding up.

"Hmmm. I don't know...like I said, he was a good-looking guy. Late twenties maybe, fairly tall, decent build. He just asked if you were home. He didn't give his name or anything. That's two guys who have come around for you now. What's going on?"

"I don't know," I said. And I didn't. "Maybe it's just a work thing. I'll call my uncle in the morning. I'm sure it's nothing."

Never one to waste her time analyzing things that don't fit into whatever moment she's having, Harley had already moved on.

"Okay! Want to watch Point Break with me? Keanu and Patrick Swayze robbing banks and surfing. Maybe we can pick up some tips?"

I expect Harley was referring to surfing, but the other part sounded interesting, too. You never know what might be handy to learn.

"If you fix the couch, I'll make the popcorn," I said.

I spent most of Monday running errands. Harley had scored a victory against the coffee machine, but only after enough failed attempts that we had run out of coffee. So I did a grocery run, a library stop, and then a pharmacy visit to replace some of the things in my bag that Alexander had returned, but now seemed tainted.

Lastly, I swung past Uncle Rupert's in time for afternoon tea. There were no new assignments for us, which was just as well as my replacement pizza delivery bag and lock picks had yet to arrive. But he insisted, by way of a very strong suggestion, that I pay an in-person visit to Marty, and see about restocking my supply of his electronic gizmos.

There was no other way around that problem. Even if I could find a supplier to replace them, they were likely much more than I would possibly be able to afford. And regardless, I knew Marty had heavily tweaked, modified, and configured them all to suit his nefarious purposes—so he would need to be involved at some point.

I dropped the groceries at the apartment and then chugged the Vespa over to Oak Bay. Marty let me stew on the landing outside his basement apartment for several long minutes. I knew it was intentional because he has security cameras covering every possible exterior angle, and any motion triggers a twittery bird-like alarm that you can hear even from outside. The alarm was silenced almost immediately, but the door didn't buzz open until about five minutes later. I passed the time checking my teeth in the reflection from the lens on the door camera. With any luck, the view on his jumbo-sized security monitor was horrifying.

"I hear you lost some of my things," he said when he finally let me in.

I was tempted to spin a yarn about being accosted by ruthless thugs, but I doubted Marty would be moved to sympathy. Aunt Stacy's advice on just telling the truth was not an ideal option either, though. I didn't want word filtering back to Uncle Rupert just yet about the whole Alexander-the-mob-boss situation. Not until we'd got that cleared up, anyway. Still, there was no point in downplaying the loss or dodging responsibility.

"Yep. I did. Everything. I lost the entire kit," I said. "I know it's a big deal. And I'm really, really, really sorry."

To my surprise, he wasn't bowled over, or reduced to tears by my heartfelt apology. Nor was he taking the opportunity to throw a full conniption over the loss of his gear. Marty typically enjoys reminding me that I'm woefully inexperienced and prone to rookie mistakes. But he seemed to be taking it all in stride. Though he didn't invite me in either.

"For what it's worth, I know who has it," I said. "There's still a chance I can get it back. But I thought you should know, just in case it turns out I can't."

"Rupert told me you'd had some sort of mishap."

"You don't seem that mad," I said. Which was true. He didn't. It was a worrying observation but I couldn't think why.

"You know, I've been waiting for you to mess up with every job you've been on. And that hasn't happened. You may have lost some gear, but you still got the job done. Which was no big deal, by the way. This Tim guy did a recovery of the data and sent it all back to his client, and a copy to ours as well. So everyone's happy."

"Even you? Wow Marty, are you getting soft on me?"

He didn't reply to that with anything more than a thin smile. It was creepy enough to get me zipping through my goodbyes.

I was just getting back on the Vespa when Harley buzzed.

"Hey!" Harley's voice was so loud I had to hold the phone a safe distance from my ear. "It's cool to see you back on your FaceBook page. I thought you'd quit that!"

"What are you talking about, Harley?"

"I just saw you finally posted something. Gotta say, though, sort of a weird choice."

"Harley. Again. What are you talking about?"

She explained, and I put two and two together fairly quickly because I'm clever sometimes. During those minutes when I'd been left standing outside his apartment, Marty had hacked his way onto my FaceBook page. An act he'd then followed up by uploading a close-up video of me inspecting my teeth. Harley said that it already had fifteen likes. So that explained Marty's sudden forgiving nature. He had already exacted his revenge.

I signed off with Harley with a promise to pick up the cream cheese she likes from the little grocer on Niagara and was about to stow my phone when I noticed that there was a group text message from Benny: *It's here. Everybody better come over right away.*

Oak Bay is only about ten minutes from downtown, but I'd run into a string of delays that included a school bus doing drop-offs, a stalled FedEx truck, and worst of all a slow parade of geese that refused to move any faster than they felt necessary. So, once again, I was the last to arrive. I found the rest of the gang standing around the table in the flower shop design room. Colin was in his school uniform and Maryam her work overalls. There was no obvious jubilation or relief in the air. But then there wasn't any sign of a Stanley Cup either.

"What's up?" I said. "Where is it? I thought you said it was here."

"Oh, it is," Tim said and sheepishly pointed to the table.

I squeezed in closer.

"Oh, dang," I said.

It was a beautiful replica of the cup. No question. It was lying on a bed of packing peanuts inside a shoe box, and could easily sit on the palm of my hand.

"Did it come with a key chain?"

9

"I mean I hate to say it...but we can't *really* be surprised. The whole idea seemed way too good to be true," Maryam said. "Only four hundred dollars for something made out of silver?"

Tim hefted the tiny trophy up and down. "I assumed it was silver-plated not solid silver."

"You can't tell just by looking one way or the other," Saffron said. "Unless there is a hallmark on it somewhere."

"What's that now?"

Saffron's face took on a glow. "If it's solid silver, then they'll typically be a stamp—a quality mark—that will certify the silver percentage. Pure silver is rare, and the stamp would say *fine silver* or the number *1000*. Sterling silver is a more common mix of other metals. The stamp for sterling is usually around *925*. Britannia Silver comes in somewhere between the two. And then there would also be the hallmark of the silversmith that produced the piece. Or if it's plated, then it might have an *EP* for electroplate stamped somewhere. However, if someone is trying to pull a fast one then who knows? I know there are some tests you can do, but the point is that you can't tell them apart just by looking at the finish."

"Ummm...Wow!" Tim said.

"How is it you know so much about it?" Maryam asked.

Saffron just dipped her head in response, and the flush on her face deepened. I realized it hadn't come from pride but embarrassment.

Colin had been begging Tim for the cup and when it changed hands, he held it close to his nose for a squinty inspection. "I think it's cool. It's got all the names on it and everything. At least I think it does. Oh wait! I'll take a picture with my phone and zoom in."

"Find nineteen ninety-three for me," Benny said. "That was the last time Montreal won."

"Who'd they beat?" Maryam asked.

"The L.A. Kings," Benny said. "Los Angeles won the first game four to one. Montreal won the last game by the same score. The three games in between all went into overtime and Montreal won them all. What a series! Gretzky was playing for the Kings at that time, along with Jari Kurri and Luc Robitaille. And Montreal had Guy Carbonneau, Denis Savard and Kirk Muller. But it was Patrick Roy who stole the show. All of them legends. Did you watch it?"

"Did I watch it? In nineteen ninety-three? Benny, I was like...five years old," Maryam said.

"Oh, right," Benny said. His shoulders slumped a fraction and looked around the room, almost as if seeing us for the first time.

"Hey! Victoria won it once," Tim said, tapping at his phone. "They beat Montreal."

"What? Victoria? We had a team in the NHL? I don't think you're reading that right." Maryam's voice was heavy with skepticism.

Tim did some more poking and scrolling. "Yep. Well, sort of. They weren't in the NHL, there were different leagues back then. This was like a hundred years ago—back in the nineteen twenties. The Victoria Cougars. Though they were called the Aristocrats before that. They beat Montreal in three games to one in a best-of-five series. But then the team dissolved two years later."

"That's even before my time," Benny said and seemed to perk up a little.

"And it's all fascinating I'm sure. But what do we do now?" Saffron said. "We've lost a day and have nothing to show for it."

"Not entirely," Tim said. "The trophy does look pretty good."

"As a paperweight maybe," Maryam said. "What else can we do with it?"

"Hey," Colin said. "We could put it on a table and then stand way in the background so that it seems bigger than it is. You know…like people do taking gag photos of themselves with the Eiffel Tower and the tower in Pisa? Only in reverse?"

"Might work for a social media post, but I doubt Alexander will see the humour," Tim said. "I just meant that this one *looks* really good. It's sort of proof of concept. I agree, I messed up with this one. But the idea is still sound. We just need to find another replica that looks as good as this one, but, obviously, done on the correct scale. It's still the best idea. Right?"

"If by *best* you mean *only*?" Maryam said. "Then I guess so. I suppose we should get googling and see what else we can find."

"Unless…" Saffron started.

"You have another idea?" Benny said.

Saffron's face reddened all over again. "I hate to even think it, really."

"Go on…"

"Maryam, I'm sorry, but when we were in our powerpods yesterday—brainstorming ideas—I didn't want to mention, but...my ex-husband, Colin's father, he's a machinist. That's why I know a bit about silver and things. He could make one."

"Oh, that's a cool idea, Mom!" Colin said. "Dad has got all these wicked computer-controlled machines where he works. They're like 3D printers, only they use metal. All sorts of different types. Lathes and stuff."

"Interesting," Benny said. "Ex-husband, huh? We wouldn't want to put you in an awkward place."

"What would you say?" Maryam asked. "Would you tell him *why* we need one?"

"I could call him," Benny said. "Leave you out of it. Tell him I want a promotional piece. Something for the front window of the shop. What with the playoffs about to start and all?"

"No, it's fine," Saffron said. "He's difficult to deal with and I'd hate to feel that I'll owe him one. But if anyone else calls, he'll just send you through the company front desk and that would take forever. I wouldn't give up on Tim's idea, though."

Benny showed Saffron to his apartment upstairs so she could have some privacy while the rest of us dug out our phones, tablets and laptops to begin scouring the internet for life-sized trophies. In no time, the conversation devolved into a series of short and unproductive statements.

"Here's one in Sweden...oh wait...no never mind."

"Hey! I found...oh. Plastic."

"How about...hmmm. Nope."

"Here's *another* one that's only three-quarter size. What's with that?"

"Wait," Tim said. "Are we all searching for trophies for sale? Like on auction sites and so on?"

"Isn't that the point?" I said.

"Yes, but what about actual trophy manufacturers? Saffron's idea of having one made got me thinking. Rather than look on eBay or whatever, maybe we should be looking for actual trophy makers?"

There were a few minutes of silence aside from the clack of keys and tap of fingertips on screens.

"There's one in England," Colin said. "But I don't think they do anything other than football trophies."

"There's one in Ottawa," Tim said. "Eight weeks delivery time though. And it's almost nine thousand dollars. It would be half that price, or less, for one sent from China, but that's a three-month wait for one of those."

"I got one in the States!" Maryam said. "Wow! They do nice work. And they've done Stanley Cups too. It doesn't say if they have any ready to go, though. What time is it in Denver? I'm going to call."

The rest of us kept searching while Maryam wandered off to the front of the flower shop, phone at her ear. Benny returned with a tray loaded with mugs, tea and cookies. The number of hits got less and less. One by one, we put our devices aside and sat in expectant silence with our tea and cookies, waiting.

It was Saffron who was the first to return. She came down the stairs with a half smile.

"What did Dad say?"

"He'll do it," Saffron said. "He didn't care what it was for, he just enjoys having something over me."

There was something cagey in the way Saffron avoided eye contact.

"And...?" I prompted.

She played with the hem of one of her scarves. "And...in

addition to the cost of the trophy, he wants to skip two months of alimony payments."

"Can he do that?" Tim asked.

"Not legally no. I'm sorry honey, it will make meeting our rent difficult. But we can maybe move in with your Aunt Simone."

"Hold on. Nobody is moving anywhere," Benny said. "There's no way you have to put up with that. If your ex will make one for us, then, of course, we'll all cover the cost. Won't we?"

Tim and I both gave firm nods, though for myself I had no idea how I'd be able to hold up my end. That replacement pizza carrier had better arrive soon so I could get back to my delivery moonlighting.

"It better be a really good copy!" Tim said.

"Oh for sure," Colin said. "He does amazing work. Well, the machines do it all, really. But still, it's cool."

"What!?" Maryam's voice had been a low murmur from the other room, but it suddenly rose to a shout. She walked in, still holding the phone to her ear.

"I'm sure it's amazing, but *fifty thousand dollars*?"

Benny gestured for the phone. "Who you got there? Let me have a word."

Maryam shook her head, but it was in reaction to the amount, not Benny's request. She handed him the phone with a stunned expression.

"Benjamin Schlesien here. Who's this? Hey. How are ya?"

Benny grabbed a cookie and then slowly paced around the table with Maryam's phone.

"Eighty-one this year. Oh, ya...? Uh-huh. Uh-huh. Is that right? So what keeps you busy down there? You don't say. Me? Still working. Running a flower shop. I know. I know.

Should've retired years ago, but you know how it is? What else should I be doing? So my friends and I are interested in a Stanley Cup, and I gather you got one. Uh-huh. Tell me about it…"

Benny wandered his way over to the far end of the design room to a bench laden with spray bottles, wires, foam blocks of different shapes, and mysterious little plastic tubes. He was far enough away to nearly be out of earshot.

"What's going on?" I asked Maryam.

She sighed. "I called the trophy shop that I'd found. They could make one, but it would take months before it was ready. And they don't keep any just lying around in stock. It's all made to order. However…they knew that one of their former clients had bought a very special custom version as an investment years ago. He'd told them to let him know if any buyers came along. They gave me his number, and so that's who Benny is talking to. I gather it's in absolutely perfect condition and solid silver."

"Sterling probably," Saffron chipped in.

"But fifty thousand dollars?" Colin said, his eyes wide to match his open mouth, slack in wonder.

There were occasional bursts of laughter from Benny in the corner. He stayed by the bench, keeping his hands busy sorting flower arrangement wires into their containers, and contently chatted away. We polished off the cookies while Saffron brought Maryam up to speed on the deal with her ex-husband.

"Well, that's great," Maryam said. "So why is Benny talking to this guy, then?"

"Because," Benny said, handing the phone to Saffron as he rejoined us. "It's good to have options."

"Options we can't afford," Tim said. "Or is the flower

business particularly good these days?"

"I do okay," Benny said. "But that's neither here nor there. We came to an agreement in principle. Harry Montana. Nice fellow. Lives outside of Seattle somewhere. A real wheeler-dealer type. Turns out I got something he can use, so we'll trade. Won't cost anybody a dime."

"What about Saffron's husband?"

"Ex," Saffron mumbled.

"Do you want to vote on it?" Tim said. "Which of the two do we go for?"

"Sure," Maryam said. "Democracy in action. Those for Saffron's?"

Saffron, Colin, and Maryam all raised their hands. Tim, Benny and I just exchanged looks.

"Oh well now, that's just great," Maryam said. "There had to be an even number of us in the elevator, didn't there?"

"I mean, if Benny has it covered," Tim said. "Then isn't it better to go with a cup that we know actually exists?"

"A split vote," Benny said. "No problem. We do both. Agreed?"

There was a moment of silence and a scattering of nods.

"Agreed," Maryam said. "We do both."

In our focused discussion, not even Benny had noticed the brief volume increase coming from the street traffic as the outer door opened. A moment later, a bulky shadow filled the opening of the design room.

"Both of what?" Valery said. For a man of his size, he could move like a ninja.

Benny opened his mouth to say something but closed it again as Valery was joined by someone a third of his size.

"I like your flowers," Polina said.

"I told you. Stay in car." Valery had even more of a scowl

than when I'd locked him on the roof.

"Yes. Yes." Polina gave a dismissive wave.

"Both what?" Valery asked again. Giving us a hard glare.

"Pizza," I lied. "Both kinds. We couldn't decide between Hawaiian and the Veggie Lovers. What's your fav Polina? That Hawaiian you sucked back the other night was pretty fine. Am I right? Which reminds me, I'd be super keen on getting my carrier bag back, and…my other things."

They both ignored me.

"Can we go?" Polina said. "The movie starts soon."

"You two a couple?" Benny asked.

"No…not that," Maryam said. She gave the pair of them a long look. "I'm betting bodyguard."

"Yes," Valery nodded. "Is dangerous job. Kirill's job. Remember what happened to him? I stop now to remind you of this."

"Can't we do anything *else* for you?" Saffron said. "Stealing the Stanley Cup? Why does it have to be this?"

"No. This is what Alexander wants. This is what you do. Or…"

"Or you'll throw us down an elevator shaft?" I said.

"Is *that* what you did with Kirill?" Maryam asked.

Polina laughed. Valery ignored all of us and stepped closer to the table to pick up our small Stanley Cup. It looked even smaller in his hands, like something you might hang on a Christmas tree.

"Alexander is concerned you're not taking this seriously," he said. "What is this?"

"Inspiration," Maryam said. "Something to remind us what we're working on."

"It's cute," Polina said. "Do you people even know where the actual one is?"

Out of the corner of my eye, I could see Colin's thumbs working furiously on the phone in his lap.

"On a plane." Colin's eyes darted back and forth between his screen and nowhere in particular. "The opening game of the playoffs starts tomorrow night in New York. It's only the first game, but they bring it for media promotion and such."

"So? What are you doing?" Valery said.

"Look, tough guy," Maryam said. She moved in close to Valery until they were nearly toe to toe. The top of her head came to his shoulder, so she had to crick her neck to make eye contact. "We're *on* it, okay? Alexander said he didn't want to know the details. So why are you bothering us?"

Neither of them blinked for what felt like an eternity.

"You don't frighten me, you know?" she said. "As I recall, when the shooting was going down, you were the one holding a phone—not the gun. What was it for, anyway? Making a movie? Something to share with your little gangster Facebook group? Show how tough you think you are?"

Valery was the first to blink. He slammed the miniature cup onto the table, gave a sharp gesture to Polina, and then they marched out of the shop without another word. I noticed the cup wobbling on the table. It was nearly folded in half.

"Are you *insane*?" Saffron said to Maryam. "Why would you provoke him like that?"

"Just pushing back a bit," Maryam said. "Besides, we could hardly tell him what we were really doing. Could we?"

The awkward silence that followed stretched on and on. Eventually, we made tentative plans to check in with each other the next morning. Saffron was going to see her ex and make sure that things would be in progress, and Benny just said he had to check on a few things and would let us know.

I still had too much adrenaline in me to navigate the scooter safely through downtown traffic. Instead, I texted Harley and convinced her to meet me at our favourite bar. It's a hotel lounge that doesn't look like much from the outside, but it has a deceptive charm. I found an empty couch by the fireplace and ordered some appetizers and drinks while I waited for Harley. I was so engrossed in replaying the encounter with Valery in my mind that Harley had to snap her fingers at me to get my attention when she arrived.

"Planet Earth to Margot," she said. "What's going on? I mean, if it's none of my business, just say so. But I know something's up."

"It's complicated," I said. "Hopefully everything will sort itself out in a few days and I promise I'll tell you everything then."

"Does it have anything to do with these guys who have been chasing you around?"

"Why do you ask that?"

"Cause..." She leaned closer. "Don't look now, but here comes the studly one."

I couldn't *not* look, of course. Though perhaps I could have spun around a bit more subtly than I did. Not that it would have mattered. The 'studly' guy, as Harley called him, was headed our way with a certain focus and conviction. As he got closer, I had no trouble seeing the resemblance to the brief look I'd had of him at the café. And as he reached us, he was slightly preceded by the stench of stale cigarette smoke which tied him to another memory as well.

"Can I help you?" I asked.

He smiled at that. "I think it's possible that I can help

you. My name is Max Kirkpatrick. I'm an agent with CSIS... and I think we need to talk."

10

"What's a seesus?"

"It's like MI5 in Britain or the CIA in the States," I said. "Only, you know, the Canadian version."

"No way! He's a spy!?"

"I guess," I said. "I don't know. Are you?"

"Just an agent," Max said with what seemed to be a modest shrug. "May I sit?"

"Shut Up!! Oh my god!" Harley yelled and jumped to her feet. "You're a *secret agent*!?"

"Not anymore, he's not," I said, conscious that every possible set of eyes in the entire lounge was now looking our way.

"Margot! He's like James friggin Bond. Oh my god! Where's my phone? I need a picture."

I tried to get her to sit down, but Harley can rarely be contained even when she's not excited.

"Yes, please sit," I said to Max. Hoping that Harley might follow as well. Which she did, but only after perching on the arm of his chair to take a selfie of the two of them. Max tried to protest, but just managed a wincing grin in the flash of her phone.

"Please don't post this," Max said after Harley had dropped back beside me and started tapping madly at her phone. He pulled out a pack of cigarettes and spun the box in one hand with nervous movements.

"You can't smoke in here," Harley said. "Why can't I post it?"

"Harley, I'm fairly sure the *entire* point of being in a secret agency is not having everyone in the world *know* that you work for a secret agency."

"Entire world? Please. I don't have that many followers. Besides, James Bond always tells everyone who he is. And even when he doesn't tell them, the bad guys always seem to know, anyway."

"Harley!!?"

"Oh fine," she sighed and put her phone down with obvious disappointment.

With Harley settled, I turned my attention back to our uninvited guest. "Max Kirkpatrick? Did I get that right? Is that short for Maxwell or Maximilian? Or something else?"

"Just Max," he said and tried out a lazy smile of the sort I imagine they teach you in spy school. One carefully designed to make the suspect feel safe and warm. It was certainly working on Harley.

"So, are you a *special* agent? Like on TV?" she asked. "You do have a bit of an accent. Did you know that?"

"I think it's just the FBI who are *special*," I said.

"Just a…regular agent," Max said. "And yes, English is not my first language. I was raised by my grandparents, who were immigrants. I grew up speaking Ukrainian… which is why I have the job I do."

"Yes, tell us more about that," Harley said. "Everything actually. Ooh, do you have a license to kill? Can you show us your gun?"

"No…license. No gun. I just work with the information section that deals with Eastern Europe."

"And how does that bring you to me?" I asked, mostly for Harley's benefit. It didn't take a genius to connect the dots. Presumably, CSIS was keeping a close eye on our local branches of organized crime, and my visits to the office building had attracted their attention. As a guess, it was pretty much a certainty, but Max immediately removed any doubt.

"It's my understanding you've come into contact with Alexander Yevgeny Mironov. He's a very dangerous man."

"Who's that?" Harley asked. "Oh wait. Is that the big bald dude? This is fun!"

"No, he's the big bald dude's boss," I said.

"That sounds like you're describing Valery Yakovlevich Mikhailov," Max said with a nod of approval. "An even more dangerous man."

"Wow. They *really* go in for the big names, huh?" Harley gave me a squinty look. "How do you know these guys?"

"It was just a pizza delivery gone wrong," I said. "Kinda ran into them at their office, and I guess I made an impression."

Max took some time to ponder that. I had to admit I was being a bit cryptic. But that was intentional.

"I see. So what is it they want from you now? More pizza?" The lazy smile was dangerously close to a smirk.

This was the moment for some hard decision-making. I knew next to nothing about CSIS beyond the rare times they made it into a newspaper section that also held the crossword. My impression was they just collected information and worked with other police agencies. Which is more or less what Max had said. Certainly, you never heard about a CSIS agent running around and arresting people or anything. I suspected that being a witness to the murder of Kirill Bondarchuk might fall under 'information of interest'. Mind you, so might the knowledge about a hapless group of individuals who were scheming about committing grand theft of the Stanley Cup. Not that we were, of course. Still, Benny and the gang, as I was beginning to think of us, had all made sworn promises not to discuss anything with anyone without agreeing to first. So what did Max already know? And what, if anything, should I be telling him?

"Do you guys have witness protection?" Harley asked. "Like you see on tv with American cop shows?"

"Do either of you need protecting? Is there something you would like to tell me?"

"I would hate that. I bet they stick you somewhere really boring. Like, I dunno, Toronto or something."

"Harley, only *you* could be bored in Toronto," I said.

"Well, I mean we went there on a school trip and we did the space needle thing, and Niagara Falls and the shoe museum, and that was all fine...but I don't know about the rest. There was a lot of walking. A lot. On concrete, Margot! Concrete! Not hiking through old-growth forests. It was savage."

There was a lot to unpack in that. But then, with Harley, there usually is.

"I'll give you the walking and maybe the shoe museum—cause for all I know, maybe they have one—but Niagara Falls is actually in...Niagara Falls, not Toronto. And the space needle is definitely in Seattle, so I'm assuming you went to the CN Tower?"

"You know what I mean."

I did. But I was used to Harley's wonderfully lurching train of thought. Max, on the other hand, judging by his expression, seemed to have lost the thread.

"We're fine," I assured him. "No problems. And I don't know anything much about these guys you're interested in. I don't know what I can tell you."

Max gave that a full half minute or more of thoughtful reflection.

"Well, that's good. I'll give you my number. Just in case something comes up—anything at all. It's very important that you don't tell anyone we've met. I can trust you, I think. Yes?"

The lazy smile was back and, from what I could tell, he kept it on all the way outside.

"Just remember," Harley said, holding the napkin that Max had written his number like it was a treasured heirloom. "I saw him first."

"That's debatable. But anyway, he's a smoker. You hate that."

"Oh right. Fair point! That is a deal breaker. Secret super spy or not." She dropped the napkin on the table and set her drink on it as a coaster. Instantly forgotten. "Movie? I scored a whole stack of DVDs someone dumped in the little free library. No James Bond, but lots of romances. We could watch Titanic! Action and romance all rolled into one!"

My new lockpicks were waiting outside in a discrete package when we got home to the apartment. They were nicely made from laser-cut steel, but hadn't gone through much in the way of finishing. I like my tools to be silky smooth, so I dug out some ultrafine sandpaper and worked on the edges while we watched Jack and Rose flirt, cavort and swim with decreasing levels of success.

"Jack did not need to drown. That door could have easily held both of them," Harley said. "It's huge. Plenty of room."

"It's not the surface area, it's the buoyancy. A solid wood door isn't that floaty. You've seen the driftwood at the beach—most of it's underwater."

"Pish posh. What have you got against Leo DiCaprio?"

"Nothing. You're just a hopeless romantic."

"Hey! I'm not hopeless," Harley said, and then slowly started beaming. "I'll prove it! Where's my surfboard? Grab some towels. C'mon, we're going to the beach."

For a moment, I thought she was joking. But then I should know Harley better than that. It was well past midnight, and I tried to argue that the door in the movie was nothing like the surfboard. But that was a mistake. She agreed I'd made a brilliant observation and so then I had to relent to stop her from taking our apartment door off its hinges.

There is a shallow inlet on the other side of downtown called The Gorge. The water there can be wonderfully warm in the heat of August when you hit the tides just right. Harley and I sometimes like to bicycle over for a swim and lounge in the sun. But that's miles away and not at all where she wanted to go.

While our apartment is just a few short blocks from the water, it's on the ocean side of downtown. Rather than a sheltered inlet, the Salish Sea opens up to the tip of Washington State and then beyond that you have a clear shot across the Pacific to Japan. The water is deep, cold, and at one in the morning, black as squid ink.

There'd been a zany spirit of adventure vibe that had helped to carry me along to the water's edge. But then I wavered. There was enough of a moon that we hadn't needed the flashlight I'd brought, but it made the dimpled strip of sand between the rocks and the water gleam like hammered steel.

"Are you sure about this?"

"Are you kidding?" Harley said, throwing off her towel

and fleece pants onto the rocks. "How can you *not* be?"

She grabbed the surfboard and ran full speed into the water. The shrieks were ear-piercing. After a few deep breaths, I gritted my teeth and waded in after her. The water was so cold it felt like I was walking through razor blades.

When I finally caught up, she was chest-deep with her arms on the surfboard, head tilted back and looking up at the stars.

"Do you think the water they were in was this cold?"

"They hit an iceberg, Harley. I'm sure it was way colder."

"It's not bad if you don't move."

"I think my shivering sort of precludes not moving."

"Seriously, just hold real still. I think your body warms up the water right beside you and then if you don't thrash around, it stays there. Like an invisible blanket. I think it's a metaphor."

"For what?"

"Life."

She said it with such comfortable, absolute certainty that I didn't want to break the spell by asking what she could possibly mean. I just mirrored her position, draped my arms alongside hers over the board, and tried not to move.

"Do you ever think we'll go to Mars?" she asked a minute later.

"Mars? We've been. All sorts of exploration robot things."

"No, I mean real people."

"Oh. Maybe. I dunno. Why?" I asked.

"That would be interesting."

"To go to Mars? Harley, if you find Toronto boring, what are you imagining Mars would be like?"

"Oh ya. That's a very good point," she said and started

making little punches into the water.

"Stop moving, you're making it cold. Well cold-er," I said. "I thought your point was to stay still."

"I was trying to get the bioluminescence to wake up."

"Is it working?"

"Not yet. All the little glow-in-the-dark critters must be asleep."

"Well, it is pretty late," I said.

"Another good point. You're on fire tonight!" she said. "Okay, it's time for science. Get on the board. You're smaller, so you get to be Rose. I'll be Jack."

Try as we might, there was no way to get both of us on the surfboard without it sinking completely. As it was, even for me, I had to tuck my arms tightly alongside my body and lift my feet to get completely out of the water and even the slightest movement had me splashing. On the plus side, all the flailing and laughing warmed us up enough that by the time we called it quits, I had stopped shivering.

My skin had settled into a numb tingle, and the night air suddenly seemed warm, so we took our time getting dressed. The moon had dipped below the horizon and the milky way overhead was now a swath of light.

"Kind of strange that secret agent dude following you around, huh?" she said. I started to answer, but she hurried to cut me off. "And those other guys, too. He said they were dangerous. You know if things get weird...I'm here for you. That's what roomies are for. You do know that? Right?"

"I do," I said. "But, no Harley. Not all roomies...just you."

Harley tilted her head as far back as she could, spread her arms wide, and then began to spin slowly in place as though she were preparing to fly off to the stars. "Cool."

11

I woke late to find a note from Harley, a text from Benny, and a missed call from Uncle Rupert on my phone. I dealt with them in that order.

Harley's message was just an unhappy face on a sticky note I found on the coffee machine. I considered a few interpretations. My favourite was that Lucifer had won another round in its daily battle to deny us coffee, and so maybe she'd popped out to buy us coffee and muffins from the café. Of course, if that was the case, then it was equally likely that she'd gone shopping for an entirely new machine we couldn't afford. Or, maybe the sad face was just because we had run out of toothpaste, or that Mars was farther away than she'd hoped. With Harley, there were always options.

Benny's text was easier to decipher. *Dear Margot. Are you free this afternoon? I need to be down in Seattle by early tomorrow morning. But I need help with something before I leave. -Benjamin Schlesien.*

I was about to send a quick: *no probs. 2 pm good?* But I paused with my thumb over the send button…it didn't feel right. That was fine for Harley, or anybody else really. Benny had taken time and thought with his text, and I should do the same. It took me a full ten minutes of editing to create a different reply—which was almost as long as I'd spent on writing anything in my life. On the one hand, I was worried he would think I was making fun. But I also didn't want him thinking I was just another one of those he'd refer to as 'these kids today'.

Dear Benny, I would be happy to help. Shall I meet you at the flower shop at two pm? -Margot Croft.

Uncle Rupert's message was far easier to deal with, as it turned out to be an invitation to brunch. This was always a welcome event, not least because Aunt Stacy made the world's best waffles, but also because an invitation always meant there was a job to do. Uncle Rupert preferred to give me work details face-to-face. A little paranoia goes a long way. Not that he wouldn't invite me over without needing a reason, but that rarely happened.

He didn't specify a time, but then he didn't need to. We both knew very well that in Aunt Stacy's mind, breakfast is at eight, and lunch at noon. Anything between those two could only logically commence at ten sharp. Harley's ministry-of-silly-walks wall clock had John Cleese's legs showing nine-thirty, so I jumped into gear.

The anticipated waffles turned out to be orange-infused French toast. I wouldn't go so far as to say that they were *better* than her waffles...because saying that out loud would be dangerously close to sacrilege. They were certainly extremely fine. After stuffing ourselves to critical levels, Aunt Stacy excused herself to take Pretzel for a walk to 'smell the flowers' and left Uncle Rupert and me to deal with the post-feast kitchen cleanup.

"So?" I prompted, as Uncle Rupert handed me a frying pan to dry.

"An easy one for you," he said. "Just a tracking chip plant. Divorce case. One side suspects the other of extra-curricular shenanigans—the usual sort of thing. I'd do it myself, but I know you could use the extra income and besides, you'll enjoy this one."

Divorce cases always make me a little sad. If people like Uncle Rupert and me are involved, then you know that it's come down to name-calling and dirt-digging and generally just as far removed from the wedding day happiness as can be imagined. I must have pulled a face.

"No seriously," he said. "There are perks this time."

"How so?"

"Turns out the wrapper works at a spa. I know you love your pizza delivery gag, but you can get a massage or your nails done, or get dipped in mud or ice water, whatever it is that spas do—all at company expense."

After last night's antics, I felt no urge for an ice-water plunge. A massage on the other hand—that did sound nice. He gave me the details, and I made careful notes. Uncle Rupert had another surprise for me in the form of a small kit with a variety of listening and GPS tracking devices.

"I saw Martin yesterday afternoon, so I thought I'd grab them to save you the trip. Might be a good idea to remember that we consider them disposable, but only after they've done their job. Not because we misplaced them. Right?"

"Got it."

"There's one more thing..." Uncle Rupert started the dishwasher to signal the end of our clean-up duties. "Something in the workshop you might enjoy."

'Something' turned out to be a new Bowley door lock. Bowley locks appear very average from the outside. Inside is an *entirely* different story. They use a unique key design that makes all their locks essentially un-pickable. In *theory*, there should be a way. But in practice, neither Uncle Rupert nor I had ever managed to open any of the Bowleys in his collection—despite countless hours of trying. There was no question of attempting to use anything but the key on this new one, either. We just wanted to take it apart to see how it worked. We were like kids at Christmas.

"I'll bet not even a CSIS agent could get into a Bowley, huh?" I asked as Uncle Rupert placed the eighth, and final, pin assembly into his sorting tray.

"CSIS? That's a new one. You thinking about a career change?"

"Just curious," I said. Now that he'd tipped me off that he could tell when I'm telling whoppers I was conscious of keeping my vocabulary along middle school levels of sophistication. Might as well avoid giving Uncle Rupert anything extra to worry about.

"You don't hear much about them, but I know it's a big agency. I think they tend to look for employees who have fluency in at least a few languages. English and French are probably just the bare minimum—being federal and all."

Uncle Rupert didn't need to point out that my high school French grades had been well short of spectacular. I could order a meal or ask for directions to the train station, but that was about it.

"What about other languages?"

"Sure. Italian, German, Russian, or any of the European languages would be good. I imagine, though, that Asia is where most things are going on. You want to learn Chinese?"

He slid the nested lock cylinder apart and then paused in thought with half of it in each hand. "I did meet a CSIS analyst a few years back. Connie Zhao. She was involved with tracking down some phone scammers from overseas. Some operation that was targeting locals who had Chinese heritage. From what I recall, she was mostly the information gatherer, and it was the RCMP that handled all the warrants and arrests and so forth. If you're interested, I think I have her contact information. Let me know if you want me to reach out first as an introduction."

"Sure," I said. "Not that I'm looking for anything else. I'm happy doing what I do. Just, you know, curious."

"Uh-huh. Well, not to dissuade you or anything, but I'm pretty sure most of her work is behind a desk with a computer or a phone, and almost none of it involves running around being sneaky. And I do know which of those things you prefer."

He handed me the lock body with a twinkle of humour in his eyes.

"Now I hope you've been paying attention," he said. "Let's see you put it back together."

After I'd reconstructed the Bowley—earning a few '*hmms*' and '*hahs*' but ultimately a '*nice job*', in the process—I had just enough time to stop for a fill-up on my way to the flower shop. I locked the Vespa to a lamppost outside and entered to find Benny ringing up a sale for a customer while simultaneously bantering with Colin.

"But *why* aren't you in school?"

"It's a PD day."

"A what? A *Petey* day? What sort of thing is that?"

"PD. Professional Development. One of those days that teachers take to learn new things about teaching."

"Shouldn't they know how to teach already?" Benny asked. He waved goodbye to the customer and then spotted me. "There's no school today. Can you believe that?"

"Kids change, Benny," I said. "Technology changes. I think teachers, like the rest of us, need all the help they can get just to keep up."

"That's all true, I suppose. Is math still the same?"

"As far as I know."

"Good. Where's your mother?" he asked Colin.

"Working. I texted her to see if I could come downtown and she said it was okay. I was going to hang out with some friends but they're having a LAN party and Mom doesn't like it when I'm on a screen all day. Besides, my friends only want to play FPS and they get boring."

Benny looked at me as though he'd swallowed a lemon. "Can you translate? I only got a fraction of that. Actually... never mind. Let me close up and we can get going."

"What games do you play, Colin? Any hockey ones?" I asked.

"No, not really. I mostly like puzzle sort of games. My Mom got me a driving wheel for my birthday though, so I've been playing the car racing games too."

"Is that right?" Benny said. "Well, we're going for a drive now. Margot's going to help me with something. If you're looking for something to do, I guess you can come with us. Why don't you call your mother and see if it's alright...if you want to, that is."

Colin's face lit up while his thumbs became a blur on his phone.

Benny hung a 'closed until four' sign on the shop door and we piled into the delivery van parked in the little laneway around back.

"You run the shop by yourself, Benny?" I asked. "Why don't you get some help?"

"No, no. It was Edna's shop. Well, Edna's and mine. It was always just the two of us. Wouldn't feel right to have someone else working there too. Even after all this time."

"So, where are we going?" Colin said.

"Not too far," Benny said. "There's a storage place out at

View Royal, just past the end of The Gorge."

Traffic was light, and it only took about fifteen minutes to reach a sprawling complex of low buildings wedged between The Island Highway and the Trans-Canada. Benny punched a code at the gate to let us through and then puttered the flower van through a maze of laneways.

"Here we are," he said, stopping alongside one of the roller doors that all looked identical to my eye. I was going to critique his choice of padlock but I figured with the gate and security cameras, the odds of anyone entering to fool with it were probably low. Besides, who would take the risk of breaking into a storage locker without knowing what was inside? I've seen some storage-themed reality shows and most lockers seem to be full of stuff that is just having a stopover on its way to the garbage dump. When I helped roll up the door of Benny's unit, I couldn't tell if that was true for him as well.

"What is it?" Colin asked.

"That, young man, is a nineteen sixty-nine Ford Escort MK1."

It was a fairly average-looking blue and white sedan with some extra headlights bolted to the front and some impressive dents and scratches along one side.

"Did you drive it off a cliff?"

"Nearly," Benny said with what sounded to me like misplaced pride. "More than a few times, actually. I know it looks a little rough, but it should make it to Seattle just fine."

Despite its appearance, after Benny removed some wires from a battery charger, the car fired up on the first try with a throaty roar.

"Hear that?" he yelled from the driver's seat. "It's got the two-litre single-overhead-cam 'Pinto' engine. Not a huge amount of horsepower by today's standards, but it's perfectly balanced and all you need."

He went on some more in that vein with various specifications. I was tempted to compare his comments with Colin's gaming jargon earlier, but I doubt he would've been able to hear me, anyway.

"Coming out!" Benny yelled.

Colin and I stood back as Benny eased the car out past the delivery van. He left the engine running and did a walk around.

"Okay," he said to me. "Can you take some pictures of it? Just all-around ones, but get the inside too. Take a bunch, and maybe a closeup of the odometer too. I guess I'll have to get one of your types of phones one day. But I like my old blackberry. It has a real keyboard, but it didn't come with a camera."

"What do you need the pictures for?" Colin asked, as I started snapping away.

"Insurance mostly," Benny said.

He went off to close the locker while I did a circle around the car to get every angle. The interior looked as though someone had scraped it clear down to an empty shell and then put back only the bare minimum. I didn't want to hurt Benny's feelings by suggesting it, but renting a proper car seemed like a far better idea to me.

"Okay," Benny said and pulled out some Edna's Flower Shop branded notepaper with an email address written on it. "Just send them all."

I was typing it in when Colin jumped into the passenger seat. "For an old car, it's kinda cool," he said. "What are these switches for?"

"Don't touch those!" Benny said and climbed into the driver's side to keep an eye on things.

"Can I go with you?" Colin asked.

"Sure kid," Benny said and gave the engine a roar. "Margot, the keys to the van are in the ignition. The gate opens automatically on the way out. We'll meet you back at the shop. Okay?"

"Interesting twist," I said. Though I was just talking to myself because Benny had already gunned the engine and driven off with a wave.

The intelligent move would have been to run after them and try to catch up before they reached the gate. But that would've involved some embarrassing explanations. I tried calling Harley, but she wasn't picking up. Uncle Rupert was certainly not a valid choice. There weren't many other options that came to mind, so on a whim, I pulled up the group chat messages and selected Tim's number.

"Hey Tim," I said. "Any chance you could talk me through how to drive a car?"

12

"You're funny," Tim said. He even threw in a chuckle to show his appreciation for my awesome wit. "Are you calling for an update? Because things are actually going pretty well."

"Sure, let's start with that," I said. Which was a good idea, since neither of us seemed to have a clue what the other was talking about.

"It turns out that there's someone outside of Montreal—a real hockey fan—who created a cup replica with a 3D printer in his garage. He's got some videos on YouTube and the result is a little rough, but the dimensions are accurate."

"And this helps us how?" I asked.

"Because the guy made the modelling files freely available for anyone to download. He made his version out of plastic, but Clarence—that's Saffron's ex-husband—can use the same file to make a metal one for us. It's a huge timesaver."

"Sounds great, I guess," I said and began a slow lap around the delivery van. It stirred some long-ago memory of a hot summer day at the beach waiting impatiently in line with a dozen other kids getting popsicles from an ice cream truck. Benny's had the same vintage feel, down to the sliding doors on the front cab. Probably didn't come with the nifty music though. "How long will it take?"

"Not long at all. There are a few steps in the process. First the machining of the entire cup. Then all the names get etched in by laser. And lastly, it gets silver-plated. But it's all automated for the most part, and he said he could start right away, so it should be ready by later tomorrow."

"Did you meet him?" I asked. "Clarence I mean. Saffron's ex?"

"Briefly. Saffron and I went to see him during her lunch break. I brought him the files on a memory stick and he checked them out and said they were good to go, no problem."

"Did he seem reliable?" I asked. Benny had left the driver's side door ajar, so I stepped in and had a seat. Tim was quiet for so long that I thought we'd lost the connection. But he was just collecting his thoughts.

"There was a guy I knew back in Iqaluit, Sam Crawley. He was a few years older and not so much a friend, but everyone knows everyone there. I remember this one time, some parents got together and paid him to take a bunch of us kids out on the land for an overnight adventure. He had all this great gear from when his father passed away. The thing about it was that Sam was more of a stay-at-home type. I learned later on that he was deathly scared of polar bears, never went hunting or fishing, and hated camping. At the time, though, he did like the offer of money. So what he did was just load us all on a sled behind his snow machine with a bunch of camping gear and then drove off inland. We were on that sled for hours and hours before we made camp. But when I got up to pee in the middle of the night, I saw him walking over a bluff with a coffee from Tim Horton's and a bucket of KFC chicken. We thought we'd gone halfway to Greenland, but we were only about ten minutes outside of town."

"I see," I said, though I didn't at all.

"Sam was a slippery character that way," Tim said. "Always friendly, super nice, but a little off-angle. He seemed happiest making people believe one thing when he was doing another."

"So…?"

"Just saying that it had an impact on me, I guess. I never got over that. It made me hate deception. You asked if Clarence seemed reliable. I guess I'm just saying that he reminded me of Sam. Alexander too, come to think of it," he said. "But as far as Clarence is concerned, I don't trust him. Though I suppose if we get a great-looking replica, then… what does it matter? Anyway, that's us. How are you making out?"

A fine question, I thought.

"Similar situation, actually," I said. "I'm also just outside of town. We came out to a storage unit to get this old car of Benny's. He and Colin just took off in it. I thought Benny wanted me along just for my camera, but I guess he expected I would drive his delivery van back as well."

Which I suppose was a reasonable thing to expect. I guess with my age, and my obvious prowess on the Vespa, Benny had reached the very logical conclusion that I must have a driver's license. But that wasn't true. It was something I'd never quite gotten around to doing. The bus service in Victoria is quite excellent. And most everything I had needed since turning sixteen had always been within walking or cycling distance. When I bought it at the auction, the staff didn't seem too fussy about much other than getting their money. I gave them cash; they gave me a Vespa. Done. Thankfully, the province did away with annual insurance renewal stickers years ago, so there was no way to tell at a glance the license plate was actually just ornamental. Unless I got pulled over or was in an accident, then who was to know?

"So, what's the problem?" Tim asked.

"I was trying to allude to that earlier," I said. "The part where I mentioned I don't know how to drive."

"You were serious about that?"

"More or less," I said. "It's not so much that I don't *completely* know how...just that I never actually have. I mean, you steer and there's a pedal to make it go and another to make it stop, right? Beyond that, I know most of the rules of the road—I've been driving the scooter for years now."

"Driving...without a license?" Tim asked.

"Apparently," I said. I pumped the gas pedal a few times and then turned the key like I'd seen Benny do. It chugged over a few times and then spluttered into life.

"Hey! So far so good," I said. "Now what?"

"I can't be a part of this," Tim said.

"I thought you were a hacker type? Don't you guys bend the rules all the time?"

"No. I don't like the term, but I'm what they call a White Hat hacker. My reputation is important in my line of work. I can't do illegal things."

It seemed like a bad time to mention our recent dealings with actual criminals. Instead, I toggled the phone onto speaker mode and then opted for a video call as well. A few seconds later, Tim's face filled the screen, hesitant smile and all.

"Look. Just pretend you were sitting here driving and tell me what you'd do. Nothing illegal in that, is there!?" I switched to the rear-facing camera option and aimed my phone down in front of me.

"I'm not sure about this," he said, and let out a long sigh. "Well, at least it's an automatic and not a manual transmission, so you can't stall it. Let me see where you are."

I gave Tim a slow panoramic of the storage units while he hummed and hawed and sighed some more. "I'm pretty sure that on private land you can get away with driving an uninsured vehicle. Maybe that means the driver doesn't necessarily need a license? But why didn't you just tell Benny and get someone else to drive it? I'm at my office and need to be here for a few hours still, but I can get a cab after work and do it."

"I've got to learn sometime," I said. "Besides, Saffron has me reading my horoscope lately. Apparently, there is a great deal of grounding energy in the world for me today, and my heart and emotions are on the same page. So that's all gotta be good. Right?"

The advice for Leos also went on and on about the importance of avoiding drama—but I was pretty sure that had been about romance, so I didn't mention it.

I hadn't intended to drive the delivery van on the road. I guess I just wanted to prove to myself that I could. But after twenty minutes of looping around the storage units, I was feeling pretty comfortable. The little van was just a bigger version of the bumper cars at the fair. Only—as Tim kept yelling to remind me—you're not supposed to hit anything.

"Okay, that last time around was the best yet," he said. "Just remember, the wheels are much further apart than what you're used to, so stay wide. And I can see you moving around—you're still trying to lean the van around the corners. It's not a scooter. Just turn the wheel."

I had found a roll of duct tape in the cargo area and had mounted my phone on the headrest behind me, so when I wasn't blocking the camera with my head, Tim had the same view that I did. Which is why he reacted almost before I was aware of what I was doing myself.

"Wait! Wait! Wait! Where are you going?" Tim said.

I didn't at the last corner for yet another practice lap. Instead, I'd kept straight on. The exit gate loomed into view as I brought the van to a lurching stop and waited for the bar to rise.

"You might want to sign off now," I said. "I'm feeling bold."

"No, no, no, no, no—"

I unstuck the phone from the headrest and ended the call for him with a little wave of goodbye. If things went sideways, I didn't want him to feel responsible.

It was all actually pretty easy. There were even a few turns where I remembered to use the blinker thingee. It was hard to see what all the licensing fuss was about. I just pretended the van was an oversized scooter and did all the same things I usually did.

There was really only one tiny incident worth mentioning. Benny's van had about the same get-up-and-go as my scooter. Which is maybe why it seemed so comfortably familiar. And also why I didn't get overly upset by the occasional honks from impatient drivers whenever I struggled to get the van back up to cruising speed after stop signs and such. On the plus side, the brakes were fantastic. As soon as I took my foot off the gas pedal, it slowed right down even better than my Vespa—something that hadn't been overly apparent in my training laps at the storage facility. The first clue that there might be something amiss didn't strike me until I pulled to another abrupt stop outside the flower shop. A thick cloud of white-blue smoke swept past me, along with a nasty choking stench.

Benny, Colin, and Maryam were all waiting on the sidewalk beside Benny's beat-up car. When the smoke thinned out, I saw Colin in openmouthed surprise. Maryam wore a slightly amused expression. Benny's was something much more scowly.

"Put the four-way flashers on and leave it there," he called to me. "It'll give the drums a chance to cool down. I'll move it around back in a minute. I'm just going to run upstairs and grab a few things."

"Is there something wrong?"

He gave a small shrug as he headed to the door. "It's no big deal. Let's just say…don't bother to set the hand brake. It's already on."

Hand brake? Never thought about that. The Vespa doesn't have one and Tim failed to mention it.

"You left the parking brake on? Is that what took you so long?" Colin said.

"There was a slight delay in leaving. I was on the phone with Tim." I admitted. Embarrassment had the words coming out a little too quickly, and I forced myself to take a breath. I skipped over the driver-training aspect of our conversation and focused on what was important. "He said the replica that Saffron's ex is making for us will be done by later tomorrow. So that's good news."

"At least you made it in time," Maryam said.

"In time for what?"

"Benny didn't want to leave until you'd got here."

"Leave? Where's he going?"

"Schedule change. The guy with the cup called and apparently, he has to fly to Texas tomorrow to see a sick relative. So it's either when he's back later next week…"

"Which would be way too late," I said. "Or…?"

"Or…now. Right now," Maryam said. "If we scramble, we can catch the next ferry and then make it to Seattle before midnight. Stay in a motel somewhere and we pick up the cup first thing in the morning."

There had yet to be any discussion about who actually would be making the trip down. Benny seemed to have taken charge. He was the one who had made the arrangements and had offered to trade whatever valuable thing he had for it. I just hoped it wasn't any of his late wife's jewelry or something like that.

"Oh god. He's back," Maryam said. She tried to duck in front of me as though to hide from whoever she'd spotted in the distance. Our height difference made that a fairly futile gesture, so after that realization sunk in, she dragged me by the arm into the flower shop, pushing Colin ahead of us.

"Have you been followed around too?" I asked. I started to give a quick description of CSIS agent Max Kirkpatrick, but Maryam cut me off.

"What? Who are you talking about? No. Valery. Valery is back. I just saw him go into the tea shop."

"Maybe he likes tea?"

"Oh please! I've been seeing him lurking around all day. At my apartment, when I was grocery shopping, and even at job sites. He's been keeping tabs wherever I go. Maybe I went too far with the mouthing off yesterday?"

"Maybe," I agreed. "Who's going with Benny, though? We can't let him go on his own."

"Of course not," Maryam said. "I'll go. I can get a day off of work so long as Valery the stalker doesn't follow me there. Anyone else up for a road trip?"

Colin's face lit up at the thought, but his excitement only lasted long enough for him to text his mother. An orthodontist appointment scheduled for the morning was set in stone.

"It's probably just as well," he said with a long sigh. "I doubt my dad would've let me go, anyway."

"What about you?" Maryam asked me. I'd gone over to the window and had been peeking up the street to see if I could spot Valery. Instead, I noticed a dark BMW with the driver's side window rolled down. I couldn't make out the occupants, but a male hand popped out to flick the ash from a cigarette. It seemed both Valery and Max were enjoying some stalking today.

"I'm in," I said.

13

Benny assured us that our destination was 'Just outside Seattle', which turned out to be perfectly true. But he'd skipped mentioning *which* outside direction that was. So it was a full extra hour of driving past the sprawling downtown core and then off towards the base of Mount Rainier and a town called Carbonado. I wasn't allowed behind the wheel for any of it, of course. There had been plenty of time on the ferry across to Vancouver and then hours in the car that followed for me to explain my ignorance of parking brakes and to recount my over-the-phone training experiment with Tim. Benny was apologetic. Maryam couldn't stop giggling.

The hilarity had waned when we crossed the border into Washington State. There's always something intimidating about customs officers. It didn't help that Benny's car had no seat belts in the back, or seats at all, for that matter. I just sat on a stack of folded shipping blankets Benny had found in the trunk and pretended to look safe and secure.

Otherwise, the trip went off without a hitch. The two of them took shifts driving, and we pulled into a roadside hotel outside Carbonado just after midnight. Maryam had made our reservations on the way down. Benny in one room, her and I in another.

"You don't mind sharing?" she asked me.

"Only if you don't mind paying?" I said. "Otherwise I'll just sleep in the car. I was doing that on the way down, anyway. There's plenty of room to stretch out and I'm on a budget."

"Courier business not bringing in the big bucks? You could always train as an electrician, you know. Apprenticeship programs mix classwork with job training so you get paid almost right away. There might be a height requirement though, you'd have to check."

"Hilarious," I said. "Have you considered a career switch yourself? Stand-up comedy? You have a flair for dealing with hecklers too. Or whatever Valery is."

I instantly regretted mentioning Valery's name. The reminder cast a pall over our mostly good-natured banter and suddenly I was exhausted.

"Let's go get some sleep," Maryam said. "And you'd better not be a snorer."

We were up early and thanks to the map on Maryam's phone and satellites in space; we were able to navigate ourselves to the address Benny had been given. The little that I saw of Carbonado was—aside from the proliferation of American flags on display—no different from any other small town outside Victoria. Rows of mostly charming detached homes with covered porches, and even a few with white picket fences. We didn't get to see the inside of any of them though, as the GPS sent us a few miles out of town and onto a gravel road that led off into the woods in a vaguely sinister way. It was a very different feeling a few minutes later when the single-lane track suddenly opened into a sprawling vineyard acreage.

"Wow," Maryam said, which I felt summed things up nicely.

Stretched along the crest of a low rise above us was a sprawling manor of cedar, rough stone, and glass. It presided over a countless number of orderly rows of grapevines that ran in undulating waves over the hillside.

We followed a single narrow lane through an archway announcing Carbon River Vineyards and up to the building above. Benny pulled us in beside an open jeep, where an elderly man was loading a suitcase. He checked his watch as he raised a hand in greeting.

"Benjamin Schlesien? A pleasure to meet you," the man said. His face eased into a smile. The deep lines and weathered skin of someone who'd spent their life not just out of doors but working hard in the process.

"Harry Montana," Benny said, and the two of them shook hands like they were school chums at a reunion. "Call me Benny. These are my friends, Maryam and Margot. Quite the place you've got here."

"Oh, just my little part of the world," Harry said with a twinkle in his eye as he shook our hands as well. "I'd love to show you around, but I'm on something of a clock today. Flight to catch in a few hours, so I'm afraid we'll have to keep this on a strictly business footing. You'll all come back again sometime soon for a proper visit, I hope. I've got a Sauvignon Blanc that'll knock your socks off. But for now, let's have a look at that cup you're after."

Harry waved us to follow, and he led the way inside with a loping stride. We filed down a short hallway and through a pair of massive carved wooden doors.

"Here's our tasting room. We open things up in the later summer and get some groups and such doing the tour come through." Harry said, ushering us into an open barn-like space. The far wall was entirely floor-to-ceiling glass, with a sweeping view past the vineyard and into the valley beyond. Morning light cut over a series of low tables and a long bar counter. Everything was made of solid timbers and lacquered to a shine. The long shelves behind the bar were mostly filled with rows of wine bottles. But here and there gaps were left for framed photos, and awards, and one larger space where the Stanley Cup sat.

"Your timing is perfect, actually," Harry said. "There's a Haida artist from up your way who makes these wonderful masks. He has one for me now. A replica he made of one of his grandfather's creations—just amazing! But I've had no place to put it. Now I do."

He had to stretch up to reach the trophy and Maryam stepped in to help lift it down and set it on the bar.

"What do you think?"

"It's fantastic," Maryam said.

"Accurate in every detail." Harry nodded.

We took turns examining the cup from all angles, and while none of us knew exactly what we were doing, we all agreed it was a stunning piece of art in its own right. Harry produced the paperwork that had come from the trophy maker attesting to its silver purity and other specifications. Then he dropped a custom-fitted soft bag over top and handed it to Benny.

"How are you getting back?" Harry said. "I can take you as far as the Sea-Tac airport if you like."

"That'd be fine," Benny said. "We can catch a bus up to Seattle from there. I thought we'd take the ferry back."

"Umm…Benny?" Maryam said. "Why aren't we driving your car home?"

I finally clued-in to what was going on.

"You're trading the cup for your…car?" My stunned incredulity came from a few different angles, though the major one was probably along the lines of wondering why

Benny hadn't just left it at a wreckers yard years ago. How was his old dented-up car worth anything at all?

"That's the deal," Harry said. "I'm happy if you're happy Benny?" The two men shook hands and Benny held out the keys.

"You might want to hang onto those. I'm just thinking that you'd mentioned you're in something of a hurry as well. The ferry from Seattle to Victoria only goes once and day and it left an hour ago. Though you could make your way up to Port Angeles. They have one this afternoon, I believe, but you won't get there in time unless you drive yourselves. I know some folks who live up that way. If you park it in the ferry lot and leave the keys tucked away somewhere, I'll ask them to pick it up for me."

"You trust us to leave the car for you," Maryam said.

Harry's face took on a slightly puzzled expression. "Any reason why I shouldn't?"

"Not a one," Benny said, and the two shook hands one more time.

"Alright then. Let's all get a move on," Harry said. "We've got a plane and a boat to catch. Do promise me you'll visit again when we can linger? And maybe you'll even find time to tell me why it is you want it so badly."

Value. It's a funny thing. One person's trash is another's treasure, as the saying goes. I was once again in the back of Benny's car, though this time I was sharing the blanket with a fifty thousand-dollar replica trophy. I was finding it difficult to reconcile that the car and the cup were somehow of equal value. I'd seen better-looking cars on my street with For Sale signs asking for a tenth of that.

"You ever hear about *tulpenmanie*?" Benny asked after

we'd pestered him long enough.

"Is that a kind of car?" I asked.

"No, it's Dutch. It means 'tulip mania'."

"You sure? Sounds like an STD," Maryam said. "Is there a vaccine?"

Benny just sighed and shook his head. "There was a time when tulip bulbs in the Netherlands became incredibly valuable. People were selling their cows, their houses, everything just to buy tulip bulbs. They don't teach this stuff in school anymore?"

"Cows?" Maryam said.

"This was years ago, back in the sixteen hundreds. People had cows."

"So you're saying we traded a cow for a tulip bulb?" I said.

"No, nothing like that," Benny said, but couldn't seem to stop his fingers from tapping on the steering wheel. "Well, actually, maybe. I guess we'll see."

We stopped twice on the way to Port Angeles. Once for Benny to fill up with gas while Maryam and I went a bit crazy getting unhealthy snacks and sports drinks for breakfast. And then later when a rest stop was called for as a result. We didn't dilly-dally too much, but even so, we barely made it in time. Benny pulled into the first available spot in the public parking lot to the right of the ferry pier. He had me take photos of where it was to send them to Harry. Then Maryam ran off to buy tickets while Benny hid the keys. Which left me to carry the cup.

It was more awkward than heavy, though it was hardly feather-light. I found that my best option was to hug it to my chest like it was a beach ball. But even that way, it kept slowly slipping down as a walked. I ended up sliding my arms underneath the cover so I could press my hands against the metal, which gave better friction but also brought up awkward memories of high-school dances.

"You need a hand there?"

Two burly guys in their thirties fell into step beside me. One had a full beard, the other thick glasses, and both were wearing New York Rangers ball caps.

"I'm good, thanks," I said, glancing back to see where the others were. Maryam was jogging towards me, waving tickets in one hand. I spotted Benny with his head bowed, walking at a much slower pace.

"Tis the season, huh?" One of the men said.

"To be jolly?"

"For playoff parties. Looks like you're getting set up," he said and bent down as we walked along to peek under where the cover. "That's a nice one. How much did that run you? If you don't mind me asking."

"How do you know it's not the real one?" Maryam asked as she moved in beside me.

He gave a full belly laugh. "Loads of reasons! Don't tell me you think you have the real one. It's a great copy, I'll give you that."

"Of course not," Maryam said, with a slight edge to her tone. "But how can you be sure?"

They didn't get a chance to answer as we'd reached the loading gate and were getting stern looks and sharp waves from the staff to hurry aboard. Benny caught us up and Maryam flashed our tickets.

We found four seats together with a view and had barely sat down when the two guys from earlier joined us.

"For one thing," the guy with the beard said, as though

there had been no interruption to our conversation. "None of you look like you're on the 'Keepers of the Cup' team. There is always one of them with the cup twenty-four-seven. The only time they leave it is when it's in the cargo hold of the plane they're on. And when it does, the cup travels around in a special shipping crate, not a bag."

"I see," Maryam said. "Is that all?"

"Well, I know the real one is in New York because I saw it on TV about an hour ago. Rangers won the first game last night. The next game is tomorrow, and then they're off to Vancouver for the next two. They had a thing going on today at the Gardens so fans could come out and see the cup up close. Wish I was there."

"You still don't know for sure this isn't the real one, though," Maryam said with something of a tease in her voice.

He gave another belly laugh. "Can I have a better look?"

Benny shrugged, and Maryam pulled the cover off.

"Ya, it's obvious. I mean, yours is perfect."

"Shouldn't it be?" I said.

"Oh, heck no! The real cup doesn't stay safe in a trophy case somewhere, it travels the world and it's seen some damage. The base is all dented and chipped. The bowl has been repaired a bunch of times. But aside from that, you can tell right away from the engraving. See, every letter of yours is perfect. That's because whoever made the trophy engraved it somehow."

"What do you mean?" Benny asked.

"On the real one, they aren't engraved like with a machine or a laser or whatever. They're all hammered in letter by letter by hand, so there are all kinds of variances between the letters. Some are real deep. Others you can barely make out. And somewhere..." he said and began turning the cup on its seat, searching for something.

"Ya, there you go. Look here. Nineteen eighty-four Oilers. The owner, Peter Pocklington, tried to sneak his father's name onto the cup even though his dad had nothing to do with the team. So he managed to get it on, but they crossed it out later by hammering a bunch of Xs over the name."

His buddy with the glasses had been busy on his phone. "Here's a close-up from the wiki page, a real mess. Now look at yours—just put a perfect row of X's all even and nice—no letters smushed underneath. Obvious."

Benny, Maryam, and I all leaned in together, nearly bumping our heads in the process.

"Oh, there are lots of other typos and mistakes, too. Don't know if yours has those or not. I'm not that much of a geek that I know them all. I'm a hockey fan—no question. And I only know so much because my son did an assignment on it for school. So we were doing all the research online and watching some documentaries and such."

"How interesting," Benny said. He almost sounded sincere, but I could tell he was as close to being violently ill as I was.

"Hey, sorry, didn't mean to say yours isn't great or anything. It is. It's perfect."

Maryam put the cover back over and she and Benny both slumped into their chairs. I took my phone out onto the deck and watched Port Angeles slip away as the ferry got underway. I could just make out Benny's car in the parking lot.

Was it a cow or a tulip? I couldn't tell.

14

According to a placard by the washroom, they built the Coho ferry in nineteen fifty-nine and it's been puttering back and forth between the US and Canada ever since. I'd only been on board once before. A high-school camping trip to the Olympic mountains. Other than feeling seasick—though that was mostly due to overeating S'mores—the only other thing I remembered was that the crossing took about an hour and a half. So I knew I had plenty of time to wander the upper deck and ponder our too-good cup replica.

We had used Maryam's phone for all our navigation needs, so I'd shut mine down the day before to avoid the roaming charges that I couldn't afford. When I judged the Coho was more than halfway across the strait, I switched it on and managed to connect to my home service provider. I ignored the backed-up queue of messages that began streaming in, as there was a call I needed to make first.

Saffron answered on the first ring.

"How's the trophy-making business?" I asked, trying to keep my voice light and peppy. "We had a hitch at our end. It's probably something your ex-husband should know about." Saffron patiently listened as I went on to explain the difference between the engraved lettering and the hammered version as best that I understood it. She said she'd call her ex right away and let me know.

Then I guiltily scrolled through several messages from Uncle Rupert asking how I was making out on the latest assignment. It was long past due for me to actually do some work, so I looked up my notes for the number of the Cadboro Bay Spa. A machine answered with a hold message to inform me they would be eager to rejuvenate my body, mind, and soul, but they were unable to take my call and that I should visit their website if I wanted to book an appointment. So I tried that instead. I clicked through to the online calendar of the masseuse in question. His first available appointment for new customers was a staggering three months away. Must be nice to be so popular. Though I imagined Uncle Rupert and the company client would disagree with that.

I scrolled around and found that while the massage slots were booked solid, there were a few options with other spa staff for mud baths, pedicures, and the like. Any of which would at least get me in the door. And I've never been particularly comfortable with the whole concept of strangers touching me anyway, even if their intentions are purely medical. The soonest I could find was for a simple manicure the following week, which seemed like a waste of an all-expenses-paid pampering opportunity. And there was the probability that if we couldn't deal with Alexander, then I wouldn't be free to make it, anyway. I clicked the 'Book Now' button all the same.

Lastly, I called Harley. Partially because she'd left me a half dozen text messages wondering where I was, but mostly just to hear her voice.

"Sup, homey?" she said. "You missed it—I watched Jungle Fever last night. Get this…the name of the character that Wesley Snipes was playing was called *Flipper Purify*. Can you believe that? So awesome. Not *really* a great romance though, way too angsty, and has no happy-ever-after ending, so that was disappointing. Halle Berry had a small part, so there was that I suppose. Can you get milk? I had those knock-off Rice Krispies things with apple juice this morning. It was terrible."

I happily let her ramble on about movies and food experiments until the drone of the engines changed to a lower-pitched rumble signalling our approach to Victoria. My phone began beeping with Saffron's return call just as we rounded the breakwater at Ogden Point, so I signed off with Harley. I realized that I'd forgotten to check to see if I could spot our apartment on the way in, something which she would undoubtedly ask me later.

"It's no problem," Saffron said before I could barely say hello. "I sent him some closeup photos of the cup that Colin found online that show the engraving...or whatever it is. He said that he could do something with the laser settings so that the letters will get etched in at random depths. It only takes a few minutes apparently, and the plating doesn't take long either. What is it now? Two thirty? He said he'd have it done by the end of the workday. I'll have him deliver it to Bennys."

"Sounds perfect. We're just about to dock now, so we'll be back at Benny's place in no time. See you later then," I said, as the inner harbour swung into view. The Coho coasted its way towards the pier and I took a moment to admire the view of the Empress Hotel, the Legislature, and all the boats moored in the harbour. We'd passed a cruise ship moored at Ogden Point and the streets were busy with rickshaws and pedicabs, and the clip-clop of horse-drawn carriages all carrying tourists. My eyes were drawn to a steady ambling flow of pedestrians on the sidewalk above the ferry parking lot. A second later, I was moving down the stairway at a half-jog to find Maryam and Benny.

"We have a problem."

"Another one?" Maryam said.

"A more urgent one," I said. "Valery is waiting out there."

"Valery? Where? Here? Are you sure?"

"He's pretty hard to mistake, even from a distance. I spotted him out on the street, leaning against his blue Audi. He's got all his attention on the ferry." I quickly related what I learned about the progress of the other cup from Saffron. "So I guess we need to decide if we want to walk out with this cup in plain sight or not?"

"With any luck, the other one that Saffron's making will be more convincing," Benny said. "She's having it sent to my shop? Alright, so we wait until then. If it looks good enough, then we can give that one to Alexander. He'll be happy and I'll just have a nice souvenir. And we can put this whole mess behind us."

"But what do we do now?" I said. "About Valery?"

"Has he been shadowing either of you guys around?" Maryam asked.

Benny and I shared a look and a shrug. "Not that I've noticed," he said.

I was tempted, once again, to mention my own stalker—Max Kirkpatrick of CSIS. But I couldn't see how that would do anything but complicate things more than they already were. Particularly when we seemed so close to the finish line.

"Alright, well, let's do this," Maryam said. "For whatever reason, he's been suspicious of me, so I'll go out first and make sure that he sees me. You guys both hang back and wait. If he follows me, I'll lead him on a shopping trip and you two can sneak off at your leisure."

"And if he doesn't?"

"Hmmm. If that happens, I'll send a text and Margot can go out next and try to get him to follow her instead," she said. "If *that* doesn't work, then...I guess he's waiting for somebody else entirely. Or maybe it's just a coincidence that he's here and he's doing some gangster stuff. Of course, you could be mistaken, and it's not even Valery in the first place?"

"I'm sure it's him," I said. "But I guess we'll see."

"I guess we will," she said. "You're okay to carry the cup, Benny?"

I noticed that he had slid the cover up to expose one section where he was absently running his thumb over the Montreal victory of nineteen ninety-three

"I'm fine," Benny said. "Don't worry about me. You two go. I'll find a cab or something and see you both at the shop later. But...you know...be safe, okay?"

"What if he's not here to follow anybody, but wants to talk, or...worse?" I said.

"You worry too much," she said, and for a horrible moment, I thought she was going to pat me on the head.

It turned out that we were both right. It *was* Valery. But apparently, I *do* worry too much. Valery sprung into action the moment he saw Maryam, but it was only to try to shield himself behind one of the ornamental trees that were spaced along the sidewalk. As Valery's neck alone was wider than the tree trunk, he gave the impression of a toddler trying to play hide and seek. Maryam pretended not to notice—which couldn't have been easy—and strode off while Valery scrambled back to his car. He briefly played with his cellphone before tossing it onto the passenger seat and then merging out behind a rickshaw to give chase at a crawling pace.

"Have we considered the possibility that he is a moron?" Benny asked.

"If he is a moron, he's a scary one," I said. "And either

way, Alexander is surely not."

"True enough," Benny replied and hefted the cup under one arm. "Alright, let's go find us some transportation home."

It's only about a ten-minute walk to Benny's flower shop from the ferry dock, but neither of us wanted to lug the trophy that far. I found a pedicab roomy enough for Benny and me and the cup.

"Do you think we traded your car for nothing?" I asked.

"Looks like it," he said. "I guess we could dent Harry's cup up a bit to simulate some wear and tear, but there's no easy fix for the engraving thing. It certainly was obvious to those fellows on the ferry."

"Is Alexander as knowledgeable as them, though?"

"We don't know that he isn't," Benny sighed.

The Vespa was where I'd left it outside the flower shop. I woman-handled the cup into the shop myself while Benny paid the driver. We agreed he'd be in touch with me and the rest of the gang the moment the other cup was delivered. He looked tired and worn out by the whole ordeal. I felt the same. I drove home with the only two things on my mind; a shower and a nap.

The shower was brief, but the nap went on far, far longer than intended. I woke up to find Harley sitting on the end of my bed, eating a bagel.

"Wakey, wakey, sleepyhead," she said. "Here. You left your phone on the kitchen table and it's been going bananas."

"Oh god. What time is it?"

"Movie time! I have three left from the pile to choose from," she said.

I glanced at the list of messages and missed calls and

threw off the covers. With a promise to be back as soon as I could, I was running for the door.

The flower shop had a 'closed' sign, and the door was locked, so I hiked around to the rear and came in through the small loading door where Benny received flower shipments. The design room was empty of people but well decorated with Stanley Cups.

Benny's replica that we'd picked up in Seattle was in the centre of the table. Beside it, Tim's undersized version that Valery had crushed in his bare hands sat looking as though it was hanging its head in shame. The new one that Saffron's ex-husband had crafted was right in front of me. It was sitting on a small shipping palette, just inside the loading door, half covered in bubble wrap.

I could hear voices from upstairs. I stepped around the palette for a closer look. It was impressive. The letters looked much closer to those I'd seen in the online photos of the real one. And the dimensions and finishing detail all looked great to my eye.

There was a difference in the sheen of the finish. Benny's had a greyish hue that brought to mind the cutlery that my grandmother only brought out at Thanksgiving and Christmas. Saffron's was as bright and shiny as a new dime. Though that was maybe not so surprising, as it was only hours old, not years and years. I expected that we would need to rough it up anyway to add some dents and dings, as the fellow on the ferry suggested. But if that was all…then I felt we'd done it! A replica good enough to pass for the real thing.

I ran upstairs with a lightness to my step. Benny was sitting in the living room portion reading a newspaper. The others were slouched around the kitchen table, nursing mugs of tea. The mood was surprisingly sombre, and I couldn't think why.

"Hey guys," I said. "It looks amazing."

Saffron gave a slow nod in agreement. "Yes, it does *look* good."

"I don't understand," I said. "What's going on?"

"So you checked it out," Maryam said.

"Ya, it's awesome. Isn't it?"

"Did you try to pick it up?" Colin asked.

Uh-oh. The size, the finish, and even the lettering were perfect. *Something* was wrong. Then it hit me: no one had moved it off the palette.

"Is it too heavy?"

"Got it in one," Maryam said. "And not just by a little heavy, either. They used a forklift to deliver it."

Tim waved his phone to indicate he had the facts. "It's supposed to weigh thirty-four and a half pounds."

"And how much is it off?"

"Hard to say, really," Maryam said. "The largest wire spools I use at work run about fifty pounds. I tried to shift it by hand on the palette and it didn't budge. I could lean it a little though. I'd guess it's probably around two or three hundred. Maybe more."

"Maybe we can get Valery to lift it?" Colin said. "He probably wouldn't notice."

"So we're no further ahead," Saffron said.

"Let's recap, shall we?" Maryam said. There was a flush to her cheeks that went with the sharpness in her voice. "We've got a tiny cup that we can play catch with. We've got another that is too perfect. And we have a better, less-perfect one that is apparently filled with concrete. We've wasted four days and I don't know how much money."

"We have an invoice from Saffron's ex-husband for twenty-five hundred dollars, plus two months to cover his alimony payments for Saffron and Colin," Tim said. "Not to mention Benny's car, or however you guys spent on travelling down and back."

"And the four hundred for the little one," Colin said.

Tim gave a dismissive wave. "No, that's on me," he said. "My mistake."

"No, it's not," I said. "We're all in this together and we'll figure it out together. Right?"

There was a grunt from the other end of the room.

"What do you think, Benny?"

"Did anybody read the paper?" he asked.

"What? No. I didn't find time for the crossword today," I said. "Why?"

"I don't mean *today's* paper. Not the crossword either," he said. "I found this one downstairs. It's the newspaper that Alexander gave us last Friday."

"With the article about the Stanley Cup that started all this?" Tim said.

"That's the one," he said. "Did anybody get around to actually reading it?"

"I skimmed it," Maryam said. "It was just a fluff piece about Tampa Bay Lightning, who won last year, wasn't it?"

"More or less," Benny agreed. "You maybe missed the bit about how every winning team gets one hundred days out of the following year to have time with the cup. For parades, promotional fan events and such. But also, each player and key support staff can have their day with it. The owners, the coaches, the trainers, the management, all the way down to the guy that sharpens their skates if they want."

"So?" I said.

"So…Clara Peters," Benny said with a meaningful look my way.

"And who is that?"

"Ms. Peters is one of the Tampa Bay scouts. She's also, incidentally, a member of the Huu-ay-aht First Nations that live around the village of Sarita. And she wanted to have her day with the cup there last summer, but it hadn't worked out because of bad weather."

"Okay," I said. "So…that's a shame for her?"

Benny folded the newspaper in half and tapped it on the armrest of his chair. "Do you know where Sarita is?"

"Nope," I said. "But I'm guessing you do?"

"It's here! Sarita is here!" Colin's voice was nearly a yell. His phone was so close to his nose that I was amazed he could see anything. "It's up by Bamfield. Google Maps says it's like…less than two hundred kilometres away."

"Which is something that I'm guessing Alexander knew all along," Benny said. "And that's the point. He gave us the newspaper, not because it was just an article about the Stanley Cup. He gave it to us because it says that Clara Peters will get her day with it. In Sarita."

"And what day is that?" Tim said.

Benny waved the newspaper as though it were a magic wand. "This Sunday. In four days."

I'd moved over to the window in thought. The sun was low in the sky and what little I could see of the horizon going north was shades of grey and orange.

"Okay, but…" Tim said. "Just what are you suggesting? I thought we all agreed that we were going to find a replica."

A car on the street below was having trouble angle parking into a small space. In the spot behind, a black BMW backed up to make room. Through its open window, a cigarette dangled from the hand of the driver. Max Kirkpatrick.

My shoulders sagged. Last week, my biggest concern had been that Harley was threatening to paint our living room with some sort of Van Gogh-inspired kaleidoscope pattern. At the time, it had actually seemed like something to worry about. Now, one little elevator ride in the wrong direction and I was suffocating under a pile of Euro-mobsters, a secret agent, and a truly ridiculous task. What a mess!

What was Alexander going to do if we failed? Come to that, what was he going to do if we succeeded? As the questions ran through my mind, I kept tripping over the word 'we'. Working alone had always been my way. Even in high school, I'd always managed to avoid group projects. Still, there was some weird off-putting comfort in knowing that I wasn't the only one who had been on the elevator. For better or worse, we were all in this together.

I turned away from the window and I found all five of them staring at me expectantly.

"Okay," I said as a growing sense of purpose began to take hold of me. "We *were* going with the replica thing. Right? But let's face it. That idea hasn't exactly brought us any further ahead. Has it? We know what we need to do to get ourselves out of this mess. So…let's just…do it!"

There was a stunned silence that followed. It was eerily quiet. All I could hear were the metronome-like tocks from Benny's wall clock and the muted buzz of traffic from outside.

The contemplative calm was shattered by a growly "No, no, no!" from Saffron.

"Yes, yes, yes!" I said. There was a zip to my tone that I

realized held a hefty dose of frustration. I was getting fed up. "We need to do two things, actually. But first, let's plan on how to steal the thing and be done with it. It's no wonder Valery has been following us around. I know Alexander said he didn't want to know the details, but he has to be wondering what we're up to. He told us exactly where and when it was going to be. Valery is no doubt reporting back that we haven't made the slightest outward effort to do anything at all with that information."

"But we can't *actually* steal it," Saffron said.

"Why not? How hard can it be? It's not locked in a vault or anything." I stabbed a finger toward Benny's newspaper. "They fly the thing all over the place. Airlines lose luggage every day. We just need to get a plan together."

"You don't think they'll miss it?"

"You said two things," Benny said. "What's the other?"

"I've just been thinking, if we fail at stealing it-" I started.

"Which we probably will," Maryam said.

"*Definitel*y will," Tim corrected.

I ignored them both. "*If* we fail, then Alexander will no doubt just give us something else to do. And the next thing might be far worse. It's never going to end. Unless we end it."

"What are you saying here?" Benny was gingerly holding the rolled newspaper between his hands as though it had suddenly turned into glass.

I'd been walking by the windows, going back and forth in small strides, getting angrier and more focused with every step. Finally, I stopped and took a few moments to give each of them—one by one—what I hoped was a look that projected steely-spined confidence and resolve.

"Let's do it.," I said. "Let's steal the cup, and—while we're at it—how about we bring down Alexander's entire organization?"

15

There was a stunned silence that followed. It seemed to drag on forever while each of them looked at me as though I'd gone insane.

Finally, Tim said, "Oh, is *that* all?"

"You can't be serious," Saffron said.

Only Colin had a smile. "Cool."

"We've been going about this all wrong," I said. "You heard what Valery was saying when he came here the other day? He doesn't think we're trying, and he's right—we're not."

"What? You think our growing collection of Stanley Cups is because we're not putting enough effort in?" Maryam said.

"Not in the right way, no. I'm not even convinced that Alexander wants the cup at all," I said. "He probably just wants to be sitting in his office laughing himself silly at the thought of making us jump through hoops. Only Valery's been reporting back that as far as he can tell, we're not doing anything aside from hanging around and having fun and maybe going on a winery tour."

"So, what are you suggesting here?" Benny said.

"I think we're wasting an opportunity to help lock these guys up forever."

"Margot, c'mon," Tim said. "These are real gangsters that are connected to god knows what or who. We can't go up against them. If the fake cup idea hasn't worked, then I think we should just keep our heads down until he gets bored with us. Maybe the police will get them for whatever crimes they're doing?"

"The authorities have been trying," I said. "I don't think they've gotten very far."

"How do you know that?"

I took a breath. It was time to come clean. "A government agent approached me. Max Kirkpatrick. He's with CSIS—the spy agency guys."

"What? When?" Maryam said. "Why didn't you tell us?"

"Nobody panic. I haven't told him anything. I guess he saw me coming out of their building and talking to Valery. So he's been following me around ever since, and I had a few words with him the other night. Other than vague probing about what my connection to Alexander and Valery is, though, he didn't ask me much. He's outside right now."

There was a mini stampede over to the window. I had to elbow my way back in to try to point out the BMW.

"Well, he *was* there," I said. The dark BMW had been replaced by a fire-red Tesla. I scanned up and down the street, but there was no sign of him or the car. "Has anyone else been approached by him or seen him hanging around? He's maybe in his thirties. Not the ugliest guy, but a chain smoker."

"Why does everyone seem upset? This is *great,*" Saffron said. "We should tell him everything. Let the authorities take care of it, like I've been saying all along."

"It's not like on TV, Mom," Colin said. "The cops are not going to swoop in and arrest everybody without any kind of proof, more than just what we tell them. Are they?"

"I doubt it," Benny said.

"But if the police are watching them, then what can we do that they can't?" Saffron said.

"It's CSIS," I said. "I think they're more about gathering

information and don't arrest anybody themselves. But either way, we have two things going for us that they don't. For one, this guy, Max Kirkpatrick, might *suspect* them of doing any number of crimes, but we know for a fact that Alexander and Valery murdered Kirill Bondarchuk. And the other thing is that at the moment we have better access than any of the authorities to try to prove it. That's the real way out of this for us."

"What sort of proof are you talking about?"

"They did something with the body," I said. "Maybe it's in a freezer in another room of their office. Maybe it's at the bottom of an elevator shaft. Whatever they did with it, it happened fast—the wheelbarrow was empty by the time I went back up."

"I vote elevator shaft," Benny said. "Then trunk of a car and off to...wherever. Forever."

"I don't know...I like the freezer idea," Maryam said. "Less messy."

"That's a point," Benny said. "Nine floors down...there's going to be some impact."

"Oh god," Saffron said. "I'm going to be sick."

"We're looking for bodies now?" Tim said.

"What about Valery's phone?" Colin said. "He was recording the whole thing. Or that's what it looked like he was doing. If we could get his phone, maybe we could get the video. That would be proof, wouldn't it?"

"How would we do that?" Tim said.

"You're the computer tech guy, aren't you?" Maryam said. "Can't you do something?"

Tim and Colin took turns explaining the few truths, and many fictions perpetuated by television and movies about the ease of accessing digital devices. I'm sure it was fascinating stuff, but I'd tuned out. Instead, I reread the newspaper article, this time with more attention to detail.

"Where is the cup right now?" I asked, cutting into the flow of something to do with Wi-Fi encryption. Benny and Saffron both shot me grateful looks.

"The guy on the ferry said it was in New York," Maryam said.

"Depends on which one you're talking about," Colin said.

"She doesn't mean the ones downstairs, Colin. The *real* one," Saffron said.

"There's more than one copy, remember?" Colin waggled his phone as a visual reminder of his online prowess. "The presentation one that travels around and then there's the copy that stays at the Hockey Hall of Fame. There's also the real original one, but that's in separate pieces in the vault."

"And where is this Hockey Hall of Fame, anyway?" Saffron asked.

"It's in Toronto," Maryam said. "Always wanted to go, actually."

"So, which cup version do we think Alexander wants?" Tim asked.

"It's got to be the first copy, the presentation cup," Benny said. "If that's the only one that travels around, then that's the one in the newspaper article he gave us. Right?"

"Why don't we ask him?" I was already pulling up Valery's number before anybody could think of a good reason why that was a bad idea. It rang so many times that I nearly thought better of it myself. But then, after the tenth or so ring, there was a click, some fumbling sounds, and Valery's deep grunt of acknowledgment. There were the clangs and whirs of working machinery in the background like he was at an automotive repair shop or something.

"Catch you at an okay time?" I asked.

"What do you want?"

"It's Margot. I need to talk to Alexander."

"Why?"

"We have some questions," I said. And then as I looked around Benny's small apartment and thought about the cups filling up his flower shop, I had another idea. "And we need some supplies."

"Questions? You ask me. I ask him," he said. "You're at flower shop? Maybe I will come in an hour."

"An hour? Time is ticking, Valery. We're on a bit of a clock here. Besides, I don't want to have to go back and forth like that. We tell you, you tell him, you tell us...on and on. It won't take five minutes of his time. Surely if he wants us to succeed with-"

"Not over the phone," Valery cut me off.

"When then?" I said.

"Not now," he said. "One moment."

The 'on hold' music consisted of more muted machinery noises. There was an echoey quality to it and then the unmistakable sound of a wood saw. I amended my earlier guess and decided Valery was at an indoor construction site. Maybe they were finally making progress on the empty floors in their building. I took the opportunity to switch my phone to speaker so the others could enjoy it as well.

"Tomorrow morning," Valery growled a moment later. "The golf club in Oak Bay. He will meet you there."

"Tomorrow morning? What time?"

More muffled conversation punctuated by a few barks of laughter.

"Quarter to six. You will have five minutes. No more. Goodbye."

Harley had a massive bowl of popcorn and a double feature waiting when I got home. I made it through *Romancing The Stone,* but I was fast asleep on the couch before the opening credits of *Fair Game* had even started—so I completely missed Cindy Crawford's acting debut.

At least before I'd gotten too comfy, I had the foresight to set my phone alarm. I didn't have complete confidence that it would wake me up, but I'd given Benny permission to kick our door down if I didn't answer in the morning. Of course, I didn't want him to have to kick anything—never mind making him climb the three flights of stairs up to the apartment. As a result, my sleep was light and restless and when the alarm went off at five-thirty, I was instantly awake. Harley had either also fallen asleep during the movie, or just opted to share the couch with me by choice. Which was normally fine, but I'd gotten squished between her, the end cushions, and the bowl of popcorn. I was still pulling stray popcorn from my hair when Benny's flower van spluttered up the driveway.

We picked up a yawning Saffron and Colin on the way. I'd told them they didn't need to come, but Colin wouldn't miss it and Saffron wouldn't let him go without her.

Despite the ridiculously early hour, the sun was already up, though still sitting low on the horizon. The smooth swells of the ocean and the snow tops of the Olympic mountains in the distance were both brushed in an orange glow. When Beach Drive angled away from the shore to cut through the golf course, we were driving straight into the rising sun. Benny had to slow to a crawl as he squinted between the wheel and visor.

Valery was waiting for us at the entrance to the golf club parking lot. He held up his hand as though he were a traffic warden and directed Benny to park in one of the curbside spots beside Maryam's pickup truck. We were still exchanging blurry good mornings when Alexander appeared. Unlike the rest of us, he was looking fresh and energetic, dressed in a natty pair of tan chinos and a sky-blue polo shirt.

"What is it you want?" he said. He was struggling with a single glove on his left hand. "I told you to bring problems to Valery."

There hadn't been much further discussion last night. The consensus seemed to be that since it was my idea to meet up with Alexander, I could be the one to lead the conversation. We never got around to hammering out the details, though, so I was pretty much winging it.

"We need a few things," I said. "And, as we know how important this cup is to you, we just thought it would be best to get things organized quickly."

"Such as?"

"We've done some preliminary work, but we've been footing the bill for everything so far. Our expenses are getting up there. We still have plane tickets to buy and such, and we're not rich business types like you."

"You need money? How much?"

"Five thousand should cover it," I said and held my breath. I was going to say twenty-five hundred, but then doubled it at the last second.

Alexander's lips twitched in what might have been a smirk. I wasn't sure what he'd found funny, but he just snapped the fingers of his non-gloved hand and held it up towards Valery. They exchanged some words in Ukrainian and Valery made a sour face, but he reached into his jacket all the same. A thick envelope changed hands. Alexander tapped it against his palm a few times before holding it out to me with a hard look. I felt like I was renegotiating my student loan at the bank.

"That's ten thousand. It was intended for something else, but I'll make a different investment. Keep your receipts," he added and then turned to go.

"There's more," I said, feeling a little giddy with my success. While the money was all very nice, that wasn't what I wanted from this meeting. "As you can imagine, we have some serious planning to do, and we need proper office space to do it. We've been using Benny's flower shop up until now, but we need someplace better. Let us use your lounge instead. The one with the big tv."

"No."

"The conference room?"

"No, nothing like this. I don't want any of you in my offices."

I was afraid of that.

"What about all those other floors in the building below you? They looked empty. How about one of those?"

He looked at Valery, who just shrugged in a 'why not' sort of way.

"Fine," Alexander sighed.

"And we need it today," I said.

"Yes, yes, yes. Valery will get you keys and whatever else. Is that it? My tee off-time is soon. Can I go play golf now?"

I held back from jumping for joy and did my best to just nod in a business-like way. Alexander strolled off, still working on his glove, while I made arrangements with a grumpy Valery to meet him at the office building at two o'clock. This was, he assured me, the earliest possible time. I didn't know how long a round of golf took to play, but I could well imagine there might be other things going on. Alexander didn't want us in sight of the clubhouse, which made me wonder who he was meeting.

"Why are we doing this, exactly?" Maryam said once we'd gathered back at the vehicles. "The money is great and all, but isn't this just digging us into a deeper hole?"

"We're already in a hole. Deep or shallow, we still need to dig ourselves out of it. If he didn't before, at least now Alexander knows we're making an effort. And we've improved our access considerably."

"I don't want to do crimes," Saffron reminded us.

"Don't worry," I said. "If it comes down to anything, that's...you know, *wildly* illegal. I'll make sure you and Colin are out of it."

"Me too, please," Tim said. "I'd rather not be part of that sort of thing, either."

"That's the spirit," Benny said with what I hoped was sarcasm.

"What was all that about needing airline tickets? Were you just pulling his chain?" Maryam said.

"Nope. You mentioned you'd always wanted to go see the Hockey Hall of Fame. How about right now?"

16

It took all of about five minutes to decide who was going where and doing what. Maryam was more than happy to book a few days off of work and Colin was almost in tears of joy when Saffron said they could go to Toronto as well. The rest of us would stay and see about establishing a new base of operations.

I handed the money, and the role of accountant, over to Benny, who I judged was likely to be the most responsible. The only hitch came when Saffron had second thoughts about the likely source of that cash.

"That's crime money though, isn't it? Like from drugs or something? I don't feel good about using that to pay for the flight."

"We don't know that for a fact," I said. "Benny told me the other day that these guys spend as much time doing legal things as illegal. Right?"

Benny nodded and shrugged. "That seems to be the way of it. From what I've read, many of these organized crime groups—motorcycle gangs, the old-school Italian Mafia types, and so on—just focus on the criminal aspect because that's where the biggest profits are. But the East Europeans are more open-minded. They'll get involved in anything so long as some sort of financial gain comes out of it."

"Simple then," Tim said. "Just use the legal half to buy the plane tickets."

I couldn't tell if he was joking or not, but Saffron seemed content with the idea. There were other second thoughts relating to Colin missing a few days of school and needing to clear things with her ex-husband. But then she remembered that her astrologist had told her that travel was in her future, and so it was settled. A quick check online showed that the next direct flight to Toronto had room for three, but took off in just a few hours. Benny gave Maryam enough to cover the flights, a hotel and some running around money. Then the three of them were piling into her pickup truck and hurried off with a squeal of tires.

"What am I missing?" Tim asked as he watched the pickup disappear up the road. "Why did you send them to Toronto? There can't be anything to learn that we couldn't have found out online. Is there?"

"Probably not," I admitted. "But you never know, and it just seemed like the best idea was to have them out of the way while we get up to shenanigans. Besides, the biggest thing at the moment is to show Alexander that we're doing something about getting the cup. Going to the Hockey Hall of Fame is definitely sending that message."

"You think he's going to follow them to Toronto?"

I looked over at the clubhouse. A grove of trees hid most of the building, but on the south side, I spotted Alexander chatting merrily with three other men as they strolled a short distance onto what I assumed was the tee area of the first hole. Valery was dividing his focus between wrestling golf bags into a cart and stealing glances our way. I was a bit disappointed to see that he was just a caddy. It would've almost been worth sticking around just to see him swing a golf club. Though with all that bulk, I imagine he was more brute force than technique. Maybe I should challenge him to some disc golf.

"I think at the moment Valery has his hands full just following Alexander around," I said. "But he's proven that he has ways of tracking us down. We lost him when we went to Seattle, but he was waiting when we got back. It will be interesting to see what he does now. I expect that if he figures out where the others are going he'll have people in Toronto he can call to keep an eye on them. But I guess we'll see."

"And you didn't want to go too?"

"Me? No, the three of us have things to do."

"Setting up this office idea?"

"Smoke and mirrors and pizza," I said, which was unnecessarily cryptic but I was distracted by the sight of Valery weaving his way out of view on the golf cart as he followed Alexander and the others into the distance, and a thought had come to mind.

"I'll explain in a minute," I said. "Small errand to run first."

I dug through my shoulder bag and found the pouch with the various devices Uncle Rupert had entrusted me with. There was a collection of bugs and two GPS trackers in waterproof boxes with magnetic mounts. I figured I wouldn't need both of them for my appointment with the guy at the spa. "Won't be a minute."

The clubhouse parking lot was mostly empty, which, given how early it was, didn't seem that surprising. I ignored a group of what I assumed to be staff vehicles. They were all older, practical models of the sort that I couldn't imagine someone like Alexander willingly *look* at, never mind ride inside. They were also huddled as far from the entrance as possible. Paying members will happily walk eighteen holes worth of grass—crossing parking lots is a different story.

Valery's Audi was nowhere to be seen among the line of high-end sedans in the prime spots by the clubhouse entrance. I could only assume that Valery had been chauffeur as well as caddy. So which was Alexanders? I narrowed it down to three possibilities; a BMW, a Jaguar, and a Mercedes. All brand new. All spotlessly clean and polished to a shine. But only the BMW had the driver's seat positioned as far back as it could go. And that only made sense if someone Valery's size had been driving. I made a show of tying my shoelace in case there were any security cameras pointed my way, which I had to assume there probably were. As I stood up, I palmed a GPS tracker inside the rear wheel well. Modern cars seem to have less and less steel in them every year, so you can never be certain, but the strong magnet on the tracker pulled it right out of my hand and it sucked onto the car with a pleasing 'chunk'.

"Eight series BMW," Benny said when I rejoined them by the van. "The Alpina Gran Coupé, if I'm not mistaken. What were you doing with it? Letting the air out of his tire?"

"I thought it might be fun to see what Alexander gets up to when he's not golfing. I planted a tracker-gizmo."

"I see. And you just carry those things around with you in your purse?"

"Go-bag," I corrected. "And yes, sometimes I do. I suppose I should explain that a little better."

Which I did.

The three of us piled into Benny's van and headed off towards Fernwood, where Tim lived. As we looped through Oak Bay, I gave them a surface view of my work with Uncle Rupert. I put lots and lots of emphasis on the part where we worked for a very legitimate accounting firm, and maybe not so much on the occasionally illegal aspects of surveillance. They took most of it in with silent nods, so I had no trouble bringing the conversation back to the smoke and mirrors comment I'd made earlier.

"We need to put on a show," I said. "The office space in their building is all about making a big splash about how we're putting in a solid research and scheming effort to steal the cup for them."

"Uh-huh. But actually…?" Benny prompted, giving me a side-eyed glance.

"Instead, I'm hoping we can use that proximity to find proof about what they did with Kirill's body, or solid evidence of any other sort of serious crime that we can hand over to Max, the CSIS guy. A body would be nice. I'll settle for digital information."

"The Wi-Fi signals in the building are terrible. Maybe if we're close enough, I could try to get into their network?" Tim said.

Benny had stopped at the light in Oak Bay village. I realized we were less than a block away from Marty's lair. It wasn't even six-thirty yet, but I wondered if Marty would appreciate my early get-up-and-go spirit.

"Any sort of equipment you need to help with that?" I asked. "I know a guy."

Tim assured me he had his needs covered, but I asked Benny to make a right turn anyway. I had him pull into the laneway behind Marty's place at the end of the block. For insurance, I asked Tim to join me as I climbed out.

Unlike my last visit, Marty was at the door almost immediately.

"Did you lose more of my gear already?" he said by way of greeting. He was wearing a bathrobe, but he was often dressed that way, so it wasn't clear if he'd just gotten up or was on his way to bed. Or maybe that's just how he dressed.

"Nope, all accounted for," I said. "I dropped by for a few other things, though."

"This isn't a candy store," he said. "You can't just grab whatever, whenever you want. If Rupert tells me you need something...then we'll see."

I kept a perky smile firmly in place and waved at Tim. Marty had started to close the door, but curiosity got the better of him.

"Who's this? Your boyfriend?"

"A new acquaintance," I said. "Marty meet Tim Angulalik. Tim works in cyber security. You know... recovering data from corrupted hard drives? Things like that."

Marty's face transformed almost instantly from a flushed sneer to a blanched slack-jawed expression. It was a fun moment for me. I hadn't been sure that Marty would remember whose network he'd recently been hacking into, but clearly, he was better with names than I gave him credit for.

"Marty is into computer things too," I said to Tim. "I expect you two would have *loads* to talk about."

Marty yanked the door sharply closed, leaving just enough of a gap for a conversation.

"What do you want?" he rasped.

I asked for two bug detectors—one pocket-sized for discretion, the other a fair bit larger but with better range and directionality and the ability to find anything electronic whether it was powered on or not. Together, they should be able to detect any sort of device; audio or video, analog or digital. I was fully expecting—and hoping—that Alexander would have our new office space under electronic surveillance. Though it would also be good to give Benny's flower shop a scan and make sure it was not. Typically, I was the one placing the sneaky devices, so detectors weren't something I was super familiar with. I had to hope that the internet would tell me how to use them, as Marty was never one to provide manuals or instruction. I also grabbed another GPS tracker to replace the one I stuck on the BMW. Not that I felt I needed it, but it was fun to see Marty in such a giving mood.

It was still way too early to go shopping for office supplies, so after a brief debate, we agreed that breakfast and a general reboot to the morning were in order for everyone. We planned to rendezvous at Benny's for ten. After dropping Tim at his house, Benny had me back at my apartment in James Bay, still on the dawn side of eight o'clock.

As early as it was, when I climbed the back stairs to our apartment, I found both Harley and the coffee machine were gone. I checked the schedule that Harley keeps on the fridge and saw that it was one of those days when she had an early pick-up to kick off her morning dog walk. Which explained where Harley had gone. It wasn't clear at all what the coffee machine's excuse was.

I contented myself with a cup of tea and the crossword from the local free newspaper. The puzzle section shares the same page as the horoscope, where I read that Leos could expect: *It's a good week to get in touch with your feelings rather than push them away. You will find that the more sensitive your approach, the farther you will get in the pursuit of your goals.* That all sounded like reasonable advice. For someone else. I like to think I'm always in touch with my feelings, and that at least today, pursuing my goals had taken on more of a swashbuckling approach, but it seemed to be working.

The crossword was one of those types that require you to have up-to-date knowledge of the names of tabloid pseudo-celebrities. So I had pretty much given up on it when a message came in from Maryam. After a mad scramble to pack the necessities, they had avoided speeding tickets and were now apparently all checked in at the airport. Which was pretty impressive, I had to admit. More text messages followed, suggesting that they were actually hoping to make it to the Hall of Fame before they closed. What with the flight time and the three-hour time difference, I wasn't personally optimistic of their chances. But all the smiley faces and exclamation points seemed to indicate that Maryam was game to try. I had to admire the enthusiasm. Which prompted me to drop the crossword with a guilty pang and jump into action.

After a shower and a change into non-popcorn-smelling clothes, I found and downloaded the entire PDF manual for the Omicron HD version 3.7 Deluxe Non-Linear Junction Detector. Then I spent a lively hour or so wandering around the apartment looking for non-existent listening devices. The biggest hurdle was that I couldn't use the detector and refer to the user guide simultaneously, as all it would do was locate the phone in my other hand. So the first while involved running back and forth between the phone at one side of the room and the detector at the other. Eventually, I got it figured out. I even found the remote control for a VHS machine that had gone to recycling years ago hidden in the sofa.

Then I packed up and headed over to join Benny and Tim at the flower shop. I even arrived almost on time at a little after ten. I showed off my newfound bug-sweeping skills to confirm that Valery and Polina hadn't left anything behind when they'd dropped by the other evening. Once I was satisfied it was all clear, we piled into Benny's van and headed to the mall to spend some of Alexander's money on office supplies.

"But why do we need *four* whiteboards?" Tim asked.

"They're huge!"

"You know how they sometimes say that 'less is more'?" I said. "This is a 'more is more' situation."

Valery was waiting for us when we pulled into the underground parking lot of the office building at two on the dot. There was still only one elevator working, and Valery had to wave a keycard at the panel inside to activate the eighth-floor button.

"Do we get an elevator key, too?" I asked.

"No. You can maybe go to the fourth floor. Then take stairs. Here is key to the stairwell door," he said and handed me a standard Schlage key designed for a six-pin cylinder. "No making copies."

"I won't need to if you give me my tools back," I said with a hopeful smile.

Valery just gave a low grunt, which I interpreted to mean 'possibly later but not right this second' and we rode up the rest of the way in silence. The eighth floor had the look of a hastily abandoned bomb shelter. There was a skeleton of steel studs marking out where walls for offices might have gone. In the spaces between was a random assortment of building materials; open cardboard boxes of fasteners of various kinds, a stack of drywall sheets held down by bags of compound, reels of cables and wires. Over everything was a thick layer of gritty concrete dust.

"What a mess," Benny said.

"The Feng Shui needs some work," I admitted.

Valery just gave us a thin smile as the elevator doors slid shut.

"Now what?" Tim asked.

The rest of the day mostly involved an equal mix of running errands for cleaning supplies and putting those materials to use. We found that while you couldn't press any of the buttons inside the elevator to go anywhere other than the fourth and lower floors, it would happily show up if you pressed the button from the level you were already on. So one of us always stayed on the eighth floor to press the call button to bring the others back up after a supply run. Text messaging worked well enough to let each other know when to press the button. The only downside was that you had to remember to lean your phone on a window ledge to get any sort of signal.

In the end, we created a working office space in the largest open area on the floor, which I estimated was directly below Alexander's TV lounge. The whiteboards took some time to assemble on their stands. We wheeled them to form four walls around a long folding table and six office chairs Benny had found at Staples. Tim had provided a few computers from his office downstairs. They were not the fastest in the world, he said, but were more than ample for online research—if only we had an internet connection. Try as he might, Tim could find no Wi-Fi signals of any sort. Whether he was ignoring my calls or was just busy, I couldn't get Valery to pick up, so I left a message to complain about our lack of service and we called it quits for the day.

Harley was waiting with takeout Indian food and a surprise when I got home.

"What do you think?" she said, gesturing towards the kitchen table as though she was auditioning for a role on The Price Is Right. "Isn't it awesome?"

I chewed thoughtfully on some naan bread before answering. "You traded our coffee maker…for a karaoke machine."

"I know! It's a good one too!"

"Uh-huh. I'm sure it is. But they're not *really* the same thing, are they?"

"Think about it!" she said, tapping the side of her head with two fingers. "*Why* do you drink coffee?"

"Hmmm. Okay. I give up. Why?"

"It's not a riddle," she said with a fair amount of exasperation. "It's a question."

In truth, in all the years I had known Harley, the distinction between the two had never once been clear to me.

"I suppose because I like the taste and it helps me to wake up?"

"Well, there you go," she said. "Same thing."

"Is it?" I was fairly sure that if Harley and I suddenly decided to start each morning by belting out ABBA songs, Mrs. Carter's broom handle downstairs would find a difference.

"Hurry up and finish eating so we can go try it!"

"Go? Where?"

"It has batteries. We can take it to the lake in the park. Ducks love being sung to."

"Ducks?"

"I read it somewhere. Probably the turtles will like it too. I don't know about that."

Sometimes in life, you have to stand firm in the face of things you don't understand. But I've yet to find a way to do that with Harley. We walked to Goodacre Lake with the karaoke machine and sang until it was long after dark and the batteries died. I don't know if the ducks or the turtles enjoyed any of it.

I know I did.

17

The good feelings created by our midnight serenading to wildlife didn't last long into Friday morning. I woke to realize two very important things. One was that I'd overslept and was going to be later than promised to meet up with Benny and Colin at our new office. The other was that Harley and I no longer had a coffeemaker.

I sent Benny an apologetic text and then tackled the second problem with a trip to the Black Canoe café around the corner. I ordered a muffin and my American Misto to 'go' and checked the tracking app on my phone while I waited. Even Alexander, or at least his car, was already at work. It was a confidence boost to see that I'd correctly guessed which car was Alexander's at the golf club. Not that there was much penalty if I'd been wrong other than the pain of having to recover the tracker from wherever it ended up—which could just as easily have been someone visiting from almost anywhere in the province. I had at least checked the license plate, I'm not an amateur.

When I puttered the Vespa into the underground parking at the office building, I found Benny's delivery van sandwiched between Alexander's BMW on one side, and Valery's Audi on the other. I wondered what Polina drove. Or did she? Valery seemed to fill the dual duties of bodyguard and chauffeur. Which prompted the question: where did he leave her when he was off doing other things? Had she been at the golf clubhouse having breakfast while the boys played a few rounds? I didn't peg her for the early riser type somehow. Maybe she'd left town altogether?

Since Marty had been so generous, I popped one of the GPS trackers onto Valery's car to make it fair. Then I called Benny, hoping for a lift up in the elevator, but he wasn't answering. Instead, I rode up to the fourth floor and then hiked up the stairs the rest of the way. Benny had the only key, and he didn't answer my bangs on the door, so I took it as an opportunity to use my new lock picks.

The stairwell doors were all equipped with an Everest series Schlage. They're decent locks with a paracentric keyway and an extra check pin to make things interesting. It's a lock that is often billed as being 'high security', but it's really not. The extra pin is always in exactly the same place and you can't over-drive it, so once you have the other pins cleared, you can shove almost anything in. I had it open in about two minutes. Which was disappointing. It was a type of lock that I was very familiar with and could typically have opened on Uncle Rupert's workbench in thirty seconds or fewer. But then new picks always take a bit of getting used to, and there was some construction dust in the mechanism —at least that was my excuse.

The reason Benny and Tim hadn't heard me was because they were both wearing headphones. They were sitting shoulder-to-shoulder, sharing a computer. On the screen was a shaky view of the Stanley Cup. It suddenly switched to show Colin and Saffron waving.

"We've got internet," Tim said when he realized I was there. He threw in a thumbs-up and then gestured to a box on the table. "There was a router wired up when we got here. We're video chatting with the guys in Toronto!"

A blue cable hung almost straight down from a freshly drilled hole in the ceiling. On the floor, directly beneath it, was a small volcano of cement dust that just missed the edge of the table.

I left them to chat away while I did a tour around the entire floor with my new bug detection gear. Cameras and microphones come in the tiniest size imaginable these days. But regardless of the size, the device still needs to have a power supply and something needs to happen with the signal, whether that's just a recording or transmission over a wire or through the air. Since they'd shown they were happy to drill holes through the floor, I paid particular attention to the ceiling. But the detection gear wasn't excited about anything—aside from all the electronics on the table around Tim and Benny.

After a few laps around the entire floor, I'd found no indications of any listening devices or hidden cameras hiding anywhere among the piles of abandoned construction materials. I also didn't stumble over any freezers tucked away that could hold dead bodies—so that was a bonus. Still, the lack of electronic surveillance I found surprising, but then maybe I was overthinking their interest. I was about to declare us bug-free when I finally realized it was right in front of us the whole time. Or at least in front of Benny and Tim. The router.

I would've thought that the logical place to connect an internet cable was by the elevator shaft. That's where they typically run the telephone lines and all that sort of stuff. There was no need to drill a hole in the floor as they did. Unless, of course, they didn't connect us directly to the outside world, but looped through their own network.

"Let's go for coffee," I said.

"I brought a thermos," Tim said

"Doughnuts then?"

Benny got the hint before I had to resort to getting them

to turn their phones back on so I could start sending text messages. Although the reception was so bad that the idea probably wouldn't have worked, anyway.

"Ya, I need to stretch my legs," he said. "Bagel place on the corner, any good? Let's give it a try."

"It makes sense," Tim said after I'd explained the likely location of a camera and microphone. We had ordered coffee and bagels to go and were sitting at a corner table by the window while we waited. "If the hidden device is PoE-capable, then it can all go over the same LAN cable. Though of course, the router has its own power supply, obviously, so it would make sense to power it remotely. Now I've run Wireshark and I don't know yet what log monitoring they're doing, but I have a custom NIDS running and I always use a VPN on my systems, so we're encrypted, of course."

"Of course. Good thinking," Benny said, though he shot me a look that suggested he understood about half of those words, which was about where I landed as well.

"Okay..." I said. "I'm less interested in them hacking us, as I am us hacking them. How do we do that?"

"We can't," Tim said.

"Is this another ethics issue?" I asked. "Because I don't want to belabour the point, but we're working to get ourselves out of this mess and it seems to me like an ideal time to maybe take off the white hat for a minute or two. No?"

"It's not that. I do admit that I'm not happy about trying to break into anyone's system without their knowledge and consent," he said. "But this is more about *can't* than *won't*."

"Which means what?" Benny said.

"As I was saying, while Margot was wandering around

with the device detector, I was running some diagnostics on the internet connection."

"And?" I prompted.

Tim gave an apologetic shrug. "As far as I can tell, it's just a direct connection to a local service provider. There's no sign that it connects to their network on the ninth floor at all. If we assume that there's a camera or microphone hidden inside the router like you say then it's using some of the extra wires from the LAN cable—there's often more than you need—and short of taking the router apart there's no way to access them. So that's it for the wire. The other way to try to access their network is through their Wi-Fi. From what I remember seeing when we were up there, they were running around with their laptops and cellphones to access the internet so obviously, they are running a wireless network. But it's weird. It's like they must have wrapped the building in a wire mesh or something when they built it. Every floor seems isolated. It's like a Faraday cage—wireless signals can't get through. So even if they are running a wireless network, I can't even detect it, never mind try to access it—which, by the way, is far more difficult than most people think."

"So we can't access their computers?"

"Nope. Well, not without physically connecting. Though I don't see how. Unless you're thinking of drilling another hole in the floor? I expect somebody might notice if we run a cable up the stairwell."

"Remind me why we care about any of this?" Benny asked.

"It's all about trying to get whatever information they have about whatever criminal things they do," I said. "If we can get tangible proof, then we can take that to the police.

Nobody wants to go into witness protection, right? So we need to have something we can give to Max Kirkpatrick and get Alexander put away. Hopefully, forever and without involving us. We just need to get onto their computers, or maybe find Kirill's body...but I'd prefer the former ."

"Alright," Benny said. "So what's at the other end of that cable, then? If part of it is going to the internet then where are the camera wires going?"

"I dunno," Tim said. "Hard to say. They probably have some sort of monitoring station up there—there are security cameras all over the building. But I can't tell more than that."

"So what do we do?" Benny asked.

"No problem," I said. "We do it the old-fashioned way. We just need to break in instead of trying to access things remotely. However, there is that security camera issue, and I guess we'll need Maryam to deal with that."

The idea of sending them all to Toronto was really just to get them out of the way and give the illusion we were doing something. At the time, it had seemed like a good idea, but then I hadn't considered needing Maryam's electrician skills.

I dug out my phone and called her number while Tim went off to collect our order.

Maryam answered and immediately launched into a full recap of her insightful conversation with a chatty security guard. It took a few minutes before I could steer the conversation back to relevant topics.

"What do you know about security cameras?" I asked. "And, more specifically, any chance you would know how to put the building security cameras in the dark for ten or twenty minutes or so?"

Another monologue followed. This time it was all about battery backup systems and needing to consult Tim on possible offsite internet monitoring. The take-home message, however, was that if I could provide her access to the basement utility room, then it should all be 'no problem at all'.

"So, when are you thinking of coming back?" I said.

"Tonight actually," Maryam said. "And we have *loads* of pictures. I'll start sending some when we get to the airport. We're booked on the five o'clock flight, so with the time difference we'll be back around seven-thirty, I think."

With the three of them having so much fun, I made a mental note not to tell Harley how great Toronto is.

"Colin wants to see the 3D film again, though. Oh, hey! We got to meet one of the Keepers of the cup too! Did you know they keep the original cup inside an actual vault? The museum is on the site of an old bank. Wild, huh? Oh, yes... Saffron wants to know if we can visit the gift shop?"

Why not? I supposed. "Just keep the receipts," I said.

Maryam said she'd call as soon as they landed and we'd figure out the next steps then. As for the next steps right now...that was easier.

"Maryam mentioned that the cup has its own social media accounts," I said to Tim and Benny as we walked back. "We need to start looking into all that. Can you guys start trying to figure out exactly where and how the cup is travelling to Sarita?"

When we got back to the building, I noticed a dark, somewhat generic BMW parked beside Alexander's flashier one. A familiar blonde was walking from it towards the open elevator as we approached.

"Sure," Tim said. "What will you be doing?"

"Hey Polina," I called out. "Wait up."

She flashed us a deer-in-the-headlights sort of look and

then immediately scampered inside the open elevator.

"I'm going to try something. See you guys up there," I called back over my shoulder as I broke into a sprint.

It was close. But I managed to slip sideways between the doors just as they closed, and all but crashed into the rear wall beside a very startled Polina.

"Thanks for waiting," I said. "I was hoping to catch you."

Her face flushed, and she clutched her purse tight. I couldn't tell if she was angry or embarrassed. Maybe somewhere in between.

"What do you want?" Polina said. She waved a keycard like Valery had at the panel and pressed the 'nine' button with a perfectly manicured finger.

I was focused for a moment on wondering if Marty had any gizmos that would mimic a keycard when Polina repeated her question. What did I want? Good question. Ideally, I just wanted to have a chance to wander around the ninth floor and see if I could spot where the cable they'd drilled through the floor was attached to. But I'd settle for a refresher on their security camera placement.

"My pizza carrier," I said. "I forgot it the other day."

"Oh," she said, and her shoulders dropped instantly. The relief was palpable. "Right."

"So you're here to pick up your bodyguard, huh? Isn't he supposed to follow you and not the other way around?" I asked. I meant it in jest, but she didn't seem to find it funny.

"What are you talking about?" The flush was back on her cheeks.

"Valery," I said.

She gave a breathy exhale and a dismissive shake of her head as the elevator whirred to a stop. We could hear the shouting even before the doors opened. Polina and I exchanged wide-eyed looks as we stepped cautiously out. Alexander's voice was bellowing from his office down the hall and we stopped where we were.

"What's going on?" I asked.

Polina held up a palm as she listened.

"Ukrainian," she said after a minute. "It's much like Russian but also different, so sometimes is confusing."

"But you understand what he's saying?"

"Oh, yes."

"...and!? What would that be?"

"Well, he's talking on the phone. He's very angry."

"Ya, I got that much. What's he angry *about*?"

"It's strange," she said. "Alexander is usually so calm."

"*What is he saying?*" I said, struggling to keep my voice level.

Before I had a chance to vent further frustration, Alexander came stomping into view. He glared at both of us in turn, softening his look for Polina but then sharpening it right back again for me.

"Why are *you* here?" he asked me. His voice was pitched just above a whisper, which I found to be far more threatening than the yelling had been.

"She came for her pizza thing," Polina said. She waggled her fingers in my direction, but some imperfection caught her eye. I was instantly dismissed, and she was giving her nails a critical appraisal as she walked off.

Alexander waited until Polina was gone before turning all his focus to me. He blinked once slowly and then stepped closer until we were nearly toe to toe. There was a scent of expensive aftershave, breath mints, and something more primal. He was so close that I had to lean back to look up at him. His jaw muscles were flexing in what seemed to be a struggle to keep himself contained.

"Things have changed," he said. "You will have the trophy for me on Sunday."

"But...but...that's in two days," I said. I meant it to come out as a conversational counterpoint, but my voice was more of a squeak.

"Yes," he said. "So stop playing games. Don't worry about this pizza box. Worry only about the task I have given you. I don't wish to make more threats. If you force me to bring your uncle and aunt or your friend Harley into it, then I will do so. Is this clear?"

"Crystal," I said. I was having trouble swallowing.

"Good. You will have the cup at Ogden Point at twenty hours Sunday."

Twenty? I did the conversion to normal time in my head. "Eight o'clock in the evening?"

"Yes. Not later. If not by quarter past, then you are too late. Understood? Good. Now go."

I didn't want to wait for the elevator in case it had already gone off to a different floor, so I retreated to the stairwell door. Despite my stunned condition, I was able to take in that the locks had been changed from the standard Schlage that was on the other floors to an unpickable Bowley, of all things. I was fumbling to release the deadbolt when he called after me.

"One more thing. Valery. I want him always with you from now until the end. Whatever...*end* that means for you."

18

I made it down the flight of stairs on numb legs. For some reason, I was more shaken up than when this whole thing started. So many questions were rocketing through my head. Why was Alexander so angry? Why suddenly did he need the cup so soon? Why at such a specific time? And most of all…why there?

Ogden Point is the jut of land that marks the entrance to the outer harbour of the city. There's a long breakwater with a lighthouse on the end that gives sheltered mooring for visiting cruise ships and emergency boats. Aside from the massive pier buildings, the only other structures are a bistro that aunt Stacy and her friends use to warm up after cold ocean dips on one side, and the Helijet facility on the other. Everything in between is just a massive industrial parking lot. Weird.

"What's wrong?" Benny asked as soon as he'd answered my knocks on the eighth-floor door.

I guess my expression gave away my thoughts all too clearly. It took longer for me to relate Alexander's bombshell than it had for him to deliver it, but then I padded mine with various musings about what it all might mean.

"I think overall nothing has changed," Benny said. "We still need to make an effort to figure out exactly when and where the cup is going to be. And we still need to come up with a plan on how we could, in theory at least, have the cup at Ogden Point by the time he wants on Sunday."

"At eight o'clock at night?" Tim asked.

"He was quite specific," I said.

"Curious."

"Isn't it though?"

We sat at the table and chewed on our bagels and our thoughts.

"Alright," I said, addressing the router as much as Benny and Tim. "Why don't you guys work on the location aspect? See how much detail you can find online about the travel timeline for the cup between wherever it is right now, and when it arrives in Sarita. Maybe we can intercept it along the way?"

"Sounds good," Tim said.

"What about you?" Benny asked as I stood and slung my bag over my shoulder.

"I'm going to check out some ideas on how we can separate the cup from its Keeper. Shall we meet up here this evening when the others are back?"

"Sure," Benny said. "What about Valery?"

I pulled out my phone and brought up the tracking app —which worked fine now that I had a Wi-Fi connection to the router. Alexander's car was just crossing the blue bridge heading towards downtown.

"Save a bagel for him," I said and made for the stairs. "And a whiteboard for me."

Before I jumped on the Vespa, I stuck my last GPS tracker onto Polina's car. Might as well know where everybody was. I'd have to remember to get at least one of the trackers back before the spa appointment or Uncle Rupert was going to have some salty things to say about my work ethic.

It was apparently a day for headphones. When I got back to the apartment, I found Harley dancing silently but energetically in the kitchen. She was in mid-production of some sort of baking project. Her wireless headphones have cat ears on the headband that flash neon colours in time to whatever music is playing. The steady pulses, and continuous head bobs, suggested electronic trance music, which was at odds with the grass skirt she was wearing.

"Hey!" she yelled when a gyration turned into a full spin and she caught sight of me. "You're just in time. The first batch is ready. I'm making those cranberry muffin things you like."

I gestured for her to take the headphones off so I wouldn't have to join her in yelling.

"Nice hula skirt," I said.

"Hah! It's *not*!" she said, her voice sparkling with glee at my mistake. "It's a *piupiu*. Atarangi is from New Zealand. She says I have okay footwork but my singing needs work. See? I *knew* the karaoke machine was a great idea!"

This was too good to let pass.

"Alright. I'll bite," I said. "Details..?"

"Okay. So I was picking up a new client over by the Y—it's a Bernese Mountain crossed with a Maremma sheepdog. *So* cute, you would not believe. Anyway, I saw a poster for a learn-to-dance *kapa haka* class and so I signed up. It's an eight-week course and I don't know if I have a memory for all the hand movements, but I *really* wanted the skirt."

"I see. You couldn't have just bought a skirt without taking lessons?"

She pulled a face as though working on a complex math problem. "Ummm…nope. That would be silly."

Harley put the headphones back on and danced her way back to the mixing bowl.

I took a muffin and my laptop onto the deck and threw myself into the task of learning everything I could find about

Leonid Konstantinovich Yakovlev. Which turned out to be quite a lot. In Alexander's ranting, there was one name that had jumped out several times—Leonid. The only Leonid that I'd ever heard of was the one that I'd read about online exactly a week ago—Polina's grandfather.

One thing was for sure, the man was seriously rich—or at least he used to be. The distinction between millionaires and billionaires is all pretty blurry for me, but if you could measure it by the number of luxury yachts, then at one point Leonid had at least one for every day of the week. Which says nothing about the various vacation palaces and so on he owned, scattered here and there around the globe. There was plenty of information about Leonid dating back from the nineteen-seventies, right up until the day he spoke out about Vladimir Putin's invasion of Ukraine. He wasn't a fan. Still, it seemed that Leonid had just dropped out of public view. There was nothing about him clumsily falling out of a window, as so many other critics of the Kremlin often did. So, at least in that regard, he had done better than many of his other oligarch comrades.

As for the business interests that paid for all his houses and toys, well, that was a mixed bag. He seemed to have gotten his start back in the nineteen-nineties during the Wild West period that followed the breakup of the Soviet Union. Oil and gas were the main areas, but by the end of the century, he'd moved away from that and diversified into almost anything you can think of. I found a list that showed his recent holdings, which ran all the way from potato farms to exporting matryoshka dolls. But it was the last item on the list that caught my attention: a hockey league.

Leonid shared his ownership of the Kontinental Hockey League—Russia's answer to the NHL—with one Alexander Ivanovich Medvedev. Another oil and gas zillionaire. Judging by the number of photos online with the two of them rinkside, they rarely seemed to miss a game. Medvedev used to run Gazprom—the Russian national gas company—at least he did until he also fell into Putin's bad books for not charging the Ukrainians enough.

I wondered if the Ukrainian Alexander that I knew and this Russian Alexander would get along. Probably not. Though I imagine they would find plenty of things to discuss. Which brought me back to Leonid. If Polina's grandfather was the Leonid that I'd overheard Alexander yelling about, then what did that have to do with anything? Was there some connection between our task of getting the Stanley Cup and Leonid owning a hockey league?

A week ago, Ukrainian Alexander had been telling us we needed to keep him happy so he could keep his boss happy. With Polina Pavlova under his wing, it suddenly seemed more than likely that the boss in question was Leonid. It was all interesting stuff. But I didn't see how it helped.

I'd told Benny and Tim that I would research ideas on how to steal the cup. But that was only for the benefit of the microphone in the router. In truth, I had no ideas at all, but I needed to at least come up with something that looked plausible enough to scribble all over one of the whiteboards. There were still hours to go before the flight from Toronto landed, and I doubted that I would contribute much to the research that Tim and Benny were doing. The best thing to do when I need to think is to move around. While dancing around the kitchen is always fun, I needed something quieter. I took my bag of discs and went golfing.

It was nearly seven o'clock when I got back to the office building, half an hour before Maryam and the others were due to land. I picked the eighth-floor lock just to see if I could improve on my earlier time and entered thirty seconds later to find Valery sitting alone. He was reclining on one of our new office chairs with his feet on the table at a dangerous angle, holding open a newspaper with a Cyrillic headline.

"Tim and Benny have gone for good," he said when he saw me.

Gone for good!? I nearly collapsed in shock from the mental image of Valery having thrown them down the elevator shaft.

"*What?*" I said. It came out just below a yell.

His brow did a funny wrinkle. "They just left. There is time to call if you want. Not that garbage you get. I sent them to Prima Strada. Good pizza! What's wrong? You're all… funny-looking."

Gone for *food*. Gone for *food*. I repeated it in my head a few times to calm my pulse. Valery's deep voice and thick accent required all my attention to decipher.

"Where are you from Valery?" I said once my heart rate had returned to nearly normal.

"Gomel."

"Which is where?"

"Belarus," he said with a slight shake of his head that seemed to indicate my lack of geography skills was a disappointment.

"How do you know Alexander? I thought he said you were all Ukrainian?"

"Alexander is Ukrainian. He is from Chernihiv. But…no. Don't call it Chernigov, he'll get very upset!" He waggled a meaty index finger at me in warning.

"Promise," I assured him. "But, why not?"

"Chernigov is the Russian name for the city. Alexander isn't sometimes fond of Russians. You understand?"

I could easily think of a few reasons that might be true.

"But isn't your boss, Leonid, from Russia?" I said it in as conversational a tone as possible. It was a spur-of-the-moment gamble. If I was wrong, then likely all that would happen would be confusion and possibly a further chuckle or two at my ignorance. If I was right, then there was the very real risk Valery would be angry at my knowing things I had no right to know. But he just gave a backhanded wave.

"Oh sure," he said. "But business is business. You can not worry about things like this. And Leonid is usually okay guy. Sometimes not."

He dropped his feet from the table and they hit the floor with a thud.

"I tell you secret," he said and leaned forward in the chair, gesturing me to come closer. "Leonid has granddaughter. You will *never* guess who!"

"Can't imagine," I lied. It seemed strategic not to spoil his surprise.

His eyes went wide, and he broke into a sly smile like the kind my Uncle Rupert would make when he showed me a new lock-picking trick. "Polina!"

"Wow," I said. "What is she doing here?"

"Hiding," Valery said and dropped his voice to just above a rumbling whisper. "Leonid has some trouble back home with the FSB."

"FSB?"

"Russian secret police. Well, not so secret. Used to be called the FSK. Before that KGB. Before that NKVD. It goes on and on. They change name, but is always the same. Same people. Same things. Bad things."

Worse than shooting people in wheelbarrows, I wondered. But I kept that question to myself.

We were interrupted by the sound of a warbling ringtone. Valery jumped to his feet, and all but jogged over to the window where he'd left his cellphone leaning for better reception.

"Pizza is here!" he said.

While Valery went to call the elevator, I had a closer look at what Tim and Benny had been up to. They had outdone themselves. Three of the whiteboards were completely covered with an impressive maze of lists, maps, and dates, all written in seemingly random colours. In between were sheets of paper fresh from the printer that Tim must have brought up from his office. They'd saved the red marker to draw connecting lines that sprawled over and between everything, like a web left by a deranged spider.

At the top of the fourth whiteboard in tiny lettering were written the words: 'Save for Margot'. I was tempted to fill the space underneath with a huge question mark, but then I didn't think Valery or anyone else would find that amusing.

One board was devoted to all the things we should have learned long ago about the cup, its physical attributes, its history, the damage, and the repairs.

The next board was all about the keeper of the cup, who is never apart from the cup aside from when it is loaded into a plane cargo hold. There was a crew of them, and one was always with it. Whether it was showing up at fan appreciation days at hockey arenas around the continent, or dropping in to visit other sporting events like the PGA, or even paying respects at the funeral of legendary players like the passing of Guy Lafleur. Which was a name that even I could recognize as Aunt Stacy had been a huge fan—at least of his hair. I was less certain if that included his other achievements. The only time a keeper wasn't in arm's reach was when it was back for a stay at the Hockey Hall of Fame in Toronto. As Colin had said over the phone, the cup had its own social media accounts. Tim had printed a few off with random dates from over the last year, beginning with one from last fall…

2:57 PM / OCTOBER 10

Welcome back!

Hey @CityofTampaBay we are back in town. Opening week in the @nhl The @Lightning become defending #StanleyCup champions once the puck drops. Stay tuned we might see you this week somewhere!@HockeyHallFame

— Kevin Reynolds (@keeperofthecup) October 10

The Lightning weren't going to be repeat champions this year, though. The most recent posts mentioned only New York and Vancouver.

The left side of the third whiteboard was completely filled with a printed map of the west side of Vancouver Island—Victoria at the bottom, Sarita near the top. The few possible routes connecting the two were traced in yellow highlighter. The shortest one was marked as being one hundred and ninety-six kilometres with a driving time of three hours and forty-nine minutes.

The other half of the whiteboard had the name 'Clara Peters'—the scout who was having her day with the cup—written in Benny's neat block letters along the top. Lines on the board connected one social media printout to the next like a spider web. The posts, comments, likes and shares from friends and relatives all worked together to give an almost minute-by-minute account of what was planned for the Stanley Cup visit to their small community.

The first tickle of an idea was sparking somewhere in my

mind, though I couldn't immediately figure out what or why. When the smell of fresh pizza finally caught my attention, I realized I had moved back to the 'keepers of the cup' board. There was an entire page devoted to the shipping crate that protected it on its travels.

"What are you grinning about?" Benny said as he offered a paper plate collapsing under the weight of a pizza slice.

"I have a plan," I said. Something in my tone caught his ear.

"But..?" he prompted.

"But we're going to need another cup."

19

"Tell me you're kidding," Benny said in a whisper. "You don't think we have enough Stanley cups lying around already? You want another one?"

"I don't want to waste your replica on my idea. It's valuable, and you sacrificed a lot to get it. Besides, we know it wouldn't fool any of one of the official Keepers of the cup for a second. What we need now doesn't have to even *look* like the cup exactly. It just needs to be a similar size, but it has to weigh exactly the same."

"So you want thirty-four and a half pounds of something Stanley Cup-ish?" Benny's eyebrows lifted, and he had a vaguely sneaky smile. "You know? I think I might have just the thing. Leave it with me."

"This is all still smoke and mirrors, though," I said. "We need to get access to the computers upstairs and soon."

"About that. I was here last weekend," Benny said. "After the whole Friday evening event, I guess I wanted to come back and see what was real in case my mind had played tricks on me. The place was deserted, as far as I could tell. So it seems these guys follow a standard Monday-to-Friday kinda work week. No cars in the parking areas underground or out back. If tomorrow is anything like it, then we'll just have Valery to worry about."

"Which is a big worry," I said. "Figuratively *and* literally. Let's see what tomorrow brings, I guess."

What I didn't share was that while getting Valery out of the way was indeed a concern—getting access to their floor was going to be at least as challenging. There was no way that I knew of to get past the Bowley deadbolt on their door that didn't involve a chunk of time and a very big drill. And getting in and out undetected was pretty much the whole idea. Well, that, and getting away with some sort of incriminating information. A point that reminded me it was long past time to get in touch with CSIS super spy Max Kirkpatrick. I wondered how excited he'd be with a gift of a hard drive or two filled with gangster data. How quickly he would be able to act on the information was another matter.

We finished the pizza, and I had to admit Valery was maybe right about the quality compared to my usual source. Though, I expect there might have been a sizeable difference in the bill to match. 'You get what you pay for', as Uncle Rupert was fond of reminding me. With a plan to meet up early the next morning, I left to try my phone and see if the Toronto tourists had landed. A breathless Saffron assured me they were all well, but exhausted. We agreed to meet up first thing in the morning.

Harley had a massive bowl of popcorn and a DVD queued up when I got home.

"It's more thriller than romance. At least that what's I'm getting from the description on the case."

"Who's in it?" I said. "Another supermodel? I slept through the last one with Cindy Crawford."

"*Way* better," she said. "Lee Marvin. He was in Cat Ballou with Jane Fonda. Remember that one? Pretty sure he got the Academy Award for it, which is rare for a comedy, never mind a western."

Movies and dog names. Harley rarely remembered what she'd had for breakfast, but ask her who starred in any film she'd seen, or better yet, the breed, gender and disposition of any dog who had a supporting role...and she'd have a detailed answer.

"Do you still have that climbing gear from that course you took last year?" I asked between mouthfuls of popcorn.

"That's a *great* idea!" Harley said. She started gesturing wildly, and the remote went flying. "Let's go! There's not many cliffs around but we could try climbing the big trees in the park. We can watch the movie later."

"Hold up," I said, as I replayed my question in my head to see if I could spot where I'd gone wrong. Any excuses along the lines of fatigue or danger I knew would be ignored. "Great blue herons."

"What about them?"

"Aren't they nesting in the trees right now?"

"Are they?"

I had no idea. But I was pretty sure I'd seen a sign barring dogs from one section of the park not too long ago for that reason. If dogs weren't allowed, then it seemed likely to have kept Harley away as well.

"Besides," I said. "I was just asking because I need to borrow the rope tomorrow for a work thing. But maybe next week we could go to a disc golf course, I know. Loads of rocks and cliffs there."

With that promise, she retrieved the remote, and the credits started over skaters drunkenly wobbling on a pond to what might have been the 1812 Overture. I made it just long enough to see William Hurt and Brian Dennehy fighting in a railyard. As I fell asleep, the characters on-screen changed in my mind. So it was Alexander who was getting pounded by Valery's fists. I don't wish violence on anyone, so the idea was more disturbing than entertaining. Harley managed to prod me awake enough to stumble into the comfort of my own bed when the movie ended.

With the lingering echoes of Tchaikovsky running through my dreams, I woke the next morning feeling as though I hadn't slept a wink. A shower and half a pot of Irish Breakfast tea did little to help. When I stumbled into our eighth-floor office twenty minutes later, I found Tim, Benny, and the Toronto crew all looking bright-eyed and energetic. Seeing as they'd only been gone a day, I doubted it was the time zone difference, so it seemed more likely they were just excited about their trip or maybe the lecture that Tim was conducting as he guided them through the whiteboards.

"Hey!" Colin said when he saw me. There was an open cardboard box with a stack of Vancouver Canucks hockey jerseys. He rummaged through and then pulled one out."We bought everyone team jerseys. Yours is the extra small. It has the captain's 'C' on it. Cool, huh?"

"What's next boss?" Maryam asked me. "Tim was filling us in on all the research you had them doing."

Captain? Boss?

I looked over at Benny, who gave an apologetic shrug. "I told them you had a plan. Besides, we all know you're the one with the ideas. The rest of us are just doing our best to keep up."

The thought that I could be the leader of anything was unsettling. Harley didn't even let me walk her dogs when she was sick, as I 'didn't project an air of authority'. I consulted my phone while I thought of an appropriate response. Alexander's and Polina's cars were both stationary at the golf course. Valery's Audi was heading this way from that direction. I figured we had at least fifteen or twenty minutes before he arrived. I looked around at the circle of expectant faces. At least I could try to give the camera on the router something encouraging to transmit.

"Okay," I said. "Well, it's now Saturday morning and Alexander expects us to somehow show up with the cup at Ogden Point tomorrow at eight. Here's where we are..."

I started by lavishing praise on the fine work that everyone had done collecting information in Toronto and here at home online, with lots of emphasis on how hard and diligently we were all working. Tim supplied some more details on the expected minute-by-minute movements of the cup over the next forty-eight hours—thanks to all the social media posts. From what we could gather, the keeper of the cup was going to be arriving in Nanaimo on the eight a.m. Sunday morning ferry. Twelve hours later, he would be back to catch the eight-forty-five p.m. return ferry to Vancouver. In between was a tight schedule that included the main celebration planned in Port Alberni, followed by a shorter visit to the community school in Bamfield along the coast. Lastly, though most importantly, Clara Peters would have a few hours to take the cup to see her aging father at his home somewhere in the hills south of Sarita.

"So our big challenge is to decide exactly *when* to make a grab for the cup. Along with that, is to figure out how we could transport it from wherever we get it, to down here by Sunday night." I ended with a hearty salute to our overlords for the benefit of the router. "Thankfully, of course, we have Valery on the team now so he can help us with the actual *how* part. Which is great, obviously. Has anyone seen him yet this morning, by the way?"

Not unexpectedly, all I got back was an array of quizzical headshakes.

"Alright, well, who's up for a bagel run while we wait?" I

gave a general sweep over the room, but focused most of my attention on Maryam. I caught a gratifying nod of understanding from Benny out of the corner of my eye.

"Why don't you and Maryam go? The rest of us will stay here," Benny said. "I'd like to hear more about the Hockey Hall of Fame. Oh...and...a blueberry for me, please."

I checked my phone app one last time as Maryam and I waited for the elevator. Valery seemed to have stopped at Starbucks. Maybe he wasn't a bagel fan.

"Bagels?" Maryam said once we were in the elevator.

I held a finger to my lips and leaned close. "I need you to tell me all you know about the security setup here. And whether we can shut it down somehow."

"Why are we whispering?"

"Just in case," I said. "Pretty sure they bugged our office area. Maybe here too?"

We waited until the elevator had brought us back down to the parking garage and Maryam and I huddled by Benny's van.

"I have an idea of how to sneak onto the ninth floor so that Tim can have access to their computers. But it won't work if I set alarms wailing or if security cameras are being monitored. So how do we avoid all that?"

Maryam did a scan around the parkade as though to re-familiarize herself with where we were. "Right. When I first worked the site here, I was around for some of that installation. The main feed for everything is in a utility room just over there behind the elevators. All the electrics to the building run through it. Phone lines, internet, security feeds, and service panels. I can show you where the room is in a second, but it's all locked up and I don't have a key."

"I might," I said. "Let's take a look."

Fortunately, Alexander's new enthusiasm for unpickable deadbolt locks didn't appear to extend beyond the ninth floor. The utility room Maryam led us to just had the same sort of Schlage set that the stairwell used. After a quick check that there were no obvious security cameras, I had the deadbolt and latch both open in probably under a minute.

That part was easy and fun. The rest was less satisfying.

"Two choices," she said. "The most certain is to shut off the main breaker for the entire building. Put the whole thing in the dark. But there's a catch...we first need to disable the security UPS battery that powers the security system in case of power loss. Also, there's a generator that automatically fires up to power the elevator and emergency building lights. I'm not sure if they have anything plugged into that system security-wise, but it's certainly possible. In addition, we'd also need to kill the landlines as most security will have an automated call out to whatever service is monitoring the instant the power goes down. There might be a cellphone component too, but with the garbage reception, I doubt it."

"That sounds like a lot. You said there were two options?"

"Or, we just take out the landlines and the internet and leave the power alone. Then, if the security system is triggered, it can wail and scream all it wants, but nobody outside the building will know. I meant that metaphorically, but of course, the physical sirens and bells will make things pretty noisy inside the building if they have things set up that way."

"Okay, how do I do that?"

"You? No! Better I do it. Wouldn't want you to touch the wrong thing."

"Believe me, I'd prefer that too, but you'll be busy," I said.

"Doing what?"

"I'll explain in a second. First, show me how to do your 'plan B' before Valery shows up."

I had Maryam show me twice to make sure I'd got it before I hurried us out. I relocked the latch, but left the deadbolt open to save time. As it was, we barely made it. Valery was already pulling into his usual parking spot to the squeal of rubber on painted concrete when we turned the corner.

"Morning," he said with what seemed like genuine glee. "You have good trip?"

This was clearly directed at Maryam, but I jumped in before she could answer.

"Speaking of trips," I said. "We were thinking we need to drive up to Sarita today to check things out before tomorrow. It would be good to do the drive so we'll know what sort of time window we'll have tomorrow. So probably be pretty boring for you here today."

"Who? All of you?"

"All for one, one for all," I said, with my best cheery 'hi-ho' smile.

"No, this is bad idea," Valery said as he ushered into the elevator. "Too many for one car. Two cars wasteful."

I was afraid he might say something like that. Any plan of accessing their computers required Valery to be somewhere far, far away. I was hoping that if he knew we were all gone, he'd go play golf or something while Tim and I snuck back to the building while the others did the drive. The other hope was that Valery wasn't quite the environmentalist his electric car suggested. If he did want to come along for the drive, then I was going to make sure Tim and I were in whichever car he wasn't.

Valery led the way over to the whiteboards as soon as we reached the eighth floor like he owned the place. Which I suppose was possibly true.

"There are two ways to get there, yes? This way is most direct," Valery said and jabbed a sausage-sized finger at the map Tim and Benny had put up. "But maybe construction. Maybe problem somewhere. Cowichan Lake can be busy this time of year. I have done houseboat vacation there. Is very nice."

I wondered what sort of vacation allowance someone like Valery had, and for that matter, what the pay structure and hiring policies of criminal organizations might be. How much did Valery and Alexander make in a year? Were there bonuses in place for killing the occasional troublesome person like Kirill? How much extra would Valery get if he had to dispose of my body? Grim thoughts.

"We go different way," Valery continued. "Here. See? Logging roads. Port Renfrew and then here, along the coast. Longer maybe, but we see. Also, very pretty drive."

"So who is going?" Maryam asked.

"Maybe...we take my car?" he suggested. It was an open question, but the shy gleam in Valery's eye had given him away even before he opened his mouth. Suddenly, all the stalkering he'd been doing to follow Maryam had a distinctly less than strictly professional feel.

"I'll navigate," Saffron said, surprising us all. "I'm not great at driving on logging roads, but I know the area pretty well. There's a yoga camp outside of Nitinat which is on the way. I've been there a bunch of times. Colin should stay, though. Something tells me this won't be a good day for you to get carsick. Does anyone mind looking after Colin for a few hours? And keep him out of trouble..."

Saffron added that last part with a sharp look toward me.

"Mom," Colin protested. "I hardly get sick anymore. I never get to go on road trips."

"You said you had some driving games you played," Benny said. "Any of them have roads around here?"

"No. The games I have are all track ones. There's this one game, though. This rally game. All sorts of real cars and it uses satellite imagery and mapping data and real-time weather and everything! You can drive anywhere in the world on it. And the game physics are supposed to be amazing. It's super expensive, though."

"Oh...I'm sure it's in the budget," Benny said. "Maybe we can do the same route faster than your Mom and the others? What do you say? Why don't you and I go do a little shopping and get set up? Just remind me to keep the receipts."

Benny's plan got encouraging nods from both Valery and Saffron. So with that settled, Valery all but skipped his way back to the elevator. I caught Maryam and Saffron exchanging raised eyebrow smirks as they followed behind.

"I have satellite in car for phone," Valery called back. "Same number. We stay in touch."

"Don't forget to time yourselves," I said, but the elevator doors were already closing and I doubt they heard me.

"Well, that was easy," Benny said. "So now what?"

"You do your plan with Colin," I said as I gave my tracking app another check. Alexander and Polina were still parked at the golf course. So I just had to wait to see Valery safely on his way and I could get into action. "Keep him out of trouble and stay busy in view of the router, in case anyone is checking remotely."

I gestured for Tim to join me and led the way to the elevators.

"How are you with heights?" I asked.

"Terrible," he said, smiling as usual. "I'd never been in a building with more than three floors until coming to Victoria."

"Terrific," I said. "Well, I guess it'll be me then."

"To do what?"

"The lock on their door is unpickable. At least it's beyond my skills. So we either need to lower ourselves down from the roof and hope we find an open window. Or we do it from the inside."

"Which means what?"

"The elevator," I said.

"But that won't go to their floor without a keycard like they have. Maybe there's a way to hack the elevator electronics, but that's not *really* my area. Otherwise, someone needs to be on the floor to call it up. Which seems like a catch-22."

"Yes, but I meant the other elevator."

"But there isn't one."

"There is a shaft, though. I'll just jimmy the elevator door and climb up. It's just an empty tunnel from this floor up to theirs."

"A tunnel that goes up and down, though," Tim added unnecessarily. "And it's a long, long way down."

I was trying not to think about that.

"Margot," Benny called from behind the cluster of whiteboards. "Where's my bagel?"

20

I took my time having a stroll to the bagel shop. The outing served a few purposes. For one, it allowed Valery to get further away. It also gave me a chance to steady my nerves in anticipation of the death-defying spectacle I was planning. And, well, bagels are always good.

I chewed on my whole wheat and checked the tracker app on my phone. Valery was already comfortably distant. They were making good time and were already almost at Goldstream on their way up the Malahat Highway. Alexander's BMW hadn't moved, but Polina's was taking a scenic tour along Dallas Road toward Cook Street Village. I needed to look at the logs at some point and see where everybody lived. But that was a curiosity for another time. The more urgent point was that none of them were here and there was work to do.

Benny and Colin were waiting for me downstairs by the flower van when I returned.

"If you're sure you don't need us, I thought it might be best if Colin and I go run those errands," Benny said.

"Good idea," I said and handed him the bag of bagels. "Just drive on past when you get back if you see the building surrounded by police cars or security people."

We exchanged meaningful looks. Mine was intended to say 'I'm serious'. His had more of a 'try not to do anything silly' vibe to it.

As they pulled away, I sent a message to Tim asking for an elevator call and then jogged to the Vespa to grab Harley's climbing gear bag from the under-seat storage. Tim was waiting by the elevator doors when I reached our floor.

"This is exciting," he said.

Or incredibly stupid, I thought. But I kept the negativity to myself. I made sure that the whiteboards shielded us from the view of the router, and then I spread the contents of Harley's bag on the floor. It was a heavy bag. There were fifty meters of climbing rope. A climbing harness. A chalk bag. A whole bunch of interesting-looking metal blocks and mechanical doo-dads on slings. And, most importantly, a learn-to-climb instruction book.

"I guess we should see what we're dealing with before I go knock out the security feeds," I said.

I dropped my shoulder bag on the floor beside Harley's gear and rummaged around to find the homemade drop-key I'd remembered to bring. Most elevators have a small hole somewhere in the outer doors of every floor. The hole allows firefighters and service people to manually open elevator doors by inserting a special key. It's not a key in the usual sense, so much as a rod made of two parts that hinge together. The first bit swings down thanks to gravity once it's inserted and then the whole thing becomes a simple lever to push against a release mechanism. Uncle Rupert had me make one years ago as an exercise to improve my skills in the workshop. But I'd never actually had a chance to use it until now.

There were a few anxious moments as I tried it on the doors of the unused elevator shaft. I finally realized I was being too gentle and just cranked on the key as hard as I could until there was an echoey 'bong' sound to signal the release had been tripped. The doors shuddered open a tiny fraction as I pulled the key out. I gingerly slid my fingertips into the gap and pulled them open a teeny bit more.

"Cool," Tim said.

"And dark," I added.

In all my careful preparation, I'd forgotten to bring a flashlight. I toggled the light on my cellphone instead and aimed it into the shaft. Straight ahead was a blank cement wall. Just to the right, an orderly stream of wires and pipes ran beside heavy metal guide rails, all of it bolted securely to the wall. There was a pair of matching rail systems on the other side seemingly hanging in mid-air until I tilted the phone far enough up and down to see where they attached to cement beams on each floor. Just past the rails, I could see the boxy shape of the elevator car suspended in the other shaft beside me. There was no sign of convenient ladders or even reasonable handholds.

"In theory," I said, stepping back to the safety beside Tim. "If I can figure out a way to climb up to the roof of the elevator car, then I should be able to reach the door release for the ninth floor. Then it's just a climb out and I can open the stairway door lock from the inside and we're in. Or you just get in the elevator and I call it up. I guess that works, too."

"Sounds simple enough," Tim said. "Good thing you know how to rock climb, I guess, huh?"

"Yes. It would be, wouldn't it?" I said, trying to avoid eye contact. I flipped through the book with the sinking feeling that beyond how to put on the harness, most of the rest wasn't strictly relevant to ascending elevator shafts. Probably some sort of emergency services guide from the library would've been a better choice.

Tim had a look at the elevator shaft while I struggled with the harness. There were loops to step into and a belt to tighten, but the straps looped back on themselves for security reasons and it took a few tries to get the book diagrams to match what I'd done.

When I turned to the next chapter, I realized I was way out of my depth, and I hadn't given myself time to figure this out properly. I could feel my anxiety levels spiking. The thought of stepping into an open shaft nine floors high without knowing what to do was playing havoc with my imagination. My hands were shaking hard enough to make the text jump. I should have gone to the park with Harley last night, Great Blue Herons or not. Like an idiot, I'd passed on a chance to learn how this all worked and instead, I'd just slept on the couch.

"You know," Tim said. "There's maybe an easier way. Isn't there a little door in the ceiling of the elevator? The movies always have one, right? We could get a ladder or a step stool or something on the inside of the elevator and you could just go climb up that way."

I'm not sure the team that gives out the Nobel prize for brilliant ideas was going to agree with me, but I was certainly going to put in my recommendation for Tim. I nearly hugged him in relief, but it turned out to be a short-lived feeling. We stampeded into the open elevator and spent a few minutes staring straight up. The entire ceiling was just a single back-lit light panel. Tim wheeled in one of the office chairs and held it braced in a corner while I stood on the seat and poked and prodded the edges of the panel. No sign of a hidden catch, release, hinge, or even any screws.

We retreated to the whiteboards so Tim could begin searching Otis elevator designs on his computer. There were a few missed calls and a single text message from Uncle Rupert on my phone that just said 'Please read my email'—which didn't sound good. Uncle Rupert prefers to have serious conversations face-to-face. But on the rare times that he has been particularly vexed with me, he has chosen to write down his thoughts so that he can edit them carefully first. I paced my way over to the windows with nervous energy. I was already angsty from the elevator project, but when I pulled open his message, my anxiety only doubled. I was right to be worried. Apparently, there had been some lively conversations with Marty. As I read through his message, Uncle Rupert expressed he was somewhat curious about why I'd dropped over at Marty's borrowing bug-hunting gear. But he was emphatically annoyed to learn that I'd brought Tim along on my visit. The rest of the email was liberally peppered with words and phrases like 'unprofessional' and 'what was I thinking?' and 'what was I doing about the spa job?' He ended with the hope that I would have a full and compelling explanation to give him when I came by for dinner that evening. As dinner invites go, it lacked his usual warmth, and I got the impression my attendance was very non-negotiable.

I checked the time and saw it was already nine-thirty. Outside the window, Saturday morning was in full swing. Cyclists and joggers were zipping along the path by the shore below. At least the eastbound ones were. Those heading in the other direction had joined the cars and buses at a complete standstill on this side of downtown. They were all converged at the red and white barriers that had come down to block traffic. I watched for a few minutes as the blue bridge rose open to allow a tall sailing ship to exit the inner harbour. With a giddy flash of insight, I realized Uncle Rupert was right. I was being very dumb.

"New plan," I said, as I marched past Tim, the chalk bag on my harness swinging behind me like a stumpy tail. "Let's go."

By the time Tim caught me up, I had already fished out

my new lockpicks from my bag and was heading for the stairwell door.

"I thought you couldn't pick the lock on their floor?" he said.

"I can't," I said. "We're going down, not up."

He followed me to the seventh floor, where I attacked the Schlage with focused intensity. Uncle Rupert would not have approved of my aggressive style, but part of me enjoyed cranking open the deadbolt that much more for that reason.

There was the same sort of abandoned feel to the seventh floor as we'd initially found on the eighth. Construction leftovers were strewn here and there all under a uniformly gritty coat of concrete dust. There was thankfully no sign of fresh wheelbarrow tracks leading off to dark corners where freezers or dead bodies might have lurked.

"Why are we here?" Tim asked.

"Because you're a genius," I said. "Or at least the folks who designed the blue bridge are. Either way, it got me thinking of how I can just walk onto the roof."

"Still confused."

"It's actually pretty simple," I said. "You're going to push the call button here on the seventh floor. When the elevator arrives, the roof of it will then be level with the floor above. Right? So if I'm up there on the eighth floor and I use my special key to open the outer elevator doors, then I'll just need to step straight onto the roof. Easy peasy. Then you take the stairs up too. When I'm safe, you press the call button there on the eighth floor, which brings the elevator and me up. Only then I'll be on the ninth floor. Then I just open the doors to that floor from the inside as I'd originally planned, and then away we go. Got it?"

Tim's usual grin went a little wider. "Why didn't we

think of that before?"

"Better late than never," I said. "First, though, I need to pop down to the basement to turn off the internet and landlines. You wait here. Give me ten minutes and then press the call button to get me back. Got it?"

It actually took me under three minutes to go down, break back into the utility room, flip the breakers, unclip the cables that Maryam had shown me, and then return to the elevator. I paced in nervous circles for what seemed an age before the elevator finally whirred back into motion. I got out on the seventh floor and gave Tim a gleeful high-five, then jogged up the stairs to our floor. Only then did I realize I should have used the drop-key to open the doors before I did the utility room visit. But with the earlier practice on the other door, it only took me about half the time. When I finally slid the doors open, though, I could hear Tim calling from below with some concern in his voice.

"How's it going up there?"

"I'll let you know in a sec," I said.

I guess I had expected the roof of the elevator to be a mostly flat and open platform. But there was actually almost no place to stand at all. Two massive pulleys were mounted on either side of the car. Each was looped by half a dozen steel cables that disappeared somewhere overhead. The rest of the space was taken up by a bunch of variously sized metal boxes that projected up here and there and no doubt housed important things. Besides that, the distance between floors was actually much greater than the actual height of the elevator car. The only pleasing aspect was the bright yellow guard rail that encircled the top on three sides. The railing wasn't very high, but it gave me at least the illusion of security, and it was something to use as a step down to reach the roof. The back and one side of the shaft were walls of solid gray cinder block. The third side was a black void where the missing elevator would run. I tried not to look as I sat on the edge of the open door and eased myself down.

After some nervous repositioning, I found a place to sit on one of the boxes and held onto the railing with both hands in a death grip. I was still wearing the climbing harness, which seemed a bit silly now, but it was also vaguely comforting. I didn't have any tools with me, but I shouldn't need them. Opening the elevator doors from the inside would be just a push on the release lever with my hand, and then I just had to open the stairway door locks to let Tim inside and he could get to work on the computers.

"All set," I called down.

Tim gave a muffled answer and then I felt, just as much as I heard, the elevator doors closing. Then it was all deadly silent until the stairway door opened and a moment later, Tim's feet came into view. I gave him a thumbs-up and told him to press the call button to bring the elevator up. He was just reaching for it when a few things happened simultaneously. First, there was a 'click clack' sound from somewhere high above. Then the entire shaft resonated with an electronic whir. I glanced up and saw Tim's expression actually changed from his perpetual grin to a look that was closer to alarm. His open-mouthed gape probably mirrored my own. This was all because the elevator didn't slowly move up as planned. Instead, it dropped like a stone.

Somebody screamed. Pretty sure it was me.

21

Harley's favourite ride when the Carnival comes to town is called The Zipper. You get locked into any of a dozen metal cages, which are all part of a conveyor belt that moves around a vertical arm. As the cages move, the arm itself spins like a propeller. And then—if all that wasn't bad enough already—the cages are free to rotate like hamster wheels. With all that going on simultaneously the g-forces tend to pile up while you get whipped around in unpredictable ways. As a result, and perhaps not surprisingly, the cages require a cleansing hose down from time to time. Harley and I both tend to scream during the entire ride but for entirely different reasons. Her yelps are from wild, giddy exhilaration. Mine are from pure, undistilled panic.

There are, however, a few differences between a ride on The Zipper and sitting on the roof of a moving elevator. For starters, even at night, the Carnival is awash with light. The elevator shaft was like falling into a coal mine. The only beacon was the open doorway that framed Tim's silhouette floating high above me like a rectangular moon. It was also a much windier ride. All that air in the elevator shaft has to go somewhere, I suppose, and it streamed past the side of the car with near hurricane force.

On the plus side, while I wasn't securely locked in place, there was also no spinning upside down involved. And when I thought about it, the movement inside the car was usually quite smooth, so really there shouldn't be much difference sitting on the roof. The other calming thought was that the elevator was brand new. The Carnival rides all had a certain battle-weariness that suggested age and neglect.

I stopped screaming somewhere around the fifth floor.

Which gave me more than half the trip down to get my heart rate under control and even grab a moment to consider who had called the elevator. The hopeful answer was that it was Benny and Colin returning from their shopping trip. The next ideal option was that it was someone from the occupied fourth floor popping into the office during off hours. But as the elevator ramped down to a smooth stop, I could already hear the muted, but quite distinct, titter of Polina's laugh. I couldn't make out the words of the conversation, but judging by the lower pitch, whoever Polina was with was definitely male—Alexander, perhaps. The car bobbed and wobbled a fraction under me as they stepped inside. I briefly debated using my phone light to check out the bottom of the shaft on the other side, in case the body of Kirill Bondarchuk might be there. But the grisly possibility kept me firmly in place.

And then the ride started all over again. For some reason, it was *much* scarier going up than down. The light in the shaft got steadily brighter until I shot past the eighth floor. I had a brief glimpse of Tim through the open doors. He had wisely retreated a safe distance away but was still wearing the same open-mouthed expression. And then it was instantly dark all over again. The whine of the electric motor suddenly grew incredibly loud, and I had only a moment to consider that as Polina was sending us to the uppermost floor, I had no idea how much clearance there was going to be between my head and whatever was at the top of the shaft. I mostly held my breath, but I may have inadvertently also panicked a little. In the eerie silence that followed, Polina's raised voice cut through the insulation of the cab.

"Did you hear that? There was a squeak or something. And there was a sound earlier, too."

Her companion replied in low tones I couldn't make out, but then Polina continued her side of the conversation in Russian or Ukrainian, so it didn't matter if I could hear him or not. I stayed glued in place until they'd either decided that any squeaks were either imagined or possibly there was a mouse problem. Then Polina stepped out and, judging by her fading voice, ran off to get something. The man stayed put, though. I could feel every footstep as he shuffled impatiently in place. It wasn't Alexander; I was certain of that. He would either have gone into his office or just calmly stood still. It made sense that with Kirill dead, and Valery otherwise engaged, they'd got a replacement bodyguard for Polina. A minute later she was back, the doors closed, and we were off again.

The second time down, I was more prepared. I even flashed Tim a quick thumbs-up as he went by. Only when we were nearing the bottom did I realize it was lucky Tim had never got around to pressing the call button or he might have had to work his way through an awkward conversation. I expected that even Polina might have found it curious to see climbing gear strewn over the floor.

But Tim had clearly pressed the button after we'd passed him the second time, as no sooner had Polina and her companion stepped out of the elevator, the doors closed and I was riding up once again.

"Won't be a minute," I called to Tim as the car slowed to a stop.

It was a stretch for me to reach the door release mechanism, but once it clunked open, I pried the doors apart and immediately scrambled out. I did a few rolls to make sure I was clear and then sprawled face-up on the floor for a full minute or more. I'd never been so happy to leave an elevator before in my life.

A muffled something from Tim got me to my feet and then it was my turn to press the call button. When the elevator rose and the inner doors opened, I found Tim holding his computer bag and wearing a very uncertain grin. He stepped out and like that; we were both on the ninth floor.

"What if they come back?" he said.

"I'll keep a close eye on the tracking app." I glanced at my phone to see that it was already close to noon. "I don't think Polina is one for stairs. Maybe we could wedge an office chair between the doors to keep the elevator here just in case? "

Tim gave a shrug. "That should be okay. It's Saturday. All the offices on my floor are closed and if there's anybody else lower down, they can always take the stairs.

"We're only going to be a few minutes, anyway. Right?"

Wrong. As it turned out.

I had hoped we'd be lightning quick, but Tim had other ideas. A tour through all the rooms revealed that there were a half dozen computers in various offices. Rather than jump through hoops trying to set up an access point to their network that he could exploit remotely, Tim wanted to take what he called the 'sneakerware' approach. Which meant physically plugging in an external hard drive to each computer and directly copying files.

I had to do some confidence-boosting and threat-reminding to help Tim past the legalities issue. And then there was some jiggery-pokery involved to bypass login screens, which was nothing he couldn't handle. But, there were a lot of files, and the computers were slow, so it was taking forever.

Since the deactivation of the security feed and alarms

seemed to have been successful, and willing things to move faster didn't seem to be working, I passed the time by unlocking every drawer and filing cabinet I could find. All I discovered was a random collection of typical office things like paper supplies and staplers, intermixed with personal things like trashy romance novels, a scrapbook of tropical vacation destinations, and expired lotto tickets.

I saved Alexander's office for last. There wasn't much to find of interest in his desk or the bookcase drawers, but the filing cabinet was a different matter. He'd left the keys in the lock, so I didn't even have to put any effort into opening the top drawer. Which seemed cavalier as it held boxes of ammunition and the chrome handgun he'd been waving when we'd first met. I slammed it closed with more force than necessary.

A more joyful moment occurred when I stumbled over my lockpick kit in the drawer beneath. It was clearly his junk drawer as it was stuffed with electrical cables, old phone chargers and even balloons and food colouring from the last staff birthday party.

I badly wanted to take my whole kit, but caution won out. Assuming Tim and I finished up undetected, then there was no point in raising suspicions. Maybe, if everything went as hoped, I could ask Max to try to retrieve it from the police collection after they raided the place. Though requesting the police to return burglary tools was just asking for trouble. In the end, I just exchanged the new tools I'd bought for some of my old favourites, which perked up my spirits. There was no sign of my pizza carrier, but that was more of an academic curiosity.

When I had run out of filing cabinets to snoop through, I told Tim to go find me on the roof whenever he was finally done. I slid open the deadbolt on the Bowley and then left the stairway door propped open—just in case. On the roof, there was a dark band of clouds brooding across the horizon to the west, but here in the city, it was still sunny and warm. My phone once again magically had full reception bars, so I took a seat on the plastic smoker's chair and opened the tracker app to confirm everyone's location. It was silly of me to have not considered Polina's car movements more seriously earlier and I gave myself a mental kick.

Alexander's car was still at the golf course. Either he was enjoying another round or maybe it had rolled into a business lunch. Polina's was now parked at the Uptown Shopping Mall. And Valery's Audi was plugging along eastward on a logging road past Cowichan Lake. I checked the time and did some math. They'd left well over three hours ago and were still at *least* half an hour or more away from Sarita. Other than stop signs and traffic lights, the app told me that the Audi had rarely dropped below the speed limit. It was clearly a far longer trip than I'd imagined. Which would've been a *huge* problem if we were actually going to go through with it. But so long as Tim found some evidence that would get the CSIS excited, then it hardly mattered.

My phone warbled with a text from Benny asking for a lift up, so I abandoned my rooftop post and went down to pry the chair out of the elevator doors. The elevator immediately whirred down, and I was grateful not to be riding on the roof. I took the stairs down to our eighth floor and pushed the call button so Benny could come up. When I'd climbed back to join Tim on the ninth, he was just packing up.

"All done," he said.

"Awesome! Anything incriminating?" I asked.

"No idea. That was just the collecting part. Now we have

to sit down and go through it all."

I did a sweep of the floor to make sure we'd left everything as close to how we'd found it as possible. Finally, I sent Tim down the stairs so that I could relock the stairway door from the inside and then rode the elevator down to the basement to restore power to the security system again. And with that done, it was like we'd never been anywhere we shouldn't have.

After all that excitement, the afternoon dragged on—for me, at least. Tim set me up on one computer while he used another and together we poured through the files he'd copied. I had little idea what I was looking for. There were no folders conveniently labelled: 'Serious Crimes We've Done' or 'Buried Body Locations', or anything remotely helpful like that. Adding to the challenge was the random use of English and Cyrillic letters. I ended up searching just for pictures and video filetypes, which brought up a dizzying array of holiday snaps and bootlegged Hollywood blockbusters. There was an entire photo folder just of Valery posing beside his car. But unless he'd stolen the Audi, I doubted they were anything that would impress Max Kirkpatrick.

Meanwhile, Benny and Colin were similarly focused on a completely different computer-related task. After a trip to a gaming store, they'd stopped to pick up Colin's steering wheel setup. Tim had offered one of his faster computers for them to use and they had loaded up amazingly realistic maps of the roads around Sarita onto a rally game. Colin and Benny had been taking turns driving like maniacs ever since. In theory, it was all 'research' of the area, but it sounded like they were having too much fun for that.

I made myself useful, and I did a run to a sandwich shop to order everyone a late lunch. When I got back, Tim was taking a turn at the driving wheel. Which could only mean one of two things. Either he'd uncovered something useful, and we were off the hook, or…

"Nothing," Benny said. "Maybe given more time, and someone who speaks their language, there might be something in there. But he couldn't find anything at all. I had a look at the spreadsheet files, but what little there is relates to this building and paying contractors. Nothing else."

"So we're stuck," I said. "If we don't have that, then… what?"

Benny just gave a tired shrug in reply. He didn't have to say it. I knew exactly what the only other option was. I grabbed some of the printed pages off the whiteboard, left them to their game, and hiked up the stairs back to the chair on the roof for some quiet contemplation.

I went through the stack of pages twice and then closed my eyes to think. All the social media posts put together gave us an almost minute-by-minute itinerary of where the cup and its Keeper would be during its visit tomorrow. If we were going to do this heist—which I suppose was the only word for it—there had to be a plan. And whatever exactly the plan might be, there was only one feasible time to execute it. It had to be done *after* the day's tour had ended. After the final time that it would be seen before being locked into its case. And then—with any luck at all—the case wouldn't be opened again until it was back in Vancouver. Or…who knew? Maybe not even until after it had flown back to New York?

If we tried to get hold of the cup any earlier in the day, then somebody was going to notice it was gone. And for sure I wasn't going anywhere near a brazen: 'Hands in the air! Everybody freeze!' kind of approach. Whatever we did would have to be sneaky. That had always been my style.

I flipped through the printouts one more time. The last scheduled visit was to be with Clara Peter's father, in the hills somewhere outside Sarita. After that, it looked like the keeper would be heading straight back to catch the ferry in Nanaimo. No stops. No time for anything else. Which, when I looked at the schedule, meant the cup would have to be in its case and leaving Sarita no later than five o'clock sharp. This also meant that we needed to have absconded with it sometime before then. How much earlier was the question? We'd need enough time to make it back for Alexander's rigid eight p.m. deadline.

The idea of hiring a float plane flashed through my mind at the same moment a weather advisory flashed on my phone. High winds and torrential rain were expected to arrive early the next morning and stay until Tuesday. The dark smudge on the horizon had crept closer and only deepened in colour. A summer storm was on its way. *Terrific.* Even if a float plane was available to hire, nobody would be flying anyway. Helicopters might, but that was a whole other logistical challenge.

My phone vibrated in my hand. I half expected another call from Uncle Rupert, so it was almost a relief when I saw it was Valery's number.

"We are part way back," he said. "Roads not so good. Wait…one moment…"

There was some fumbling, and then Saffron's voice came on.

"Well, the Cowichan Lake route is the faster way," she said. "It took us just over four hours and we didn't stop. Even to pee, I might add. Now we're taking the lower road and it's definitely going to take us even longer. We've stopped for a break and I thought we should call, so you'd know."

"That's too long," I said with a sinking feeling. "Way, way, way too long. It has to be done in like three hours maximum, and ideally less."

There was the crunch of footsteps on gravel, as Saffron presumably strolled to put some distance between herself and Valery.

"What are you talking about? Too long?" she said. There was a thready waver to her voice that sounded like she was at the end of a tether. "You said this is all just for show, isn't it? You were supposed to be finding…computer things!?"

"It didn't go so well," I said. There was no point in not being honest. "We didn't find anything at all."

"Nothing? *Nothing?* Oh, my god. So, so, so…what are we going to do?"

"I don't know."

There was a silence that dragged on and I thought she'd hung up, but apparently, she'd just been collecting her thoughts.

"This is *your* fault," she hissed. "We should have gone to the police right away. Now we've been interacting with these people. And the police *know* we have. You said this government agent had been following us around. They probably think we're criminals now. And if they do, then they're right. Aren't they? We *are* trying to be. And it's all your fault!"

I was trying to think of a point to argue, but I realized she'd hung up. In the time our phone call had lasted, the approaching line of clouds seemed to have darkened even more like a ripening bruise.

It was easy to empathize.

22

With heavy steps, I trudged back down to the eighth floor. The mood there wasn't much of a pick-me-up.

"I don't get it," Colin said, in something approaching a whine. "You're like, more than *twice* as fast as me. Even when we use the same car on the same road."

"You have to start using your handbrake," Benny replied. "It's important on all those tight turns. And you need to try to countersteer like I showed you on the bigger corners. The car needs to drift around them sideways-like. You keep trying to just steer like you were on a racetrack—that's why you end up in the trees so much."

"It's too hard. All that *opposite-lock* and *Scandi-flick* you keep talking about...I don't get it...I give up," Colin said. He pushed his chair back from the wheel and stomped off towards the windows.

Benny sighed and added a shrug in a 'kids these days—what are you gonna do?' kind of way when he saw me.

"Where's Tim?" I asked.

Benny gave an even deeper sigh, and his eyebrows dropped. "He left. I think the panic is setting in. With nothing on their computers to show any crimes...he went down to his office to pack up. I don't imagine there's much holding him here, so I guess he's probably making a run for it."

"I see. What about you?"

Benny worked up a slight smile. "Oh, I'm still here. I've been neglecting work lately, but I've got my flower shop to run. But before I get back to that...I guess we're going to make a play for the cup, after all? Last resort?"

I dropped into Colin's empty chair and spun myself in slow circles.

"I can't see it working," I said. "I have an idea for the *how*…but not for the *when*. There just isn't enough time to get the cup here by eight o'clock tomorrow. Not if we do it the smart way and avoid confrontation. I know we have Valery, but an aggressive hold-up approach might lead to someone getting hurt. None of us could live with that."

"Of course, we may not live anyway," Benny said, with a slight joking twinkle in his eye that helped soften the words.

It was my turn for a deep sigh.

"I'll call Alexander and explain," I said. "Saffron has a view that I'm the one that got us deeper into this mess. I'm sure she's expressed that thought to Valery, so maybe I can convince Alexander she's right and I'll take all the blame. Who knows? It might be fun working full time for a criminal organization."

"You think that's going to be a solution Alexander would go for?"

"It's worth a try. I don't have a business to run or any other real responsibilities at all. Not like the rest of you. And I have a few skills Alexander will probably find useful. If I pledge my allegiance to him in perpetuity, maybe that will give the rest of you some leeway."

"That's very noble of you," Benny said.

It's certainly very something, I thought. I consulted my phone for the time and remembered I was due at Uncle Rupert's.

"If you come up with a better idea, please let me know. In the meantime, I have a dinner date I'd rather not attend. But..." I trailed off with a shrug.

Benny assured me he'd keep a chaperoning eye on Colin until Saffron, and the others returned.

Dinner was a sullen affair. Despite Aunt Stacy's wonderful cooking and her lively attempts to keep a conversation going, both Uncle Rupert and I spent most of the meal in gloomy silence. I could feel him shooting me meaningful looks from time to time, but I mostly avoided eye contact and spent my time focused on herding peas around on my plate in hopes of giving the illusion I was eating.

"Well," Aunt Stacy said. It was only one word, but she managed to layer on enough spin and nuance to her inflection that it might as well have been a throne speech. She followed it up by smoothing her folded napkin onto the table with the palm of her hand. For Aunt Stacy, this was roughly the equivalent of slamming doors or screaming. She'd clearly had enough of the two of us and began clearing the table without another word.

I was just pushing back my chair to help when Uncle Rupert started making a few drawn-out throat-clearing noises.

"I was talking to your mother earlier today," he finally said. "She has a job idea for you. One of the charters she's been doing brings bikers into the mountains somewhere up by Pemberton on the mainland. They're looking for someone to help manage it. Could be good for you."

"I already have a job. And I like it fine right here. Thanks all the same," I mumbled.

It was like being fourteen all over again, arguing about where I should go to high school—up north where my parents could take turns pretending to be attentive or down here where I wanted to be.

"Yes, well. Your mother...and I...thought you might benefit from having some other work experience besides what you've done with me. Expand your resume a bit. And it might do you some good to spend time out in nature."

"I can do that here," I said. "This is my home."

"Of course it is. Don't be silly," Aunt Stacy said with a squinty look at Uncle Rupert. "You don't have to go anywhere or do anything you don't want to. You never have, and certainly, no one is foolish enough to try to make you now." She planted a kiss on my forehead and then slid a ridiculously huge slice of apple pie in front of me. I ate it all.

With an uneasy truce in the air, I left them both with long hugs and then stopped to skip stones near Ogden Point on my way home. The sun was still theoretically above the horizon, but the clouds were thick enough that it might as well already have been dusk.

In the gloom, it was a challenge to find flat rocks. On top of that, the wind had already begun to pick up, so the swells were choppy and the most I got was a double skip after half an hour of trying. An otter eventually poked its head up and gave me a hard glare, so I stopped and retreated to the Vespa. As I perched on the edge of the seat, I brought out my phone and scrolled my way to find Alexander's number.

"I've just spoke with Valery," he said. "He tells me you are working hard. This is good."

"There's a storm coming in," I said. "Did he mention that?"

"So?"

"If it gets too windy, then the ferries may not run. If they don't run, then the cup won't come over to the island. So it might not-"

"Stop! This...logistics is not my concern or my problem. I

told you this. I have always been very clear. Now, I want you—all six of you—and the trophy at Ogden Point at twenty hours tomorrow."

"I'm at Ogden Point right now! Why here?" I asked. "Why then? And why the cup at all?"

I thought they were reasonable questions, but he'd hung up, so I was just talking to myself. I didn't even get a chance to share my idea of offering to work full-time in exchange for the others being let go. Somehow, I doubted he was in the right mood to consider it.

My view of the ocean was momentarily blocked by a family of passing tourists. The father held a cellphone up at arm's length, while the mother and kids video-chatted away with an elderly woman on the screen. Nothing like sharing your vacation in real time. My eyes followed the group as they veered off away from the path out to the breakwater and instead headed towards the bistro. Beyond them, the huge expanse of parking lot that stretched off to the pier buildings was largely empty. The main docks were vacant as well. Only in the small harbour behind the protective arm of the breakwater were a few tugs and the cluster of the yellow pilot boats that guide the cruise ships when they visit. Why bring the Stanley Cup here? Why steal it in the first place? I replayed my questions in my head again and again until a tiny thought took hold. Because…because…*Leonid.*

It *had* to be. If Alexander wanted the cup for himself, then we could meet anywhere and at any time. But what if it wasn't for Alexander? The only person that Alexander seemed eager to please was his boss. The rush of goosebumps that covered me had nothing to do with the evening chill. It had to be for him. Leonid, their boss. Leonid, the hockey team owner. Leonid, the man who had wanted Kirill dead.

And then my head snapped back to where the tourists

had disappeared into the bistro as another idea struck me like an avalanche. What if the reason I hadn't found the video or photos on Valery's phone of Kirill's murder scene was because Valery hadn't been *recording*...he'd been *streaming!?* A live video chat with Leonid! They were having a live call of the whole event so that Leonid could see for himself that the job of murdering Kirill had been done. And right in the middle of that...with exquisite timing, the six of us had shown up in the background to throw a pizza box into the gears. Leonid must have been more than curious. And no doubt he'd be left wondering just what sort of sloppy show Alexander was running over here.

I pulled out my phone and searched for the cruise ship schedule. There isn't much else that goes on at Ogden Point that is time-sensitive that I could think of. The ships stop on their way to or from Alaska and passengers have a few hours to check out Victoria. Harley and I see the pedicabs, rickshaws, and horse carriages coming past our place all the time in James Bay. I like it. Reminds me we live somewhere that people think is cool enough to visit.

There was only one cruise ship stopping tomorrow evening—the Norwegian Sun. What was particularly interesting was the 'amended' notation. I clicked on it and read that the schedule had been modified. Due to a port closure in Sitka, Alaska, the Norwegian Sun would be visiting Victoria three days earlier than planned. So *that's* what happened to our original timeline! The certainty that I was right had me on my feet and pacing rapid circles around the Vespa.

Leonid was going to be here in Victoria tomorrow evening. Maybe his running afoul of Putin had him feeling the pinch? He had given up owning his own fleet of yachts and was now slumming on cruise ship tours. Or maybe even he just lived on one year-round? I'd heard of people doing that. Maybe especially people who were hiding from the Russian secret police.

And what better way to ease the boredom than having your own Stanley Cup? I guess? I mean, what do you give to the guy who had everything? And it made sense that Alexander wanted all six of us there to hand it over. Leonid had seen us witness Kirill's execution. We were loose ends. But if we all showed up lugging a stolen trophy, then Leonid could see that we were team players. In a twisted way, Alexander was actually trying to help us. My elation at finally understanding what was behind the ridiculous task had given me a tingling rush of adrenaline. I was almost dancing around the sidewalk in excitement. Alexander was trying to assure Leonid that we were no threat to his organization and so not worth having executed. It was almost sweet of him.

It was also almost a great plan. But it fell tragically short because there was just no way possible we could get the cup. Not in time, anyway.

I checked the Norwegian Sun website and skimmed the rest of its schedule. After Alaska, it headed down to Panama, the Caribbean, and Bermuda, on its way across the Atlantic for a winter of fun in and around the Mediterranean. If Leonid was a permanent guest on that ship, then he wasn't back in this part of the world until next year.

It all felt right. But it also didn't change anything or help in the slightest.

With a last look at the empty pier docks, I fired up the Vespa and puttered home.

"Hey! *It's Complicated,* tonight," Harley called out when she heard me come in.

"That's for sure," I said. "More than I can explain."

"What? No, I mean...*It's Complicated.*"

"You said that."

"I know I did. So what's to explain? You can be confusing sometimes, you know that, right?"

I forced myself to take a long, deep breath.

"Let's start again," I said. "You go first."

"Okay. Our movie tonight is the last of the DVD haul—*It's Complicated.* Meryl Streep's in it, so you know it'll be good. You know...you look like you need to sit. You do that. I'll go make the popcorn."

It was a sign of something seriously unbalanced in the universe when it was Harley who was finding me confusing and not the other way around. But I followed her suggestion. I set my bag on the coffee table and flopped onto the couch, somewhat hoping it would swallow me whole.

"Did you keep that napkin from the other night?" I said as I fished for my phone. "I guess the only thing left to make things more complicated is to call Max Kirkpatrick."

"Who?"

"Max Kirkpatrick," I said.

"Oh...William Baldwin," she said, giving weight to my thoughts. "No, this one tonight has *Alec* in it. So many Baldwins! Too many, really. Anyway, you're thinking of William. He was okay in that show *Northern Rescue*—it's a shame they only made the one season. But I think Stephen is the best Baldwin. Remember *The Usual Suspects*? *So* good."

"Harley! Wait..." I said. "What *are* you talking about? Max Kirkpatrick is the CSIS guy. The spy we met at the lounge last week. Remember? James Bond? He gave us his number on a napkin. I keep forgetting to ask you for it. You kept it right?"

"You really are muddled tonight, aren't you? No, Max Kirkpatrick was the name of the bodyguard in that Cindy Crawford movie we watched the other night. *Fair Game.*"

"Remind me. I slept through most of it," I said, suddenly finding myself completely alert.

"Okay. Well. There's this renegade KGB assassination team that is hunting Kate McQueen—that's Cindy Crawford. And then, Max Kirkpatrick—that's William Baldwin—is a cop who protects her."

"He played a bodyguard?"

"Yep. I mean, he was a cop, but ya. Like I said, she was being hunted by the KGB and he has to save her. And they fall in love. Of course."

"Of course," I mumbled. "The KGB. And he's protecting her. And they fall in love."

It hit me like a proverbial ton of bricks.

I jumped to my feet and screamed, "Harley! You're a friggin genius!"

"I *know,* right!?" she said, matching my intensity. "But, just for clarity…in this moment, it's because…?"

With a rush of complete clarity, I saw everything. One thing after another suddenly made absolute sense.

Holy smokes. Kirill—you loopy romantic. Alexander—you sneaky, sneaky, sneaky little weasel.

"Because Alexander *didn't* kill anybody," I said, grabbing Harley's hands with mine in excitement. "At least not that night he didn't. And because you're right, Max Kirkpatrick *isn't* a CSIS agent. He's friggin *Kirill Bondarchuk.*"

23

"This is...*awesome*!" Harley yelled.

We were both jumping up and down with hair-flying, eyes-wide grins of excitement. I couldn't imagine what Mrs. Carter downstairs thought we were doing.

"Is this a remake?" she panted after a pause to catch her breath.

It took me a few moments to realize Harley still, understandably, thought we were talking about movies.

"No. And...yes," I said. "In a sense, it is a remake. I think Kirill is obviously a fan of the original."

"Kirill. Right. You're saying that's who we met in the lounge telling us he was Max? He's very *method,* isn't he? Who is playing the Cindy Crawford role?"

"Polina Pavlova. Only in this version, she's the granddaughter of a Russian billionaire."

"Oooh. Nice twist. I like it," Harley said. "I don't know her work either, though. Has she been in anything I might have seen? I need to watch more independent films."

"Think of this more as...live theatre," I said. "And it's playing right now."

"It is? Cool! When can we go see it?" Harley asked and started jumping up and down all over again.

I had to guide us both back to the sofa before she had enough focus to listen to my explanation. Considering how convoluted my week had been, I fully expected I would have to have to run through it all for her several times in a few different ways—but I was wrong.

"So you and some other people in an elevator interrupted a mock execution by euro-gangsters, and now you have to go steal the Stanley Cup?" she said.

It was almost a shock to hear her say it so plainly.

"Yep. That's pretty much it. Actually, that's exactly it."

Anyone else would have then wanted to delve into the rationalizations and legal aspects behind the who's and the why's and so forth. But then Harley isn't just anybody. She just jumped up and did a little victory dance to celebrate her understanding. "Cool," she said. "How can I help?"

It was a great question. Not that I wanted to get Harley involved in any of it. But it prompted me to think about what to do next. Before moving forward, though, I needed to take a small step back. I needed some proof that it wasn't all just in my mind. Proof that the name Max Kirkpatrick from a box-office flop and that of someone claiming to be a CSIS agent wasn't just some odd coincidence.

I hauled out my phone and brought up the tracking app. There was a history function and a heat map that showed where the vehicles spent most of their time. Polina's—or more likely Kirill's BMW—was usually parked at an apartment complex not far from Uncle Ruperts.

"Where did you get the DVD haul again?" I asked.

"Near Fisherman's Wharf. It was a pain because I didn't have my backpack with me that day and I had to drop by your aunt's place to borrow a bag to carry them all," Harley said. "Wait! Is that a clue?"

"Maybe," I said. "Maybe the movies used to belong to Kirill. Or maybe it's just something random. Give me a second here, though. I need to call someone."

I brought up Tim's number. He finally answered on the fifth or so ring. Maybe he was busy packing.

"Quick question," I said. "This morning. When you got into the elevator to come up to the ninth floor…after all the rest of it. What did you smell?"

"What did I smell?" Tim said.

Harley was gesturing wildly at me. I didn't understand why until she cupped her ear with one hand, pointed at my phone with the other, and simultaneously managed to give an exasperated shrug. I switched my phone to speaker mode.

"Ya. Did you smell anything?" I repeated.

"Ummm…I dunno," he said. "Did you?"

"Yes," I said. I didn't want to lead him to any conclusions. "I know we were both a little distracted, but I do remember something that way."

"Hmmm, okay. Well, I guess there was maybe… perfume?"

Polina's signature fragrance. Something like sultry wood, vanilla, and a hint of spice, and no doubt crazily expensive.

"And…?" I prompted. "Anything else?"

"Oh, right! Definitely cigarette smoke. I do remember that."

Bingo, I thought. Kirill, the chain smoker.

"Okay. I need you to do me a favour," I said. "Just don't leave town. Not yet anyway. I'll explain tomorrow when I know more. And I'm not going to ask you to do anything crazy aside from maybe pick up Saffron and Colin at some point. Can you promise me that?"

My next call was to Benny. He also took his time to answer, but I could hear the whir of the coolers, so I knew he was hard at work in the flower shop. I put the phone on speaker again and laid it flat on the coffee table. Harley dragged over the milk crate she kept DVDs in as a stool. Our heads nearly bumped as we leaned over the phone.

"Remember the night we met?" I asked Benny.

"Well, that's hardly an easy one for any of us to forget, is it? As much as I'd like to."

"Yes. But you were there because you were delivering flowers addressed to Polina Pavlova."

"Well yes! I haven't become senile in the last few hours. How old do you think I am?"

"Sorry Benny," I said. "I was leading up to my question."

"Which is what?"

"Do you remember *who* ordered those flowers?"

"Huh. Okay. Well, no, you got me there. Not off the top of my head," he said. There was a drawn-out exhale. "But… hang on a second."

Harley flashed me a big smile and leaned closer. "This is fun," she whispered.

There was the sound of a metal drawer opening followed by paper shuffling and finally the fumble as Benny picked up the phone again.

"Found it. Young guy paid with a credit card, I remember now. Huh. Well, that's interesting…" Benny's voice trailed off momentarily. When he spoke again, there was a hint of amusement in his voice. "I'd ask you to guess, but something tells me you already know."

"Just a hunch," I said. "Kirill Bondarchuk?"

"You got it in one. How about that? The dead guy."

"Well, you'd *think* that, wouldn't you?" I said.

"Can I tell him? Can I? Can I?" Harley burst out. And then she immediately began to do exactly that, before I could object, or even before Benny could ask who Harley might be.

I had to admit that Harley had absorbed all the key facts. And she even managed to limit herself to barely a handful of embellishments. Even so, her enthusiasm got the better of her more than a few times and there were numerous backtracks to add forgotten details whenever Benny got lost.

I took the opportunity to close my eyes and playback some different details that I'd forgotten. The cigarette butts I'd found in the parking lot that day at the disc golf course. More cigarette butts were on the roof of their building beside the chair that I'd mistakenly assumed had been left by construction workers. All Kirill. Clearly, Alexander had decided to keep him busy in the days after his fake death. And what better way than to have him follow me around to make sure I wasn't thinking of doing anything silly like involve the police? The CSIS thing was inspired. Much better than pretending to be an RCMP officer or a city cop. It wasn't like anyone would be tempted to ask a spy to show identification or be dressed in a uniform.

And then there was the memory of the three shadows I'd seen running past the stairway door right after the fake assassination. Valery, Alexander, and Kirill. Kirill who'd then waited smoking cigarettes in his car to watch me search in the bushes for my cellphone.

Benny's voice brought me back to attention. He had steered the conversation with Harley back to more practical matters.

"Me? I'm Margot's bestie," she said, flashing me a thumbs up. "We even go surfing together. Not real surfing, couch surfing, only with a surfboard. You know I was thinking… have you been to New Zealand? You have!? That's awesome. Cause you have a *great* voice. How's your footwork? You should *totally* come with me to my *kapa haka* class. It's fun!"

Benny had been to New Zealand? Why not? I suppose. Though I hadn't pegged him as a world traveller. What was it Alexander had called him that first night…? Benny the jet?

I was getting another tingly rush, though this one was mixed with a feeling of embarrassment. How slow had I been to put Benny's life in perspective? All that he had done over the last week and I hadn't once asked him any of the right questions.

I got up to fetch my laptop and started a long overdue search on the internet. Benny wasn't much for social media and most of the references dated back to the nineteen sixties and seventies. But there was plenty of them. Benjamin Schlesien—better known at the time by his rally driving companions and fans as both 'The Rocketman' and 'Benny The Jet'—was a three-time winner of the Canadian Rally Championship and had numerous international victories, including a few in New Zealand.

It was turning out to be an evening stuffed full of revelations. But this was the first one that actually might mean something in the form of salvation.

"Benny," I said, dropping back onto the couch. "Can you drive from Sarita to here faster than Valery?"

"Are you kidding? *Colin* can drive faster than Valery. Maybe even you too—if you remember to take off the handbrake."

"Yes, okay, point taken," I agreed, feeling my face flush. "But can you do it in under three hours?"

"No," he said. And then, after a long pause, "...and maybe."

"What does that mean?" I said.

"The no means that we can, within reason, go pretty much as fast as we like on the logging roads...but a good part of the drive is on pavement, through populated areas. Colin and I tried some of the sections with his game. If the entire route was closed to people and cars like a proper rally course would be, then no problem at all. But it's not. And we don't want to crash into an RV on a blind corner or clip somebody walking their dog. To say nothing of just general traffic once we hit the denser areas."

"But you said *maybe*?" Harley said.

"Ya I did, didn't I? Well. Back in the day, I was involved with a local driving club and they used to maintain a training loop up that way. It's on crown land and not strictly legal, but it was built so that drivers could have a course to use without worrying about other vehicles or people. It doesn't appear on any map, though I know you can see it on some satellite photos as Colin loaded that area into his game as well."

"And that helps us how?" I asked.

"Maybe it doesn't. I haven't been involved with the club in many years. Not since Edna..." Benny trailed off for an instant. " She was my co-driver. Best navigator in the world."

I had a mental flashback to the photo that Benny had up in his apartment. Edna beaming with youth and excitement. And what I now realized was a rally crash helmet under her arm.

"But if they've kept the route clear," Benny continued. "Then one section of it runs through a valley of Carmanah Provincial Park. It cuts more than fifty kilometres off the distance between Sarita and here. So...in theory. With the right car. A decent navigator. And a bit of luck. Ya sure. I could drive it in well under three hours."

The right car. Dang, it.

"We traded your rally car away, didn't we? That's what that was, right?"

"Yep. Didn't think I'd be needing it again, and it was a

waste of money paying for the storage like I'd been doing. It was never Edna's favourite car, anyway. Might be handy right now though…I guess if this Max Kirkpatrick isn't a real CSIS agent after all, then we don't have anyone to bail us out, do we?"

"I think we need to do our own bailing," I said. "And if I'm right about everything, then it's not Alexander we need to fear. It's his boss, Leonid. If we could bring him the cup—all of us together—then I think we actually might get ourselves into the clear."

"Aside from the felonies, of course," Benny said, but then hurried to continue. "Alright, let's give it a try. Why don't I see if I can reach someone from the old days who might still be with the rally club? Find out if that training route is still maintained. And if it is…maybe I can borrow a car that will do the job."

"Okay," I said. "I'll call Maryam. I need to hear what she has to say about everything that they all saw up in Sarita. I think Saffron sent me some pictures too, so I'll look at those. And I guess I'll call Valery too. I need to work through an idea I have with him on how we could actually go about getting our hands on the cup."

"This all sounds great," Harley said. "You guys get on with those things. I'd hate to give up our karaoke thing, so I'm going to see if I can find those bagpipes I was storing in the bike shed. Maybe I can trade them to get our coffee machine back, cause it *really* sounds like we're gonna need caffeine tomorrow."

24

I woke from a night filled with strange dreams to the sound of my phone vibrating its way off the edge of the bedside table. In my sleepy state, I got my hand snagged in the pillowcase. When I lunged to grab the phone, I ended up cleaning off the entire table; phone, water glass, reading light, alarm clock, *everything*. I couldn't remember if the glass had been half-empty, or half-full, but either way, there was a wet crash of breaking glass.

I keep my bedroom meticulously neat. The only way I can deal with the chaos that the rest of the world brings is by having my bedroom as my oasis of order. Everything, from the paired alignment of the socks in my bottom drawer to the evenly spaced queue of pencils on the shelf over my desk, is always, always, always exactly perfect. On a day when so many things could go wrong, it was a destabilizing start. Maybe I was just getting my bad luck out of the way? Probably Saffron would know my horoscope. If I made it through to the evening, I would ask her.

I carefully fished out my dripping wet, but still vibrating, phone from amongst the shards of glass.

"Good morning," Benny said, "Did I wake you?"

"Maybe. What time is it?" I mumbled. When I pressed the phone closer to my ear, I could hear a rumbling background noise of rushing wind and engine throb, punctuated by the steady beat of squealing windshield wipers. "Wait. Where are you?"

"Nearly seven, and I'm just past the Malahat summit

heading towards Nanaimo," he said. "Should be in Comox in a few hours. I got in touch with someone I used to know up there, and he had some good news. That training loop I was talking about is still being used. They clear it every spring so it should be in good shape. Though with this storm coming in, it'll just take one downed tree to put us in a rough spot."

"Why are you driving to Comox?"

"There's a car up there I need to borrow. It's old, like me. But together we'll do the job."

"An old car? Why an old car? Can't you drive Valery's or Alexander's? Something, you know, more…recent?" I said. Though I was actually thinking—*something safer?*

"If all we had to do was drive in a straight line, sure. I need something small and light with a manual transmission. Believe me, I'll be able to go much faster in a car I know well. Not to worry, it'll be fine. I'll get the car and then meet up with you outside Sarita later in the day. I do need you to grab a few things from the flower shop for me. I guess I should have hidden a key somewhere, but I guess that's not a big problem for you. Is it?"

I made him repeat it all three times to make sure I had it all etched into my memory. With assurances that we'd stay in touch to coordinate the when and where of our rendezvous, I hung up and sent off matching text messages to Maryam and Valery. They had still been together when I'd reached them last evening, having just dropped off Saffron. We'd had a three-way conversation that covered a few ideas but ended with the promise that I would text them if I'd heard from Benny that operation 'Stealing Stanley' was a go.

It's on! Benny's flower shop, eight am. Bring road snacks.

It took all my willpower to just leave the mess on the floor. I somehow managed to grab clean clothes and tiptoe to the bathroom for a stealthy shower without dropping to my knees and wasting time restoring order.

When I crept out later, I found Harley asleep under a pile of blankets on the couch in the living room. Lou, the coffee machine, had returned. I didn't know when or how Harley had brought it home, but it was now in pieces strewn over the table beside her. Whether she had taken it apart or was trying to put it back together wasn't clear. Her laptop was paused on a YouTube repair video. I left her a sticky note on the top of the screen:

Gone to get Stanley. If I get in trouble: 1) very important—don't let Uncle Rupert post bail! 2) rent is paid until August. 3) remember Tuesday is garbage and food waste day. PS - be careful, there's broken glass on my bedroom floor—don't ask. You're awesome. XO -M.

Traffic was light, though that wasn't so surprising for early on a rainy and blustery Sunday morning. The scooter tends to wobble in high winds, so it was a white-knuckled ride the whole way over to Marty's lair in Oak Bay.

He kept me waiting for nearly ten minutes, so we were apparently back to our usual barely speaking terms level of interaction. I didn't make any funny faces into his security camera this time. I just stood quietly and tried to look as apologetic as possible. It must've worked, as he eventually cracked open the door just wide enough to pass me the small device that I'd texted, emailed, and voice-messaged him about.

The gist of all of those communications was pretty much the same. *I'm an idiot. I'm so sorry. Tim knows nothing about you. Honest. Did I mention I'm sorry? Also, an idiot? I'll make it up to you somehow. And…by the way…can I have another USB kill device? Pretty please?*

I could have avoided all that if Alexander hadn't hidden, or thrown away the ones he'd taken from me. But when I'd found my tool kit in his office, there had only been my lock-picking tools, so I was reduced to grovelling to Marty.

With my dignity slightly dented, I pocketed the USB stick, jumped on the scooter, and wobbled my way back towards downtown. The Vespa isn't keen on damp weather and it was popping and spluttering dramatically by the time I pulled into the alley and parked at the rear of Benny's flower shop. It even let out a little sighing wheeze of relief when I turned off the motor.

Benny's shop had a deadbolt and latch on the rear door, but the roll-up loading door was secured only by a single Master brand, number 40 style disc lock. Well…*secured* is maybe too strong a word. Despite the rain making my hands and picks slippery, I had it open in all of about twenty or so seconds. I made a mental note to make Benny a gift of something better one day.

Even though it was at Benny's request, it still felt strange to be breaking into what was effectively his home. I switched on the lights and found that apart from a new and curious smell of molten steel, the design room was, at first glance, unchanged from my last visit. Benny's beautiful replica trophy was still occupying the centre of the long table. Just beside it, Tim's damaged small version was serving as a paperweight on a stack of the patterned sheets that Benny used to wrap bouquets. The coolers were humming away and Benny's work table was neat and tidy. As I moved further inside, though, I spotted one very, very notable change. Something quite violent had happened to the overweight trophy from Saffron's ex-husband.

It had been cut open all the way from top to bottom. Most of the cup was still sitting on the shipping pallet, and if you viewed it from the right angles, it still appeared completely whole. But a wedge-shaped slice had been removed and was now sitting on the platter of an old-fashioned weigh scale sandwiched between two of the coolers.

I stepped my way closer, having to navigate around a scatter of work gloves, earmuffs, a protective face shield, and a brand-new gas-powered machine equipped with a huge cutting disc. When I neared the scale, I saw that Benny had sawed out a slice of the heavy cup as though it had been part of a wedding cake. The noise of the saw must've been terrific. The small balance weights on the scale indicated the piece he'd cut and trimmed was showing thirty-four and a half pounds. I'd asked Benny for something that was the right general dimension and exact weight of the real trophy, and he'd delivered! Perfect.

In addition to the trophy piece, there was a list of things Benny wanted me to bring from his locked filing cabinet upstairs. I hefted the slice off of the scale and parked it near the front door before heading up to his apartment.

With the obvious reverence that Benny held for the filing cabinet, there had to be more inside than just the items he'd told me about. So nerves and my imagination had me oddly fumbling with my tools. It took a full minute or more before the lock finally popped open. I had done far better last time, just with Benny's paperclips.

I pushed the negative thoughts from my mind and focused on the cabinet in front of me. Now that it was unlocked, I hesitated for a few moments, resting one hand on top of the cabinet as Benny had done. Then, with a deep breath, I slowly pulled on the handle.

I don't know what exactly I was expecting. Inside was a jumble of souvenirs from Benny and Edna's days in the rally world. Right at the front on top of a bed of trophies, medals, and certificates was the first item on my list—a battered cookie tin. The driving gloves and worn leather boots he'd asked for were stuffed under a folded jumpsuit near the back.

I was just sliding the drawer shut when I spotted a pair of keys lying on one side. I fished them out and quickly confirmed they were a match for the cabinet and then left them in the lock for Benny to find.

With the boots and gloves stacked on top of the cookie tin, I headed towards the stairs. A triple horn beep from outside had me detour to the window. Below me, Maryam was waving through a crack in the driver-side window of her pickup truck. Meanwhile, across the street, Valery was finishing up an awkward back-and-forth parallel parking of his Audi, windshield wipers going a mile a minute.

I found some kitchen-sized white garbage bags downstairs and wrapped the things from the filing cabinet in a double layer. Then I swaddled Benny's sawed-off slice of the cup in a shipping blanket from a stack in the corner. It took two trips to carry the bundles out to the pickup. I handed Benny's package to Maryam for safekeeping in the cab. The cup piece I squeezed in under the tarp that covered the rear bed. There was a relatively dry spot to wedge it between a stack of traffic cones and a massive spool of wire.

"I got doughnuts, coffee and a full tank of gas," Maryam said when I opened the passenger door. "You ready to go?"

"All set." I started to climb in, but she held out a hand.

"Better Valery comes in first," she said. "The springs on this thing are really old and he's so big that the truck leans over unless he sits right in the middle."

Terrific. So I waited in the rain until Valery finally trotted over a minute later.

"Satellite," he said, waving a little box at us. "Now we can call from anywhere."

I had to admit that I'd forgotten we'd be out of cellphone range after Port Renfrew. It sparked a thought in a *better to have-and-not-need than to need-and-not-have* sort of sense.

"One sec," I said and then I dashed across the street to lean down beside the rear wheel of the Audi. There was no point in trying to be subtle about it. I knew Valery had to be watching me curiously the whole time. When I ran back, Valery started screaming. His eyes were wide and his mouth flapped open and shut as he frantically tried to scoot away from me, crushing Maryam on the other side.

"No! No! No!" he shrieked.

"Why not?" I said.

"Relax," Maryam said with a muffled giggle.

Valery was taking ragged breaths that only gradually slowed. "But why? What?"

"Just my own kind of satellite device," I said. "It's a GPS tracking puck."

"Oh my god," he said, his massive shoulders slumped down in almost comical relief, "You scare me *so* much. I thought maybe was bomb."

"Don't be such a baby," Maryam said and threw in an extravagant eye-roll.

When he shifted his way back to the centre of the bench seat, I noticed he made sure to keep some space between my thigh and his, though I noticed he didn't give Maryam the same courtesy. That she didn't seem to mind was interesting, but there were more pressing things on my mind.

"Alright," I said. "Let's get this show on the road."

We took the lower route along the coast, which meant that

the coffee and doughnuts ran out before we were barely past Langford. It was the same way that Valery and Maryam had returned the day before. It was longer and slower than the alternate highway loop that went through the mountains past Lake Cowichan. But I thought it prudent to get the most up-to-the-minute view of the route as we could. The only real road issue was that the wind and rain, combined with the high tides, meant that just past Otter Point and later at Jordan River the low-lying sections were awash with standing water and driving spray. It wasn't yet bad enough to require Maryam to do more than slow to a crawl. But the day was just beginning and the worst of the storm was still to come.

It took us a staggering six hours in total to reach the outskirts of Sarita. Even discounting the time for snack stops, pee breaks, lunch, and a last fill-up in Port Renfrew, that still left over five hours of actual driving time. How was Benny thinking he could get from here back to the city in close to three? It didn't seem remotely possible, shortcut or not.

We reached a junction with the road that connected Sarita to Bamfield and Maryam pulled to the side.

"Now what?" Valery said.

"We know from all the social media sleuthing that Clara Peter's father lives somewhere on the road we just came down. So all we have to do is wait and follow them when they come by," Maryam said.

"You should use your magic satellite connection to call Tim," I said. "I should have thought of this earlier, but ask him to have a look at all those social networking accounts he'd found. We should probably check to make sure that the cup is actually here at all. Maybe the ferries didn't run, or… something else happened. But if everything went as planned, and they're on time, then we should only have about an hour or so to wait."

"Hmph," Valery grunted. "We should have bought more doughnuts."

Part of the reason I hadn't thought to check with Tim earlier was that deep down, I'd secretly hoped that something *had* gone wrong. If that were true, then maybe Valery would vouch for us, having at least tried our very best. And maybe Alexander, and more importantly, Leonid, would be convinced to forget this whole idea. No such luck, however. Valery got through to Tim almost immediately and after a short pause he was flashing a smile and waving a thumbs-up.

"Is all good. Pictures even. Look. Keeper guy. He is driving black Chevy Suburban." Valery pulled a frown. "Not electric. But is good car. Lots of room in back."

"Ask Tim if he can tell whether they're still holding to schedule," I said.

More back-and-forth conversation followed while I blankly stared at the front windshield and contemplated exactly what sort of experience went behind Valery's 'lots of room in the back' remark. Maryam had thankfully turned off the monotony of the wipers and it was a welcome change to watch the random patterns of the raindrops.

"Is good," Valery said. "They move things up to get back for ferry sooner in case roads are bad. More time for us."

"How much more time?" I asked.

"One moment," Valery said and relayed the question to Tim. "Not long. New postings say ceremony is finished. This Keeper person with Clara Peters now. They go visit her father."

"And then *what* again, exactly?" Maryam asked. "I got my part down. Don't worry about that. But I still don't really get why you brought that piece of Saffron's trophy."

"God is in the details. You know at the beginning of Raiders of the Lost Ark? The temple scene bit where Harrison Ford swaps the Idol for a bag of sand?"

"What about it?"

"We're going to swap the fake cup piece for the real Stanley. The weights are the same. If we do it sneaky-like, then he won't notice. All we have to do is follow them and be ready to give them a lift when their car breaks down. And then you drive off like we talked about."

"And you're sure that's going to happen?"

"Yep," I said with more enthusiasm than I felt.

"As I recall, Indiana Jones wasn't so lucky in that part of the movie."

"Ya well...he got the weights wrong, didn't he!?" I was tempted to add that Indy would've been fine if only he had *me* with him. But that just made me worry all over again about what sort of massive rolling boulder of a problem I might be overlooking.

"And so how long do we wait here, then?" Maryam said.

Aside from a few small trucks when we passed Nitinat Lake, there had been almost no traffic at all on the logging roads since Port Renfrew. So the blast of oncoming headlights was something of a shock. There was the drumming sound of aggressive tires on wet gravel, and then a dark vehicle flashed past. I got the impression of two people in the front. A man driving, and someone smaller in the passenger seat.

"Black Chevy Suburban," Valery growled. "That's them. Go! Go! Go!"

25

"Go!" Valery repeated. He had put one hand on the dashboard and the other on Maryam's thigh and tapped them both in time with his words.

Despite Valery's urging, Maryam kept her eyes fixed on the driver's side mirror and waited a dozen or so seconds before finally putting the truck into gear.

"Just wanted to make sure they didn't notice us turning around to follow them," she said. The truck tires spun wildly on the wet gravel and we surged forward.

One nice design feature of logging roads is that the intersections are all wide open affairs. Those long trucks need room to maneuver. Many of the junctions we'd passed were big enough to land a small plane, and this one was no exception. So there was no need for any three-point turning nonsense and Maryam accelerated all the way through a wide U-turn.

"That was close! We didn't make it here by much," I said. "Five minutes later and we would have missed them completely."

"Five minutes sooner and we might have got bored," Maryam said. "Let's look on the bright side, this gives us more time to do whatever it is you need to do."

Valery nodded in agreement. "They are here. We are here. All is good. You worry too much."

"We're conspiring to commit a felony," I said. "It seems to me that a little worrying isn't such a bad idea."

"Maryam is right. 'Look on bright side'. I like to 'take it

as it goes'." Valery said. "This is also saying?"

"Ya, well, so is—'luck favours the prepared'," I mumbled and checked the time on my phone—three p.m. on the dot. There was no doubt plenty of sunlight somewhere above the clouds, but down here on the ground, under the dark clouds and driving rain, it felt like midnight. I wondered how Benny had been making out. We had exchanged a few texts before I'd lost the signal in Port Renfrew hours ago. The plan had been for him to call Valery's satellite phone as soon as he found cell coverage around Sarita, but that had yet to happen.

Maryam had the truck flying along until the taillights of the Chevy ahead were at a comfortable distance, and then she slowed to match their speed. They were almost always in sight. Only around the tighter corners did the lights sometimes disappear from view—but rarely for long. As the road straightened to wind leisurely past a series of small lakes, Maryam fell back even further. A few minutes later the road began to climb and twist its way out of the valley and once more she hurried to catch up.

"There were two of them in the car. At least two," I said. "I thought maybe Clara Peters would be in her own car."

"Is that a problem?" Maryam said as we swung a little too far on a corner and she had to fight to keep the wheels of the truck off the soft shoulder. The intersections may have been roomy, but the roads themselves were rarely wider than what a single logging truck required.

"I don't know," I said. "I guess we'll see."

We'd lost sight of the Suburban and Maryam sped up even more until we flew over the crest of a rise. The trees opened up and suddenly there was nothing but a long straight stretch of empty road ahead.

"Shoot," Maryam said braking hard. "Where did he go? I didn't see any turnoffs. But there must be one somewhere. Or he drove like a fiend. Do you think he saw us following him?"

"No, no," Valery said, squinting into the distance. "Makes no sense. There must be other way."

Unlike the spacious intersection for our last U-turn, Maryam had to do a dicey back-and-forth dance on the narrow road to get us turned around. When the pickup was finally pointed back towards Sarita, she crawled along, all of us straining our eyes through the rain at the wall of trees on either side.

We kept on until we finally made it back to the valley and past the first lake—which was *definitely* well beyond the point we'd last seen them.

"We must have missed it," Maryam said and coasted to a stop.

She executed another awkward multi-point U-turn and then had us roaring back the way we'd come. It was much faster than she'd ever gone previously, or what seemed remotely safe. I glanced at the speedometer that was bobbing around the one hundred kilometres per hour mark and tightened my grip on the passenger door grab handle. I only relaxed when she suddenly braked and we were down to a crawl as we passed our previous turnaround point.

"There," Valery said and pointed ahead off to the right side of the road. "Just there. We turn around too soon."

Maryam nudged the truck forward, and we all leaned forward, squinting. Just ahead, a narrow track, barely wider than the truck itself, angled off from the road and into a gap between the trees.

"You think?" she said.

"Wait here. I'll have a look," I said.

The truck swayed from a sudden gust of wind. Outside, the rain continued to sheet down. Even though we were completely stopped, it felt as though the pickup was still at cruising speed. I zipped up my rain jacket, flipped up my hood, and cracked open the door just wide enough to slip out. Even so, wind and water briefly whipped into the cab.

I landed on the soft shoulder of the road, a slurry of gravel, sand and good old-fashioned dirt. I realized that in my haste to leave that morning, I'd made an exceptionally poor footwear choice. Even over the wind, I could hear the sucking noises from my Converse sneakers with every step. By the time I'd slogged into the trees, they were soaked through.

Under the shelter of the forest canopy, the rain was more of a steady drip and the ground was firmer. Protected from the deluge, I saw what looked to be fresh marks from muddy tires. I was debating my tracking skills when I noticed an aging wooden signpost nailed to a tree. Maybe it had once been painted, but now was weathered down to just the carved letters of the name: Peters.

I flashed Maryam a thumbs up and then held out my hand in the 'wait here' gesture. Then I double checked that I still had Marty's USB stick in my pocket before starting up the road. *Show time*…I guess.

How far the Peters homestead might be situated from the road was an open question. But it didn't seem wise to drive up in the pickup truck in case we ran straight into it. On the other hand, for all I knew, it might be kilometres away…though with the social media posts about the return trip timing, that seemed unlikely.

It turned out to be about a ten-minute hike. A trickle of rain had somehow found a way to pour steadily down my neck, and my shoes squelched the whole way. With my head down and my hood pulled shut, I probably would've walked straight into the Suburban were it not for the Keeper being thoughtful enough to leave his motor running and the headlights on. As it was, I nearly stumbled into full view.

The road ended just ahead at two low buildings positioned around a parking area. It was just big enough for a vehicle to safely turn around. The structure on the left was a long lean-to style construction that gave shelter to neat stacks of firewood. On the right was the main cabin. It was a small but well-kept construction of cedar logs over a stone foundation. The roof held its own mini-forest of moss and ferns. Warm yellow light filled a pair of windows and wood smoke drifted through the surrounding trees despite the wind and rain.

I stepped off the road and silently moved closer, slipping from one tree to the next. I could see an aging Volkswagen Microbus tucked in between the two buildings. Just beside it, the Suburban idled with its tailgate raised and its rear backed flush to the front porch.

I was just thinking that I might not get a better chance and was about to make a quiet dash for the Suburban when a heavy weight landed on my shoulder.

As I was, more or less, in the middle of nowhere, and surrounded by a dark and windy forest full of gloomy shadows, the back of my mind had already been considering things like cougars, bears and all the rest. So it was all I could do not to collapse to my knees screaming in panic. Instead, I just stopped breathing altogether and froze.

"Benny called," a deep voice whispered. "He wants to know where we meet. Is good question, no?"

I'd forgotten how stealthy Valery could be.

"Are you *insane*?" I hissed. "I swear I'm going to put a

friggin bell on you. I just about peed my pants!"

"You need bathroom? Go behind tree. Lots of trees. I won't look."

I would've had more to say, but voices from the cabin sent us quickly retreating out of sight. We ran a short way back down the road and then off to one side, behind a massive tree stump. I stopped with my hands on my knees, my heart still hammering away from Valery's scare. After a few deep breaths, I stepped to where I could just peer over the rise of the stump to see what was going on at the cabin. With our height difference, Valery was standing several paces further downhill in order to achieve the same effect.

Over the constant splatter of rain striking leaves, I could hear laughter. A moment later, a heavyset man in a formal black jacket came into view. He closed the rear hatch of the Suburban and then made a two-step dash through the rain to reach the driver's side door. We heard the engine turn off and then watched as he removed the white gloves he'd been wearing. After placing them carefully on the dash, he rummaged for what looked like a paperback novel and then reclined the seat.

"What's he doing?" Valery whispered.

"Getting comfy apparently," I said.

"He must be inside with trophy. He must always be with trophy. Colin told me this."

"I guess it's a small cabin. He's giving the Peters some alone time together with it."

"This is allowed?"

"How should I know!?" I said—trying and failing to keep the exasperation out of my voice. "Apparently that's what he's doing."

"Is problem. Yes?"

"Well, it's certainly not ideal, and definitely not what I'd planned."

I heard Valery splutter his lips in thought. "Come, tell me again this plan."

Reluctantly, I followed his lead back down the road—it was like walking behind a building. At least with Valery being the biggest thing around, I suppose I didn't need to worry about the other wildlife.

He stopped a minute later when we'd rounded a corner and were well out of earshot.

"It's simple," I said, fishing out Marty's device from my pocket. "This thing needs to get plugged into a USB port. It's a new car. There have to be USB ports somewhere, ideally up near the dash, maybe between the front seats. There might be others in the back too, but I think for this to work, it probably should be one that is as close to the front as possible."

"And it reprograms car?"

"More like *de*programs," I said. "I don't know exactly how it works, but it's supposed to overload or short-out, or just generally fry the circuits."

"So, no more phone charging?"

"No more *anything*. It's supposed to take out the whole system. Or at least all the dash electronics, which should be enough."

"That's it? Just put into USB port?"

"Not quite. That's just the first part," I said. "I can activate it with my cellphone, but we don't want to do it here. He needs to be back on the logging road somewhere far away from anybody else, so we can rescue him."

"Okay...so we wait until he goes back in for trophy?"

"And then what? Just watch him drive away? We need to

be on the road somewhere with Maryam. I was going to stage an incident. Have her in her electrician get-up with construction cones set up to force him to stop and do it then. The device only works on Bluetooth, so I have to be close enough to it with my cellphone to make a connection."

"Is problem," Valery said.

"The social media posts said they would spend at least an hour here visiting Mr. Peters. I figured it would be easy to sneak into his vehicle and plug it in. But then I didn't expect him to spend all that time just sitting in his car. So I can't just wait until he goes back inside to get it when they're done."

"But I could," he said. "You go back to Maryam and truck. My phone is there. Call Benny."

And like that, he snatched the USB stick from my hand and was dashing back towards the cabin as quietly as a cougar. There was no point in chasing or arguing because it was the only idea that had a chance of working.

It was much faster going back down, and I didn't think we'd been as long as we had, but when I finally reached the pickup, it was already after four o'clock and Maryam had worked herself into a nervous mess.

"*There* you are!" she said with a wavering sigh. "You were *ages*. I was fine before, but sitting here all alone was terrible. There hasn't even been a single car or anything passing by. Not one! It's creepy. What's going on? Where's Val? Should I move the truck?"

She had pulled further off the road and the pickup was now completely blocking the entrance of the drive that led up to the cabin. While my original plan with the traffic cones probably would've worked, I realized it was simpler and almost foolproof for her just to stay parked where she was.

"No," I said. "Valery is trying to deal with the first part.

Just stay right here. It's perfect."

I picked up Valery's phone and punched in Benny's number. He answered before the first ring was finished.

"It's Margot," I said. "We're nearly all set up here. How are things with you?"

"Oh, just tickety-boo," he said. "A few delays along the way, but now I'm tanked up and ready to go. I'm in Sarita now but once I leave I'll lose a cellphone connection. Where are you exactly?"

"I don't know. We're about a kilometre past some lakes on the road toward Nitinat. You can't miss them."

"Margot!" Maryam said.

The connection to Benny had been cutting in and out, so I held a hand to my other ear to block Maryam out as I strained to hear what Benny was saying.

"Margot!!" Maryam said louder and with more urgency. "They're coming!"

I looked up and saw headlights flashing at us through the trees on the track from the cabin.

"Gotta run," I yelled into the phone and threw it at Maryam. "You know what to do?"

"Just be a good Samaritan," she said. "I get the easy part."

"Just remember that if this actually works, then you have to stop when you reach that intersection. Long enough that I have time to jump off, anyway."

I ran to the rear, put a foot on the bumper, and threw myself over the tailgate into the bed of the pickup. As I crawled under the tarp, I fumbled for my phone and then desperately scrolled and tabbed through to find the right app.

Either Valery had managed to get the device plugged in,

or he hadn't. And either my phone would be close enough to make a connection, or it wouldn't. Both things had to work, or we were done.

I had just reached the space behind the front cab when I heard the approaching roar of a big engine in low gear. Desperately, I began jabbing a wet finger at the red 'activate' button on the phone app over and over. But the growl of the engine just grew louder. It sounded like it was right on top of us. I wondered if the driver was just going to off-road his way around when several things happened in very rapid succession.

First was a quick tap-tap of a horn together with the squeal of wet disc brakes. Then there was a brief pause before a muffled explosion, a piercing scream from Maryam, and finally complete and utter silence.

26

It all sounded very exciting.

I really wanted to stick my head out for a look, but I did as I was supposed to do, which was put my phone away, crawl under the shipping blanket beside Benny's sawn-up piece of the cup, and wait.

I felt the pickup rock under the closing slam of Maryam's door.

"Hey! You okay?" she called out.

There was an indistinct buzz of a man's voice answering in the distance. As Maryam moved away, her voice faded, and over the drumming of the rain on the tarp over my head, and the gusts of wind, I couldn't make anything of their conversation beyond the fact that they were having one. I blame Harley for the direction my imagination took in filling in the words I couldn't hear.

Maryam: Hark! Good sir! Are you in need of aid? Whatever has transpired?

Keeper: Fair maiden, you are a beacon of hope! All around me has inexplicably fallen under a veil of darkness. I know not why!

Maryam: What a mysterious shame. I often feel that the more complex technology becomes, the more there is that might run afoul. Surely there is no clearer example of this than that which lies before us now?

Keeper: Wholeheartedly, I embrace this truth! Perchance...faulty wiring carries the burden? Certainly, in no way should I consider any outside factor or ill-intentioned shenanigans to have played so evil a hand.

Maryam: You are wise indeed to have reached this, no doubt, accurate conclusion.

Keeper: Your words are a gentle balm that does much to ease the sting of my predicament. Lo, I must declare this vehicular failure to be a cruel strike that cuts me to the very marrow. For this very moment, I must away with expedient haste to catch a ferry in Nanaimo. In truth, I find myself now to be in something of a pickle.

Maryam: Indeed, a thornier pickle I have not seen! Alas, I am sorrow itself, for my destination, this foul evening lies elsewhere.

Keeper: Curse the gods! I confess I am saddened and quite more than a little anxious for my situation. Whatever shall I do?

Maryam: Nay, good sir! I beg of you—belay such thoughts! I shall hear no more! It would enslave my conscience and labour my soul to abandon you in such a state. Nearby is the village of Sarita, is it not? Perhaps at the marina, you might there arrange alternate transportation? I can afford a small detour such as this for someone in clearly so desperate a need.

Keeper: You are truly the very embodiment of kindness. I should take up your offer with joyful enthusiasm were it not for the shipping crate in the back of this vehicle. It would be incautious of me to disclose more but be assured that its contents are of great value and from it I have sworn to never be parted.

Maryam: (laughing warmly) Take heart, stout fellow! Tis but the work of an instant! As you can plainly see, my own conveyance is a pickup truck, aged perhaps, but with ample room to surely transport a crate such as yours. Let us affect the transfer this very moment and fly forth as though carried upon the wings of destiny.

Oh ya, Billy Shakespeare had nothing on me.

No doubt, their *actual* conversation was far less like an incredibly bad high school play, but apparently, I'd more or less nailed the gist, as the next clear sound was the trudge of a pair of footsteps and the lowering of the tailgate.

I squeezed myself deeper into the driver's side corner and pulled the shipping blanket over my head. Other than the voices of Maryam and the Keeper I couldn't hear anyone else. It seemed that Clara Peters had remained up in the cabin with her father. As for Valery? Who knew? He'd obviously managed to get the USB device installed. Presumably, he was ghosting his way back down the road and scaring the bejeebers out of the wildlife.

There were bumps, and sways as the truck wobbled while they loaded the crate. I heard the roll of the wheels and the twang of bungee cords as they pushed it under the tarp toward me. Then the tailgate slammed shut and there was some futzing around as they used some of Maryam's loose gear to wedge the crate firmly in place. The tarp got some final adjustments and then I heard the doors open and close. Maryam started up the engine, the exhaust rumbled, the suspension squeaked, the rain pelted down, and we were off.

The instant the pickup started moving, I was out from under the blanket and inch-worming my way to the rear of the truck bed. Thanks to Colin and Tim's research, I'd seen loads of photos of the shipping case. It was a rectangular black custom-made box on wheels with metal corners and edges like the ones you see used by roadies for rock concerts. There was a pair of handles at either end and two clasps on one side—each with a padlock. I had unzipped my toolkit and got to work even before Maryam had properly started her multi-point U-turn.

By the time she had us heading back to Sarita, I already had a corner of the tarp released, both locks off and the clasps open. With cold hands, wet tools, a moving platform and no small amount of nervous panic going on, I had to think Uncle Rupert would have been pretty impressed. Maybe not so much about what I was doing specifically, just that I'd been able to do it at all.

The tricky part was the actual swap of the real cup for Benny's stand-in weight. I had the wind and rain and the natural swaying of the truck to mask any sounds or movements. While the back of the cab didn't have a window, I wondered if when the lid of the crate was open, it would be visible in the passenger side mirror. I kicked myself for not asking Maryam to make sure the crate went to the driver's side instead.

I dragged the piece of cup cushioned by the shipping blanket closer. With a deep breath to steady my nerves, I moved into a low crouch and pushed open the case. The combined wind from the storm and the movement of the truck made the lid shudder and dance in my hands as though it were a kite.

Even in the dim light, I could see the lining was a velvety royal blue that darkened as rain splattered down. The cup was lying on its side and was so brightly polished it almost seemed to glow from an inner light. I found myself staring at it in wonder. Part of me couldn't quite believe it was real. And the rest of me couldn't believe I was about to take it. But it was. And I did.

With my shoulder against the lid, I grabbed the bowl end with one hand, the base with the other, and pulled. Thirty-four and a half pounds is heavier than it sounds. And it wasn't just the weight, but the sheer size as well. Had I been really clever, I would have practiced in the flower shop with the replica we'd got from Seattle—but there was no time to worry about that now. The truck began to angle downhill and pick up speed as we started the drop back into the valley with the lakes.

I meant to ease the cup down gently, but the truck was bouncing, the wind was howling and everything was slick from the rain. I just got the base clear of the crate when the whole thing slipped from my hands. It landed mostly on its side, and mostly on the shipping blanket. Even so, there was a resonant thud from the impact that shook the truck bed under my feet. I froze in panic, but Maryam kept her speed, and I didn't hear any shouts of alarm.

I gave a long exhale and then scooped up Benny's cut piece. The weight was the same, but it was easier to grab. I lowered it into the case without dropping it. The piece filled only a small part of the cup-shaped hole inside, but as long as the Keeper didn't try to shake the whole case and notice it rattling around, then it should be okay.

Maryam managed to hit another pothole, and I stumbled to catch my balance. The lid slipped from my shoulder and the wind and gravity worked together to slam it shut with a terrific 'bang'. This time, I *did* hear a shout.

I dropped to my knees and hurried to close the catches and replace the padlocks. I was wrapping the shipping blanket around Lord Stanley's cup just as the truck began to slow. I could imagine the conversation that was likely happening up front. The Keeper, no doubt, demanding that they immediately stop to investigate, and Maryam stalling for time with any excuse she could think of not to. He appeared to be winning the argument as the truck gradually went slower and slower. It was too risky to hope that I could hide in the truck bed with the real cup. And it looked like we weren't going to make it back to the intersection for a safe stop, either. The only choice was to jump clear. Right now. Or at least as soon as it was safe. And then just hope that I'd be able to slink off the road into hiding before I was spotted.

With the cup swaddled in my arms like it was the world's largest baby, I crawled awkwardly over the back of the truck and got my feet on the bumper—well, briefly, anyway. My plan was just to step off whenever Maryam had slowed down enough. Instead, we were still zipping along quite briskly when the rear of the truck bucked from yet another pothole. With a squeak of wet rubber on chrome, my feet slid out from under me.

My heels kissed the ground and I was instantly slammed flat on my back—crushed between the wet gravel road and the thirty-four and a half pounds of silver trophy on my chest. Pretty much every molecule of air in my lungs got instantly squeezed out, and I was left staring into the rain, through watering eyes, and gasping like a stranded fish. Over my ragged attempts to breathe, I could hear the pickup continue to coast along.

I could barely move, and certainly couldn't stand, so I just wheezed my way into a crawl. The cup had come free of the shipping blanket, so I grabbed it by the bowl end with a shaky hand and dragged it behind me. A few agonizing seconds later, I made it to the shoulder and then collapsed into a roll down a short embankment.

I slid to a stop and lay with my eyes closed, listening hard between gulps of air. Somewhere in the distance, the truck doors opened and I could just make out fragments of a short conversation. I was too frazzled to have any fun trying to guess what they might be saying, but it ended with the crisp snap of the tarp being adjusted, some laughter, and then the truck was once again driving on toward Sarita.

A minute later, I'd recovered enough to push my way up into a sitting position and take stock. I was right beside the lake, just below the shoulder of the road, and barely a meter above the water's edge. The cup was nowhere to be seen.

"You've *got* to be kidding me," I said aloud and crawled painfully to my feet.

I was already pretty much soaked through, so I hardly noticed the difference as I waded into the lake and began to pace back and forth parallel to the shore.

With each pass, I had gone a little deeper into the lake and the water was just above my waist when the high-pitched whine of an engine behind a dazzling display of headlights flew past. There was a long skid of locked tires and then the sound of running feet.

"Margot!?" a familiar voice called out.

Benny!

"What are you doing down there? I saw the shipping blanket on the road. You okay?" he said when he reached me.

"Mostly okay," I said. "Little battered. Kinda chilly."

"Odd time for a swim. Where's everyone else?"

"You must have passed Maryam. She's giving the Keeper a lift. Hopefully, she'll be back soon. Valery...him, we left in the woods up the road a little way."

"And the cup?"

"Well, ya, it's here...somewhere."

"What? In the lake?"

"I guess," I said. "I had it a while ago. It must've rolled away. Why did they have to make it so round?"

"I'm surprised it didn't float."

"It doesn't. Colin was telling me stories about some of the cup winners testing out that theory in swimming pools.

Sinks like a brick," I said, just as my shin made sharp contact with something hard. My feet were so numb that I couldn't tell at first if what I was pushing was the cup or just a log, but then it started to roll. I got one foot under the top bowl part and managed to raise it up until it broke the surface. Even through the gloom, the silver edge that broke the surface glinted brightly.

"Wow," Benny said. "That's really it, huh!?"

I dragged it closer to the water's edge until Benny could reach it. It had easily tripled in weight, and water fountained out from between the bands and around the base. Benny hauled it a short distance up the shore and waited for it to empty.

"Wow," he said again. "Just think of all the greats that have touched this...Guy Lafleur, Maurice 'Rocket' Richard, Jean Béliveau, Frank Mahovlich, Patrick, Kirk...so many."

"And now another great," I said. "Benny 'The Jet' Schlesien."

"I don't know about that," he said with a gruff tone that didn't quite hide a slight smile. "Alright. Let's go."

Benny led the way up the embankment, the Stanley Cup tucked under one arm, his other around my shoulders.

"Better grab that shipping blanket. There's not much in the car to dry off with, and the heater isn't the best."

There's not much in the car—was an understatement. Just like the one that Benny had traded away, the front seats of this one were also lightly padded bucket seats with multi-point harnesses rather than seatbelts. In the rear...there was no seat whatsoever. Just bare metal. And anything else that wasn't strictly necessary had been removed. Not only wasn't there much *in* it but there was also wasn't much *of* it.

"Benny...it's tiny," I said.

"What? How do you mean? It's a nineteen sixty-eight BMC Mini Cooper S. That's the size they are. Borrowed it from Joe Paczynski, the carburetor's tuned like a dream. Come on, get in."

We put the cup in the back seat area where it seemed to nearly fill the space. I took off my soaked jacket and laid it under for some cushioning, which seemed like the respectful thing to do after having tossed it into a lake. The shipping blanket was drier, but I kept that for myself.

The engine fired up with a roar, and the road ahead was instantly awash with light. Benny flipped some switches, and the headlights dropped to more normal levels of intensity.

"I guess we go find Valery while we wait for Maryam?" he said and pulled away.

"What's the time?" I asked. "I haven't checked, but I think my phone took a swim as well."

"Five minutes to five," Benny said.

"Oh boy. We've got the trophy. We should just go." I said. "I mean, I don't see how we can get there in time, anyway. Still, probably better to try without Maryam than to miss it with her."

"The things I asked for are in her truck?"

"Yep."

"Then we wait," Benny said.

There was a familiar note of finality in his voice. It was one that I'd often heard from both Uncle Rupert and Harley. The result was always the same—no arguing from me would change anything. So I didn't try with Benny either.

I just huddled in my seat and grit my teeth, conscious that every passing minute felt like another nail in our coffin.

27

We found Valery about two hundred metres past the dead Suburban walking south towards Victoria. Benny tapped the horn as we approached, and Valery lumbered to one side. As we pulled to a stop, he gave us a little hopeful wave. He looked like the world's most un-likeliest hitchhiker.

"Did you get the USB back?" I asked after rolling the window open a crack.

"Of course," he nodded. He had to bend over almost in half to be able to look back at me. "Is amazing this device of yours. I want one. May I keep it?"

"Why? It just makes electronic things stop working."

Valery laughed, a deep rumble like the sound of a distant freight train. "No, no. So much better. Airbags go bang! So many airbags in car. Very exciting."

That would explain the noises I heard and maybe Maryam's scream as well. I imagine that was a shock for everyone. On the plus side, it also explained why it had taken so little time for Maryam to convince the Keeper she should drive him to town. A dark dashboard is one thing, exploding airbags are another.

"I push Suburban so is not blocking road to cabin. Did you see? Is better for Clara Peters I think. You have cup?" Valery asked.

I opened the door and got out so he could lean in to inspect our prize. He was still doing that when Maryam's pickup truck flew into view. She pulled in behind us with a slide of locked tires.

"Wow, the roads are super slippery," Maryam said as she jumped out to join us. She gave the car an eyebrowed raised appraisal. "It's...cute?"

"How's our time?" I asked Benny.

"Eight minutes after five," he said. "We should probably get a move on sometime soon. You have my things for me?"

I hobbled to the pickup for the white garbage bag-wrapped bundle in the cab and brought it to Benny. The gloves and boots he put into the car straight away to keep them dry. The cookie tin he held gently with his fingertips like it was a bomb. He seemed to have stopped breathing.

"You okay Benny?" I asked.

He nodded slowly. "Who's going to sit in the navigator's seat? You or Maryam?"

"I will do it," Valery said. "I'm very good with maps."

"You? You're not coming. You're driving the pickup back," Benny said.

"What? No, I come with you," Valery said. "I stay with the cup."

"I can just leave my truck somewhere and come back to get it tomorrow," Maryam said. "It's no problem."

"Of course, it's a problem," I said. "Look at the car? Valery all by himself wouldn't fit. Where are the rest of us going to go?"

"Good point. Okay. Why don't Valery and I drive back in my pickup and you two go with the cup? We'll be hours behind you, but at least the cup will make it."

"I stay with cup," Valery said.

"Val, be reasonable..." Maryam said.

"It's far roomier inside than you might think, but it's more of a weight issue," Benny said.

"We won't be able to go fast enough?" I asked.

"Not so much that. True, it will take a little longer to get up to speed and it will definitely make cornering *much* more interesting, but it's the slowing down I'm worried about. The shortcut route apparently hasn't changed from when I used to drive it and Colin had it loaded up on his game, so I'll be okay through that section. But the rest of the logging roads are a blur in my memory. It's been a long time. I'll need proper navigation information or we're going to end up in the trees pretty fast."

"What does that mean?" I said.

"It means that I need someone to tell me exactly where I am and what's coming up just ahead. Does the road go left or right? Is it a sharp turn, or a long one? If it's straight, then for how long? Things like that. I figured I'd be okay just visually, but it's darker than I expected with the storm. And we're going to be heavy—really heavy—so I'll need much more warning than I thought. I need Edna." Benny cradled the cookie tin to his chest.

"Can I have cookie?" Valery asked.

"Royal Dansk butter cookies," Benny said, gently tracing the words on the lid with a fingertip. Then he continued after a long pause, "Edna's favourites."

"Just one?" Valery asked. "I'm very hungry."

"There are no cookies in here," Benny said. "Just Edna."

"What?" Maryam and I said together.

"Her ashes. Somehow never got around to spreading them in the ocean as she wanted. And then I lost the keys."

There was a long moment while the four of us stood quietly.

"Maybe she's been waiting all this time for a reason?" I said.

"Maybe she has at that," Benny said. His face slowly

broke into a warm smile. He held my eyes for a moment. "I've never driven without her, and I wasn't going to start now."

"So...?"

"I guess if Timo Mäkinen can drive the Ouninpohja stage of the 1000 Lakes with the bonnet open, then Edna and I can probably manage this."

"I don't know what any of that means, but I trust you," I said. "There's someone else I trust, too. And I've had an idea."

Maryam found a pullout a short distance further ahead and tucked the pickup truck in behind some trees. Valery took out his phone and satellite link for me and I left the three of them to figure out who was going where while I made a call.

"Dude! Did you get the cup?" Harley said.

"Yep."

"Cool. I *knew* you would. Listen, I have *great* news myself! You'll never guess. I got the coffee machine working! Maybe I should get a job doing something like that? I mean, walking dogs is fine and all, but sometimes I feel I'm stifling my creativity, you know? What do you think? It took me all day, and I had to put it together and take it apart again, like *fifty* times. But now it works! Only I had to test it...like a lot. Like, *every* time. So now I'm a teeny bit wired cause of all the caffeine and I doubt I'll sleep tonight, so maybe if you're up for it we can go surfing when you get home? The waves are probably going to be wicked with all this wind. What do you think!?"

Oh god.

"Harley, you didn't have to *drink* every cup," I said.

"Of course I did. Someone had to. Coffee is expensive, and you weren't here."

"Right. Okay…well, maybe the caffeine will help? I need to ask a huge favour," I said.

I got her to open my laptop and bring up the tracking app. When I gave her the number of the puck I'd taken back from Valery's Audi, there was a squeal of excitement.

"I see you! Holy smokes, you guys are like…*far!*"

"Can you zoom in until you're really close? Then all you have to do is tell us what the road just ahead is like?"

"Easy peasy."

"Okay. It should stay centred on the screen for you as we move," I said. "I have another call to make, so I'll ring you back in a second. And Harley…maybe eat and drink something that *doesn't* have caffeine in it."

I hung up and punched Tim's number. It rang and rang and finally went through to messaging.

"Tim," I said. "We have it. We're leaving now. Get Saffron and Colin and be at Ogden Point by eight o'clock. Okay? We all need to be there. Please."

When I turned back to the car, I saw that Valery had somehow shoehorned his way inside to where the rear seat used to be. He was sitting awkwardly, with his feet together and his knees nearly touching either side of the car. Across his lap was the Stanley Cup. Up front, Maryam was on the navigator's side, buckled in with Edna's cookie tin on her lap. Benny had put on his boots and gloves and was fastening his own harness in the driver's seat.

"Um? What about me?" I said.

"Sorry about this Margot. There's only one space left, I'm afraid," Benny said. "You'll have to ride in the boot. It's the only way it'll work. Maryam needs to sit up front to balance the weight. So it's either in the back or you could drive Maryam's truck back, I guess."

"No, I have to come. I have to meet Leonid. But why can't the cup go in the trunk?" I said. Not that I necessarily wanted to sprawl on Valery's lap, which seemed like the only other option.

"The cup is too big, the trunk is too small," Maryam said. "We tried. Honest."

"But I'm *bigger* than the cup," I protested.

"Yes. But, you...bend. And look!" Valery said, trying to shift his bulk to one side. "There is no seat here for me. Is gone. So is open to boot. See? We can talk. You can breathe."

Terrific.

I called Harley back, put Valery's phone on speaker mode, and handed it with the satellite link through the passenger window to Maryam.

"Harley, meet everyone. Everyone...this is Harley. If anyone is looking for me, I'll be in the trunk," I said. Then I stomped away to the rear of the car, opened the tiny hatch, and somehow squeezed myself inside.

Previously, I would have said, if anyone had asked, that the most terrifying ride I had ever been on was with Harley at the fair. But that was before this. The Zipper has the advantage that at least it's over in a matter of minutes. The ride in the trunk of Benny's Mini, however, just never seemed to end.

Throughout the ordeal, over the high-pitched whine of the engine and the frequent cries of hysterical panic from both Maryam and Valery, I could hear Harley's rapid but calm flow of words over the phone. She was amazing at telling Benny exactly the right information at exactly the right time. The only hitch was that her directions were confined to 'lefts' and 'rights' and 'straights'. The tracking app told her nothing at all about the ups and downs of the road, so there was no end to the stomach-lurching surprises when the car became completely airborne. I would float weightless for a moment as the engine revs screamed even higher and then get flattened by the impact when the wheels touched back down and the suspension compressed to its stops. Which seemed to happen every few minutes or so. For the better part of two hours.

And then, the roaring drone of the tires magically disappeared as though someone had flipped a switch. It took me a moment to realize we were finally back on pavement. Something that Benny—judging by the sharp pitch change of the engine—just took as an invitation to go even faster. Now and then there was the bleep of his horn, which usually accompanied a yelp from Maryam and a groan from Valery. But to Benny's credit, he always kept us on the road and as far as I could tell, we didn't hit anything or cause any accidents.

When the car began slowing to the occasional stop, I knew we were close to town and had started hitting traffic and stoplights.

"We're not going to make it," Maryam said.

"It's going to be close," Benny said. "We've still got all of downtown to get through."

"Wait," Harley's voice rang out. "You want to get to the pier by our place, right? James Bay?"

"That's the goal," Benny said.

"Okay! Great. So the marina in Esquimalt—Sailor's Cove—is *way* closer to you? Right? So go there. It's the one with the fish and chip place. Margot and eat there sometimes," Harley said. "They do this one Caribbean-style thing where they blend halibut, cod, salmon and tuna all together with sriracha. You have to try it—it's *ahhmazing*!"

"I know the place," Benny said. "We're not far at all."

"Why?" Maryam yelled. "We're not looking for a restaurant!"

"I could eat," Valery mumbled.

"Because like I said..." Harley explained. "Margot and I go there from our place. It's like almost *right* across from the pier. We take a water taxi. And I know one of the guys that drives one. Hang on, I'll call you back!"

There was a click, and the phone went dead.

"I need phone," Valery said. "Alexander should know."

I took stock of my bruises and worked at a cramp in my calf while Valery chatted away in Ukrainian. Benny kept us zooming along at a brisk pace, seemingly trying to toe the line between being as quick as possible, but not quite so fast that would trigger anyone to call the police.

"Cruise boat is leaving soon," Valery said. "Alexander said we must hurry."

"Coming up to the highway now," Benny said. "We need to decide if we're driving through town or heading over to Harley's marina. Thoughts?"

"The highway, surely," Maryam said. "We'll be on the wrong side of the harbour otherwise. Nobody's going to be crazy enough to drive a boat across in this weather."

The phone rang and Valery answered, but didn't do much more than listen. When he hung up he said, "Harley knows crazy person. She says he will be there. What do we do?"

"Seems like a gamble either way," Benny said. "But we're going to hit more lights and traffic the closer we get, and I don't want to cause an accident. Besides, we wouldn't be here at this time at all without Harley's navigational help. I vote we give her idea a go."

I was actually going to call out and suggest we didn't. Not because it was a bad idea, but just because if it failed, I didn't want any burden of guilt to fall on Harley. But before I could shout for attention, Benny skidded us through a hard right turn and announced that we were marina-bound.

He seemed to have decided that we were close enough that any calls to the police for his excessive speed wouldn't be answered in time, because he only increased the pace. When we entered the residential maze close to the marina, the tires shrieked non-stop as Benny had us continuously sliding sideways from one corner to the next.

There was another moment of complete weightlessness, and then the car slammed back to earth one final time. We screeched to a stop to allow the smells of exhaust and burning rubber to catch up. Benny switched off the engine and for the first time in hours, everything was mercifully silent.

"Well, we're here," Maryam said. "What's the time?"

"Seven fifty-two," Benny said. "We have eight minutes. Cutting it a bit fine."

"There's a water taxi and a guy on the dock," Maryam said. "I'll go see."

I had to wait for Benny to open the trunk to let me out. And then I needed all his help just to stand up. My legs had cramped. I was bruised all over. And I was shivering with cold. Valery seemed to be having trouble standing vertically as well. He tucked the cup under one arm like it was a football, and the pair of us hobbled along after Maryam while Benny went to retrieve Edna.

"There's a problem," Maryam said when we reached her on the dock. A yellow, black and white checked water taxi bobbed at its moorings beside her. A man covered head to toe in rain slickers stood barring the door. "He doesn't think it's safe."

"I don't," the man said. "When Harley called a minute ago, I didn't see the waves were that big. It would be dangerous to try to cross right now."

"I'm sure you're right," Benny said, as he moved in beside me. He handed me the cookie tin while he pulled out his wallet. "Let's see...we started with ten thousand... plane tickets... hotel... travel expenses... souvenirs... office supplies... gas... and that saw... hmmm. Would twelve hundred and thirty-seven dollars for three minutes of work be worth considering?"

"All aboard," the man said.

"I thought it might. And we'll need a receipt."

28

Compared to what we'd all just been through, the crashing waves and the pitch and roll of the ferry seemed more like the soothing rocking of a cradle. Harley's friend probably assumed we were all seasoned veterans of the open ocean because he was the only one who seemed particularly anxious. Maybe he was just distracted by the thought of twelve hundred dollars, or maybe it was the Stanley Cup Valery was holding.

"You guys must be big hockey fans?" he said as the little ferry bucked and spun on its way across the mouth of the harbour. "How much would one like that cost?"

"Oh, you won't find another quite like this," I said. "Trust me. We tried."

Valery nodded in agreement. He was sitting with the cup base wedged firmly between his feet, one hand on the shoulder of the barrel, while he held his cellphone in the other and chatted away in Ukrainian.

Benny was directly across from me on the opposite bench. He had Edna in the cookie tin on his lap and seemed to be half asleep. Maryam stood behind the driver with one arm casually wrapped around a vertical pole. She swayed with the movements of the boat and stared blankly out the windows like she was a morning bus commuter.

"Is good," Valery said to me when he'd hung up. He raised his eyes from the cup to meet mine. "Alexander is very depressed."

"I sincerely hope the word you're aiming for is *im*pressed.

And don't you mean Leonid?" I said.

"Him too."

"Tell me. *Val*. Why is it that you and Alexander have such thick accents, but Kirill doesn't?"

Valery's mouth cracked into a tired smile. "Oh well, Kirill...is easy for him. He was born in Kviv but moved here when small. Very small. He helps me with tricky words. Is good guy."

I couldn't help but crack a smile. Valery's English needed some polishing, but I'd yet to hear him get his past and present tenses confused. Kirill still being with us in the here and now. When he saw my smirk widen, Valery recognized his blunder.

"Is big secret," Valery said. His voice had dropped to a whisper. He looked even more scared than when he thought I'd had a bomb. "I say too much."

"What's he talking about?" Benny asked with a yawn.

"Sneaky little secrets," I said. "I'm looking forward to hearing all the details myself—but it's a conversation that will have to wait, 'cause I think we're here."

A massive wall of steel suddenly filled most of the sky. The hull of the Norwegian Sun loomed over us like a protective shield. In its shadow, the swells and gusts of wind dropped to nothing, and we plowed through smooth water all the way to a small floating dock.

The tiny ferry landed with a gentle bump and the four of us piled out, almost crashing straight into Tim.

"You made it!" he said. "I've been calling you for hours, but you never answered."

"My phone and I took a swim. It's a story for later."

"Alexander sent me over. Saffron, Colin and...everyone are all waiting at the café. But there isn't much time...we gotta run."

And so we did. At least at first.

We were jogging in a tight group when we reached the top of the dock ramp, but as we hurried across the expanse of the parking lot, we began to spread out. Tim, not having spent a good portion of the day in the trunk of a rally car, easily pulled into the lead. A few steps back were Valery and the cup, with Maryam trailing just behind.

Then there was me. The best I could manage was a stumbling jog. My entire body was stiff. I was shivering, and bone-weary, and only slightly faster than Benny. He had tried to keep up, but after a dozen steps, it was clear his knee wasn't up to it.

"Off you go," he called. "I'll be along in a minute."

I was torn. But he had Edna, and I still had a mission to finish with little time to do it. So I gave a wave of encouragement and hobbled on.

The bistro is on the upper floor of a glass-walled cottagey building above a tasting room. When I finally reached it, I tried to bound up the stairs, but it was more of a slow plod. Every step was a painful reminder of the day.

There was a welcome rush of warm air after I'd fought the door open and stepped inside. It was almost entirely empty. Any cruise ship customers had cleared out, and the storm was keeping otherwise reasonable people at home. Many times I've enjoyed Sunday dinner at the café with Uncle Rupert and Aunt Stacy, and it's usually bustling. A waitress I recognized was hovering uncertainly nearby, holding a menu.

"Hey, Colleen. Can I get an Earl Grey tea, an order of those veggie slider things, and maybe a bowl of chowder, please? There's a friend coming just behind me. Can you make sure he's okay getting up the stairs? I'll be with those guys," I said and pointed across the café."

I sloshed my way over to a cluster of five occupied tables. Tim, Saffron and Colin were at one, while Valery and Maryam were sitting close by at another. Valery pulled out a chair and gestured for me to join them, but I stopped and took a moment to look at the other tables instead.

Sitting alone, slightly apart from everyone else, was Polina—playing on her phone and looking bored. Closer to me were two stone-faced men in matching dark suits flanking a slightly nervous-looking woman holding a construction worker's tool bag. At the final table, was Alexander and the man I recognized from the internet photos as Leonid Konstantinovich Yakovlev. The big boss. The remains of their dinner had been pushed aside to make room for Lord Stanley's Cup.

The pair of them were peering so intently at the inscriptions on the uppermost band that they barely noticed when I dragged a chair over to join them. There was a half-eaten order of fries on the table, so I grabbed one and started to chew noisily.

"What are you doing?" Alexander said sharply, though his stern look softened as he took in my wet and haggard appearance. "You don't look so good."

"Oh, don't worry about me," I said. "I have a spa day coming up."

The frown returned, and he gave a dismissive backhanded wave. "Move. Go sit with them."

It was all-or-nothing time.

"Nope. I'm way too tired to shout," I said, helping myself to another fry. "And we need to have a conversation."

Leonid snapped his fingers and both of the guys in suits

jumped up as though their chairs were on fire. I held my breath as one of them hurried over towards us, but Leonid just tapped the cup with a carefully manicured finger and mumbled something in Russian. A moment later, the cup and the woman were both being rushed out the door.

"What's going on?" I said, but Alexander just shook his head.

Leonid half rose in his chair to watch them through the window. Only after they'd hurried over to a white panel van and disappeared inside did he sit back down and turn his attention to me.

"What conversation?" he said in barely accented English.

"Right. Well. Okay. The way I see it," I said. "To put it on strictly business terms...all of us here have conducted a transaction. Now some of those terms were never crystal clear. I just want to tidy things up between us now so that there are no misunderstandings going forward."

The door banged open and everyone turned to see Benny and the waitress enter. It was hard to tell who was on whose arm, but both were smiling and chatting away.

"Going forward?" Leonid prompted.

"Right," I said, turning back. "You see, the six of us have all worked incredibly hard—with substantial legal and physical risk, I might add—to get you what you wanted. Or...what Alexander said you wanted. And I think that proves you have nothing to fear from us."

"Nothing to fear?" he said, and then added something in Russian or Ukrainian that got a smirk from Alexander.

"You say a lot of big things for someone so small," Leonid said. Then he raised his voice to carry through the room. "Am I to understand that you speak for all of your...group."

I glanced over at the others. Benny was taking the empty

chair at Tim's table. He held the cookie tin in his lap with one hand and gave me a thumbs-up with the other.

"We're with Margot," he said. There were enough nods from some of the others that Leonid seemed satisfied.

"Very well," he said and stretched out his arm to clear his watch from his sleeve and check the time. "I have a few minutes only. I asked them to wait, but one mustn't be rude."

"You asked *The Norwegian Sun*...to wait?"

"Yes."

He layered the word with more than a hint of genuine confusion, as though cruise ships were no different from taxis. Which, maybe in his world, they weren't.

"Okay great? I guess? So, anyway, I just want us all to be super clear that the six of us are done with anything to do with you or your organization. From this moment forward, we all just pretend that none of us ever met and nothing ever happened. Because..." I said and turned my eyes to Alexander with what I hoped was a meaningful and insightful look. "In many ways, nothing *did* happen. Did it?"

It may have been a trick of the light, but I believe Alexander blanched a little. Certainly, he took some time clearing his throat.

"Yes, well, these were always the terms I had stated," he said. "Though I admit your abilities were surprisingly effective, and I was thinking of proposing a...working relationship."

"No, no," Leonid said, and he banged a hand flat on the table. Alexander flinched, but I was too tired to react. "This is fine. I accept your terms, only...of course, you are not finished."

I had my mouth open to ask what he was talking about, but we were interrupted once again when the door banged open. This time, it was Leonid's henchmen returning with the cup. They hurried over and set it reverentially back on the table in front of Leonid.

Both Leonid and Alexander leaned in once more to inspect something on the upper band.

"Very nice," Leonid said. He seemed to relax back into his chair as though at the end of a long journey. "Polina, dearest. Come and see."

As Polina made her way over, Leonid smiled and even tugged to loosen the tie at his throat as though we were all kicking back after a long workday as old friends.

"My son-in-law, Polina's father—may he rest in peace—played for three seasons. This is long ago, way back in the nineteen sixties. He was a young man at the time, of course, and never more than a backup goaltender. But he played. And he was with the Toronto Maple Leafs in nineteen sixty-seven."

"The last time the Leafs won," Maryam said, and shot Benny a teasing look. "They defeated Montreal if I remember right."

Benny gave a slight smile. "They haven't won it since, though, have they?"

"Come and see!" Leonid said. "It's on the top band. Every thirteen years, they remove the top one to make room for a new one at the bottom. And then it goes to be retired at the Hockey Hall of Fame in Toronto. Have you been? It's wonderful."

"Not personally, but I've heard good things," I said, wondering when we were going to get back to the bit where he'd said that our job wasn't yet finished.

"So it was necessary that the fix be done before the band was retired and forever out of reach. And this silversmith, this woman you found, did a wonderful job, Alexander. Well done!"

"What fix?" Benny said, rising from his chair to join the huddle.

"Look here," Leonid said, and pointed. "You see? Nineteen sixty-seven. Polina's father. Anton Pavlov."

"Wait, hang on," Benny said. "Sixty-seven? How did someone from Russia play in the NHL back then?"

"Papa wasn't born in Russia," Polina said. "He was Canadian. My grandparents were chess players who defected when they were on a chess tour or something. Papa was born here. He met my mother when he came back to Russia to coach hockey after everything was open. Way later."

"Okay..." Maryam said. "But I'm still not following. What was there to fix?"

"His middle name was Andreievich," Leonid said. "They made a mistake. They put the letter of his middle name in the wrong place. It should have been ANTON A. PAVLOV. But, until just a minute ago, it was ANTON PAVLOVA."

"This is girl's name," Alexander said. "Last name in Russian for men never ends with 'A'. Only for girls."

"Super," I said. "So now you have your trophy all fixed up and a waiting cruise ship. I guess you should be taking your souvenir and heading off, right? Can we all say goodbye then?"

Leonid gave a low chuckle. "I like you. You're fun. No, no. I'm not taking the Stanley Cup! That's ridiculous. You can't keep such a thing. And why would you, anyway? It's a wonderful symbol of the sport for everyone to enjoy."

"I don't get it. So...what then?"

"Well, this is why your work is not yet finished. Now

that it is fixed…you must give it back."

29

"You're telling me this is all because of a fifty-year-old… *typo*!?" Saffron yelled and leapt her feet. She'd reached some sort of breaking point. Her hands were clenching the sides of the table and her knuckles had gone white.

"My loud friend makes a good point," I said. "Why didn't you just call them and ask to have it fixed?"

"I did. Of course, I did. But, they don't like to do that. And when they do, it's just with an 'X' stamped over top. PAVLOVX is…not much of an improvement." Leonid raised a finger and his two henchmen snapped to attention. He gestured from the cup towards Saffron. "Bring it her so she can see."

The pair stepped forward and together carried the cup over to Saffron and Colin's table.

"The little mistakes, the dents and the scrapes are all part of the story," Leonid continued. "It all adds to the character. And for the most part, I completely agree. But this mistake… no. I had to have this changed. And now, thanks to you, it's done! Wonderful!"

Colin's face was one of near rapture as he stared open-mouthed at the Stanley Cup on the table in front of him. Saffron was still spluttering. I guess she'd been holding back all week and had finally reached her limit. And while I was tempted to agree, I was also reminding myself that this was a man who had ordered someone to be killed. Not that Alexander and Valery had carried out the assignment, but Leonid had expected that they would, and he believed that they had. It would be foolish to think that was the first and only time he'd made such a request.

"Saffron. Maybe we should take a moment to remember Kirill Bondarchuck?" I said gently. Her spluttering stopped, and she went a little pale at the memory of what started all this in the first place. Colin reached out a guiding hand, and she sank slowly back into her chair.

"Ah yes, Kirill," Leonid said with what might have been a trace of sadness. "Polina, as you know, I am very sorry about that. I was too hasty. You see, I have had something of a problem with the Russian secret police lately. Vladimir and I are no longer good friends. So when Polina's safety was threatened, I reacted. I'm thinking now, Polina, maybe it's best that you join me on the ship. There's nothing for you here anymore. And well, true, most of the other passengers are more my age. I'm sure you'll find ways to enjoy yourself. Bingo night is quite fun."

Polina had turned a frightening shade of white. I helped myself to another fry and turned to Leonid. "What did Kirill do to upset you, anyway?"

"He posted photos on his Facebook page." Leonid lifted his shoulders and raised his hands in a shrug of disbelief. "Photos with Polina showing exactly where they were for the entire world to see. They were supposed to be in hiding. So I was upset. But, as it turns out...nobody much, besides my people who monitor such things, took any notice at all. Apparently, he had very few followers."

"Yes...well...ask any teenager. Social media can be a minefield," I said, giving Polina a long look. The dejection was almost heartbreaking. I decided I could probably forgive her for eating my pizza. "By the way, Leonid...have you heard about Polina's *new* boyfriend?"

I flashed Polina a smile, and she gave something of a deer-in-the-headlights look in return. There was an interesting tense silence that followed that I probably shouldn't have enjoyed as much as I did.

"Max Kirkpatrick," I continued. "Super nice guy. Not a hundred percent clear what he does for work...but I'm sure you would two hit it off. Probably have *loads* to talk about."

"Polina, is this true?" Leonid said with a smile of pure joy. "Oh, that's wonderful news. Honestly. I felt terrible for having Kirill...well, let's not dwell on that. You've moved on!? That's what's important. Why didn't you bring this Max fellow along? Never mind. If you're happy staying here, then of course you must stay. Come, come, you can walk me to the ship and tell me all about him."

Leonid dispensed quick nods of what was either satisfaction, or farewell, or maybe some mix of both. Then he snapped his fingers and abruptly rose from his chair. With Polina on his arm and his two bodyguards flanking close behind, he headed off without another word. Alexander's eyes followed the little group across the parking lot until they reached the loading gate. Only when Leonid had gone through and Polina was making her way back did he close his eyes and release a long exhale.

"Okay, I have news," Tim said, waving his phone. "You guys were talking about social media a minute ago, which got me thinking to check. Kevin Reynolds—that's the Keeper you stole it from-"

"Only borrowed apparently," I said.

"*Borrowed.* Fine. Anyway...I've just read that he was delayed leaving Sarita. There was some issue finding a vehicle big enough for the crate, and as it turns out, there was no need for him to hurry at all because the high winds shut down the ferries. I was just on the website and all the crossings are cancelled, at least until tomorrow morning."

"So where is he now?" Maryam asked.

"If the timing of the last post is accurate, he's only just left Sarita about half an hour ago. They're taking him to a hotel in Nanaimo for the night. The Smuggler's Inn. It's run by a cousin of Clara Peters."

"From here to Nanaimo is the short side of the triangle. You know…if we hurry, we might even be there before him," Maryam said.

"I didn't want to say anything, but I doubt the Mini is up for much more," Benny said. "The tires are shot, one of the discs is locking, and the entire rear suspension is blown."

"I have car. I will do it. I will bring cup back to Keeper," Valery said, lurching to his feet. Then his face slightly reddened, and he took a moment to examine his shoes. "Maybe…Maryam comes too? Then after leaving cup, we go to Sarita. Get her truck?"

"Sounds like a plan to me," Maryam added with something of a sly grin.

Nobody jumped to argue. We were all probably just relieved that someone else was offering to do the job.

"Won't you need me to sneak it back into the crate somehow?" I said, without much in the way of enthusiasm.

"No, no. Time for sneaking is over," Valery said. "I just give back."

Just hand it back.

I had to admit that his plan had the advantage of simplicity. And really, what was the Keeper going to do? Call the police to say that he'd somehow lost the Stanley Cup and an unidentified, though extremely large, individual had returned it? It seemed more likely the Keeper would be quite happy to pretend he'd never lost it in the first place. Assuming that he hadn't already opened the crate and taken action. The sooner the cup was on its way back to his care, the better.

As I turned to the others, I could see that whatever happened to the cup next would first involve prying it away from Colin.

"This is so cool!! Can I touch it?"

"Carefully," Benny warned. "This is history you're looking at."

"Well then, I guess you guys might want to hurry," I said.

"Agreed?" Valery said, shooting Maryam a hopeful look. "We go?"

Between Polina and Kirill-Max on one hand, and these two on the other, I was beginning to think they all should have gone on *The Norwegian Sun* for a romantic cruise somewhere. Though I suppose having Leonid onboard might have spoiled the mood.

Valery and Alexander exchanged a flurry of words and volleyed a few shrugs back and forth.

"Okay," Alexander finally said when they'd reached some sort of agreement. He rose from the table and directed a look at Benny. "I'll drive these two to get Valery's car, which is at your shop. You wish to come?"

"No, I'm good here, thanks," Benny said.

Alexander gave a quick nod in response and then, without another word or even a backward glance, he left us. Valery pulled the cup away from a reluctant Colin and then, with it tucked under one arm and Maryam hanging off the other, they followed after Alexander.

I got up as well, but it was only to shout a reminder to do

something about the fingerprints.

Maryam flashed me a thumbs-up in acknowledgment and slipped out the door.

Saffron hesitated and then suddenly swooped in for a hug. "I didn't *really* doubt it," she said. "And I don't blame you. Leo's are always so intense. It makes it so difficult for the rest of us to get close. It's your fire element."

"That would explain it," I said.

"Of course, as a Capricorn, true harmony is just not in our stars. I blame Neptune, of course."

"Neptune. Of course," I echoed.

Colin just rolled his eyes and gave me a brisk high-five.

"I guess I should get these guys home as well," Tim said, tilting his head towards Saffron and Colin. "I suppose we all owe you a word of thanks, Margot. You got us out of this mess. Let's stay in touch." We exchanged an awkward handshake that turned into a half hug. As he headed for the door, his perma-grin was firmly back in place.

With everyone gone, Benny and I moved to a table near the window and shared a few minutes of contemplative silence. Outside, *The Norwegian Sun* had already pulled away from the pier and was disappearing into the dusk—a small city on the move. With the fading light, the sky above it had softened from the mottled dark bruises of storm clouds of the day into a uniform, silky black. Even the sporadic bursts of wind-driven rain against the café windows seem to suddenly be less intense. The calm was interrupted when the café door flew open.

"Dude!" Harley yelled. "You'll never believe what happened. I was heading over here and I ran into the *same* guy that I bought the surfboard from in Tofino. Remember? Same guy! So random! I was walking over and I recognized his van and made him stop. Anyway, he's in town visiting his sister. And get this...it turns out that she—his sister that is—runs this wicked cool women-only surf school. *The Surf Sirens*. Cool huh? So I booked us both in for lessons next weekend. It's up by Jordan River. Oh, my god! You were *just* there! You guys passed it driving down. Did you see a sign? Surf Sirens? Jordan River? How'd your thing turn out, anyway? The cup thingee? Oh wait, don't answer yet...did you order the veggie sliders? They're *so* good here. Am I talking a lot? I've had so much coffee today. Honestly...you would *not* believe!"

"Harley," I said when I thought she'd paused long enough to squeeze it in. "This is Benny. Benny...Harley"

"Oh, my god! *Benny*! It's so nice to meet you. Like face-to-face. Dude! You drive *so* fast. Margot's app thing said your top speed was like a hundred and sixty. *One sixty*! On logging roads! That's *insane*. I *have* to do that. Can we do that? Will you take me? Please say yes. Oh! And the *kapa haka* class is tomorrow night! You're coming, right?"

When her expectant silence began to drag on, Harley started bobbing up and down in her chair. Despite Benny's eyebrows having been raised as high as I'd ever seen them go for the entire time Harley had been talking, there was a comfortable warmth to his smile.

"Oh, yes," Benny said. "I wouldn't miss it for the world."

We stayed, ate sliders and drank tea, until they finally shooed us out a little after ten, long after closing. The three of us were waiting beside the road for Benny's taxi when his phone started ringing. Valery must have been inspired by Benny's driving because he'd made excellent time. Benny put his phone on speaker and the three of us huddled together to listen.

"It was easy," Maryam said. "We beat them to the hotel by a fair bit. Then Val and I were sitting in the parking lot wondering how to go about finding out which room he was in when an SUV pulled up and out jumps the guy. Val recognized him right away. Anyway, he was opening the rear hatch and we see the crate, so Val runs over with the cup to give him a hand unloading. I guess the guy hadn't opened the crate since you did the swap. You should have seen the look on his face. *Total* confusion. He whipped out his keys right there to see what was going on. And as soon as he had the lid open, Val just reached in to grab that piece you'd left. He put the real cup in its place and then walked away. Nobody even said a word. It was amazing."

"Wow," I said. "So he didn't like...call the cops or anything?"

"Oh, believe me, I was thinking about that the whole drive up," Maryam said. "But, like, what would you do if you were the guy? I mean, particularly—as it turned out—that he had it back before he even knew it was gone! What's he gonna say? It's hard to imagine a story he can tell that isn't just going to make him look pretty silly. When we left, the guy was just staring open-mouthed at the cup in the crate and didn't even look our way once. And I polished it end to end the whole drive up and Valery wore gloves...so there are no fingerprints to find. So we're good! We're on our way now to get my truck. I'll call you tomorrow!"

"I guess that's it then?" I said after Maryam had hung up.

"The end of something," Benny said, raising one hand at a yellow cab as it slowed, and clutching the cookie tin in the other.

"Which is always the start of something else," Harley said.

30

A few days later, I was on the Vespa happily cruising along Dallas Road under a crystalline blue sky. The storm was long gone, and the silvery finish of the ocean was so smooth it seemed chrome-plated. I was fresh from my overdue visit to the spa, finally managing to use one of Marty's tracking pucks for its intended purpose, and gaining some buffed nails in the process.

When I swung the scooter into an empty parking spot below Beacon Hill, I spotted Benny waiting near the stairs that led down to the beach.

"How is it that whenever we get together, you're always the last to arrive?" he said, with a teasing twinkle in his eyes.

"I have an excuse this time." I held up my hands and waggled my fingertips. "Spa appointment. I wanted to look my best."

"Hmmm," he said and gave my nails a squint of appraisal. "Manicure, huh? Very nice. What makes me think you were actually up to something else?"

"I can't imagine," I said. I even threw in a shrug of innocent confusion. "Are the others here?"

"Yep. The whole gang is down at the beach already. Valery too. I just came back up because I wanted a quick word with you first."

"Everything okay?"

"Oh, yes. More than fine. I was just thinking...with everything that's happened. It all kind of woke me up a bit. I've maybe been on my own for too long. It might be time I had some help in the shop. You know...bring in someone younger to bring a little creativity and fun." Benny's smile broadened, and it was true, I saw a spark of energy behind his eyes that hadn't been there a week ago.

"Oh, Benny...I don't know. I'm not sure I'd be much use..." I trailed off when I saw his brow furrow into a patient frown. It was similar to the look Uncle Rupert gives me sometimes when I say something especially dumb and he's waiting until I figure it out on my own.

"Right....you're not asking *me*. Are you?" I said with a slowly dawning realization. "It's an *amazing* idea! I'm sure Harley would love that. I mean, she has her dog walking gig, but that's only a few hours a day. When it comes to creativity and fun, she's all that and more. But are you sure that you're prepared for the amount of those things that Harley can unleash?"

"I'm keen to try," he said. "She seemed very excited when I asked her, but she insisted that I check with you first. Something about 'overlapping worlds' that I didn't quite follow."

I did though. I knew exactly what she meant. And it was a fair point. As usual, when it came to social things, Harley knew me far better than anyone—including myself. There was a protective bubble that I'd created around Harley and me. Other than Uncle Rupert and Aunt Stacy, I never let anyone in. Maybe it was time to let that bubble expand. At least a little bit.

I gave Benny a small nod and a bigger smile. "It sounds like a fine idea."

"Good then. We'd probably better hurry before she freezes to death," Benny said as we started down the stairs. "She was already in the water before I got here."

We found Colin and Maryam with Valery looming beside her, loitering in the middle of the beach. Nearer to the shore, Tim and Saffron were scattering handfuls of flower petals from a hemp bag into the water.

Waist-deep in the ocean, Harley was standing in a flowing white bridal gown that I recognized as one she'd found at the thrift store and sometimes used on Halloween. The train was several metres long—it billowed and flowed all around her with the gentle movement of the swells.

"Everyone looks so sombre," Benny said as we negotiated over the rocks at the base of the stairs. "We need to lighten the mood."

"Tim!" Benny called out as we crossed the sand toward them. "We still good for Friday?"

"Wouldn't miss it," Tim said. "Maybe Colin wants to join us? If that's okay with you, Saffron? Benny had me sort out some new computer gear for him. I even got a driving wheel and all that. Maybe the three of us could do some racing?"

"Friday is fine," Saffron said, giving Colin's hair a rumple.

"Friday? No!" Valery said. "You do this another day. Friday is hockey game night. Vancouver. New York. Game five. All of you will come."

"Val," Maryam said, drawing out his name with a rising pitch to her voice as she leaned closer to him. "Try making it into a question. You're not sending Kirill out for coffee or something. You're asking friends to come over."

"Question? Okay...we have lounge, you know this. Sometimes I have trouble following puck. So big TV is good for hockey. Maybe we see cup. You will all come...yes?"

Valery said, then looked at Maryam for approval.

"Close enough," she said, reaching up to give the knot on his tie a small realignment.

"Sure. Sounds nice," Benny said, then shot me a questioning look. He knew my stance about wishing to sever any contact with Alexander and Valery and their organization. But it didn't seem that Maryam came without Valery anymore and despite the strangeness of how we'd met, I somehow wasn't ready for our mismatched group to break apart.

"Awesome," Colin said. "But how about Saturday for driving, instead Benny? Can I Mom?"

"Sure, after hours. I still have a business to run. Why don't you guys come for dinner or something?" Benny suggested, then he nodded out towards the water. "We can chat later, though. Edna loved her ocean dips, but I'm worried Harley might be turning blue."

If the water temperature was getting to her, it didn't show. Her face was as calm and serene as the surrounding water.

"Thanks for coming everyone," Benny said. "I didn't want to do this alone. And, well, it's because of all of you that the time is finally right for me to do this at all. Harley, are you ready?"

"Of course. But you're sure you don't want to spread them yourself?" she called back.

"I'm sure. And I have no words to say that Edna doesn't already know well. This feels right to me," Benny said, rocking back on his heels with a wide smile.

I waved for the others to move closer and called out, "Whenever you're ready, Harley."

Harley gave a little nod and then lifted it high into the

air. She slowly tilted the tin as began to turn in place.

"The light that burns twice as bright burns half as long - and you, Edna, have burned so very, very brightly." Edna's ashes began to drift down to the water, spiralling out around her like a veil.

"What was that? A Lao Tzu quotation?" Saffron whispered.

"Maybe originally," I mumbled back. "Rutger Hauer said it in *Blade Runner.* We were watching it last night."

"Is that the one with Harrison Ford?" Tim said.

"Hush," Maryam chided. "You three babble more than Val."

Harley had stopped spinning. She lowered the empty tin and stood fixed in place staring out to sea. The train of her wedding dress had spiralled in around her and I was worried she was stuck.

"Everything okay Harley?" I called.

"Shhh. I think I saw an otter."

I glanced back to see that Valery had lingered a few respectful paces further up the shore. I realized that the rest of us—huddled together beside Benny—were standing just as we'd been during the fateful elevator ride.

Since I wasn't burdened with a pizza carrier, I linked my arm through Benny's instead.

Acknowledgements

While I had great fun with Margot and friends in this pretend (mis)adventure, the real history of Lord Stanley's Cup is filled with *much* more incredible tales. It was forgotten in a snow bank (when changing a tire), abandoned at a photographer's home studio (the photographer's mother used it as a flower pot for months before anyone thought to wonder where it was), and kicked into the Rideau Canal by the winning team in 1905 (because when you're drunk almost anything seems like a good idea). It's even been stolen once or twice—though it's always been recovered. More of these colourful stories, and of course, the original cup itself, can be found at the Hockey Hall of Fame in Toronto. I am indebted to the welcoming, knowledgeable, and very patient staff of the HHOF for all their assistance in answering my many questions and freely sharing their experiences with me.

The writing part of storytelling happens mostly in solitude. Everything that comes before and after that requires an enormous amount of help. I'm grateful to many friends and family, near and far.

I'd like to thank my brother Michael and father Gerard for never failing to provide tireless and timely support, and my mother Barbara for teaching me how to read in the first place. Thank you to Martha and Andreas for their encouragement and positivity.

I'm indebted to my critique partner, Nicole Wilbur, for her invaluable aid in pointing out the redundant, misplaced, or confusing. For anyone interested in a behind-the-scenes exploration of the craft of writing there is no better place to go than Nicole's YouTube channel: https://www.youtube.com/c/NicoleWilbur

Many thanks to my wonderful beta-readers: Ian Christie, Marie DesRosiers, Kat Kavanagh, Taylor Kennedy, Cornelia Nihon, Anna Russo, and Daryl Smith. Thank you to Robin Spano for her years of guidance, support, and inspiration.

I'm grateful to my children, Kai and Miah, for their boundlessly joyful curiosities that serve as a daily reminder that we all need to be true to ourselves and follow our dreams.

Above all, thank you to my wife, Kariann. Without her unwavering support (and faithful 5 a.m. coffee service) no words would ever have been put to paper. A map needs a compass, and she is my North, my South and every point between.

About the Author

Christopher Courtin was trained as a wildlife biologist but soon discovered that making up stories about animals was much more fun than actually studying them. For many years that story-telling interest was expressed in the world of documentary film where he worked as a writer, videographer, and editor.

He lives in Victoria, BC, Canada.

Visit his website at BlackCanoeCafe.com to keep up to date on the latest Margot and Harley news, sign up for the newsletter, or just spend some time at the virtual version of the Black Canoe café.

Manufactured by Amazon.ca
Bolton, ON